ANCIENT DESIRE

FORGOTTEN BROTHERHOOD BOOK FIVE

ANCIENT DESIRE

FORGOTTEN BROTHERHOOD BOOK FIVE

N.J. WALTERS

Entangled Publishing
644 Shrewsbury Commons Ave
STE 181
Shrewsbury, PA 17361
rights@entangledpublishing.com

Amara is an imprint of Entangled Publishing.

Edited by Alethea Spiridon
Cover design by LJ Anderson/Mayhem Cover Creations
Cover photography by 4x6 and liuzishan/Getty Images

Manufactured in the United States of America

First Edition August 2022

At Entangled, we want our readers to be well-informed. If you would like to know if this book contains any elements that might be of concern for you, please check the book's webpage for details.

https://entangledpublishing.com/books/ancient-desire

For everyone who believes in the magic of dragons… and drakons. And for my readers who love the Forgotten Brotherhood and keep asking for more.

Author's Note

The world is rich in mythology. Every culture in the history of time has left a legacy—written and unwritten—for those of us who came after. As a writer, I draw on those myths, legends, and beliefs and twist them to create something totally new. So, while you may recognize many familiar creatures, gods, or belief systems in this series, this world is something totally new. Expect the unexpected. It can, and will, happen. This is a work of fiction, as told to me by the characters portrayed within the pages.

Maccus Fury sat up in bed, his sharp gaze tracking around the darkened room. No one had gotten past the protective wards covering every wall of his home. Morrigan, his woman, his reason for living, was asleep beside him, her rest unbroken.

What had disturbed him? Had someone tried to break in? His lip curled at the thought. Not many would be stupid enough to try. He was the leader of the Forgotten Brotherhood—the most dangerous men in existence. They weren't the monsters lurking under the bed. They were the ones who killed them.

They were stone-cold assassins, men who had nothing left to lose, but they all lived by a code. Kill only those that truly deserved it and let their gods sort them out. Kill them before they killed you. Never, ever, betray a fellow assassin.

An icy shiver snaked down his spine.

Morrigan stirred beside him. "What's wrong?" Her voice was sleepy, her green eyes filling with growing concern. "Is it Lucifer?"

The leader of Hell had wreaked havoc with the Brotherhood before the threat had been nullified. "No. This is different." He rolled his shoulders and lay back down beside her. "Whatever it is, I'll deal with it when the time comes. Go back to sleep."

"But I'm not tired." As she walked her fingers playfully up his chest, his body surged to life, a wave of lust and love filling him.

"Neither am I." But even as he kissed her, the echo of power vibrated inside him. Something or someone was waking.

Trouble was coming.

Chapter One

"How much farther?" Raine Carson asked as she trudged over the uneven terrain, hands extended for balance and to catch herself if she fell. The ground was wet, making the dead leaves on the forest floor slippery.

"Almost there." Her guide had said the same thing every time she'd asked for the past two hours. She checked her watch. Over four hours had passed since she'd met the man and left her vehicle behind.

"I didn't realize it was so far off the beaten track." Mack Evans ignored her and kept carving a path through the thick woods. The man was inexhaustible, even though he was older than her. Given the lines on his face and the strands of gray in his hair and beard, she put him somewhere between fifty and sixty. If he could keep up this pace, so could she.

She was in decent shape, but teaching at the University of North Carolina at Chapel Hill hadn't prepared her for this relentless trek. "Suck it up," she muttered, even as the muscles in her legs quivered. She was dressed in layers of clothing, and the inner one was sticking to her skin.

At least the scenery was gorgeous. The Great Smoky Mountains National Park was spectacular, even in early spring when many of the trees were still naked after the winter, their bare limbs reaching to the sky. The wind moaned as it twined around them. A thick, white, misty haze hung over the mountain in the distance. The birds were quiet, a heavy silence permeating the air. She shivered and quickened her pace as she lost sight of Mack's red plaid jacket.

"Don't get freaked out," she muttered to herself as she stepped over a downed log and took a deep breath to settle her nerves. "Just because this is like a scene from a horror movie, that's no reason to let your imagination run wild."

That accusation had been leveled at her all throughout her childhood. She daydreamed too much, let her thoughts run to vivid fantasies. She gripped the straps of her backpack, gritted her teeth, and kept putting one foot in front of the other.

"Just up here," Mack called.

"Finally." Relief washed over her, the tension in her shoulders all but melting away. Even the trembling of her legs couldn't stop the excited butterflies from fluttering in her stomach.

The small clearing was a semicircle that surrounded a tall, thin gap in a rock face. "That's the cave?"

Mack grunted as he swung his pack off his back and leaned it against the rock face.

"You're sure it's in there?"

He gave a curt nod.

Mack wasn't much for conversation, but he was sharing his discovery with her, and for that, she'd forever be grateful. This could make her career.

The sensible thing would be to set up camp, document the surroundings, and then venture into the cave. She swung her pack off one shoulder so she could dig out a flashlight.

"How far back is the statue?"

"Not far." Mack crouched down and fiddled with the fastenings of his bag.

The afternoon sky was darkening and the temperature dropping. "I'm taking a quick look inside." Mack's grunt could've been approval or disapproval—impossible to say. "I'll help set up camp as soon as I'm back."

The flashlight beam pierced the darkness of the cave. Taking a fortifying breath, she squeezed through the opening. Her pack scraped against the wall. She should leave it, but a sense of anticipation tethered her, pulling her forward. The stone beneath her feet crunched against the soles of her boots. She kept one hand pressed against the damp wall to help guide her as she ventured deeper.

Her heart was pounding, as it often did before she made some significant discovery. A subtle vibration seemed to emanate from all around. A warning. Her mouth went dry, making swallowing difficult. "Just a bit farther." She hadn't come all this way to chicken out because of a spooky atmosphere.

The path widened. A rock broke away from the wall and tumbled to the ground, the sound echoing all around her. She jumped, her breath catching in her throat before wild laughter bubbled up. "Just a falling rock caused by water and erosion." Or maybe it was a critter. Oh God, was this a bear's cave? The last thing she wanted was to disturb a sleeping black bear. It didn't smell, so that was a good sign. At least she hoped it was. Bear habitat was outside her scope of knowledge.

Raising the light, she traced the edges of the corridor. There was a turn ahead. "If I don't find anything around there, I'll go back."

Screwing up her courage, she rounded the corner. The world dropped away as she stumbled forward and fell to her knees. The stone statue had to be more than twenty feet long, maybe even twenty-five, and stood at least eight to ten feet high, even though the creature was lying down, the head and long tail curled around it.

"A dragon." There was reverence in her voice as she tentatively reached out. Swallowing heavily, she stroked her fingers over the cool, hard stone.

The detail was exquisite, each scale incredibly defined. It would have taken years—maybe even a lifetime—to create something of this magnitude. The dedication it would've taken, the blood and sweat, to lovingly carve each groove and curve by hand was enormous. This had huge significance to whoever had made it.

Why in a cave? Why wasn't something this magnificent out in the open where everyone could have seen it and been awed? From what she'd studied about the native peoples who'd lived on the land, this didn't seem to fit with any of their legends. Most dragon myths in North America were focused on water serpents. Maybe this was more in keeping with the Thunderbird legends—giant, almost prehistoric-like birds that hunted livestock and sometimes people.

She raised the light higher, taking in every line, every muscle, every scale. "You're gorgeous." Raine pushed to her feet, a sense of wonder pulling her closer. The head was on the ground, tucked into the body. It was wedge-shaped and flat on the top with an elongated jaw. Like the body, the face was detailed. It was amazingly lifelike, exuding a sense of power even at rest.

"You're also going to make my career." She was already imagining the book, the lecture tour. This was only the beginning.

She ran her fingers over the long line of the dragon's jaw. Why was its mouth closed and not open to expose the sharp teeth? It'd been done that way on purpose. And why sleeping and not in a more powerful pose? She had so many questions and no obvious answers.

Excitement thrummed through her, a song that lifted her spirits. This was what she loved, what she lived for. Tracking down myths and legends was her life's passion, but it was rare to find anything other than stories passed down through generations, maybe the legendary creatures depicted on clothing or pottery or small ceremonial pieces. This was substantial. This was real.

"No one will believe me until they see you."

She frowned and leaned forward, shining the light on the dragon's eye. There were no signs of tool marks, at least none she could see. Tucked away inside, the weather wouldn't have worn the stone down. The lines were crisp and new, as if the sculptor had finished yesterday and walked away.

Was this a hoax? But why would someone go to such trouble? It made no sense.

Likely, she wasn't seeing things properly. She needed more light. And maybe the sculptor was just that good. Archaeologists and historians tended to believe earlier peoples hadn't had the skills of modern man. And while that was true in some cases, in others, they'd been far more advanced.

"You're going to be famous," she told the dragon. There was so much to do. She had to make detailed notes, take pictures, and get accurate measurements. This guy was going to be the star of the book she was going to write.

Caught up in the excitement, she leaned forward and pressed a kiss to his cool, hard cheek. The ground beneath her trembled and rolled, followed by a loud rumble. "What in the world?" The stone eye of the beast shattered and a pale pink one stared back at her.

Her scream was drowned out by the explosion that rocked the world. She fell back, the flashlight slipping from her hand as she covered her head to protect herself from falling debris.

. . .

Lucius did his best to ignore the voice tugging him from sleep.

He wanted to be left alone. Over the centuries, only a few had dared to violate his chosen resting spot. The "fuck off" vibe he emitted, even while sleeping, was usually enough to send them running.

But not this person. This person dared touch him.

Human. He inwardly curled his lip. He had little time for them. They were a violent species, always warring with those who were different, those they feared. Not all of them; he had to give them their due. He'd met some wise and welcoming men over the course of his long life, but they'd been few.

The ground shook beneath him, followed by an explosion and a high-pitched woman's scream that pierced his soul. His heart thumped hard against his chest. Still, he didn't move. Dust filled the air as rocks tumbled to the ground around him. Several bounced off his back, more an annoyance than anything. If the entire mountain fell on him, it wouldn't be enough to harm him.

He strained to hear the woman, reaching out with his preternatural senses. Was she still alive? Sadness filled him, making him frown. Why would he care if she lived or died? She wasn't his business.

The resolve that had sent him into the Deep Sleep of his kind was rapidly burning away under the brunt of his curiosity. Another reason to ignore the intruder. He was done with this world.

A deep cough was followed by another. Relief flooded him. Disgruntled over this unreasonable caring, he closed his eye, determined to go back to sleep. Her groan vibrated through his entire body. Was she hurt? *Sleep*, he reminded himself. Problem was, he was awake, and his innate inquisitiveness had kicked in, demanding answers.

"You're okay." The voice was strained. Was she talking to him? Impossible. There was only one heartbeat. "You're okay, Raine."

She was talking to herself, as she must have been earlier, since she was the only one trapped in here with him.

"Was that an earthquake?"

It wasn't any natural phenomena that caused the cave-in. That he was sure of. As a drakon—the son of a dragon sire and a human woman—he had a measure of control over all the elements, even though his affinity was with the earth. Whatever had happened just now was man-made.

A low grumble rolled out from him, causing the ground to shudder. The woman—no, Raine, as she'd called herself—gasped as several more rocks tumbled to the ground. The hitch in her voice, the stench of fear surrounding her, quieted him. For some unknown reason, he didn't want to cause her harm.

"That was nothing more than an aftershock. You can handle this," she told herself. "The entire path can't be caved in." Boots scrambled over the floor, growing fainter. She was leaving.

Fear, not relief, clutched his heart. Every muscle in his body clenched as he fought a growing need to go after her, to bring her back.

Mine!

The single word thrummed through his blood, pounded in his brain. No, she wasn't his. He didn't need or want a woman, especially a human. The ones he'd known had either shunned him for what he was or welcomed him because he was a novelty, because they hoped for power or money through their association. That's when they hadn't been actively trying to kill him, which had been most of the time.

"Hello?" Her pulse was racing, the thudding sound echoing in his ears. Her breathing was fast and shallow, edging on panic. "Mack? Are you there? Can you hear me?"

Anger roared through him, hot and thick. Who was Mack?

"Help!"

"Ms. Carson?" The voice was faint, but unmistakably male.

"Oh, thank God. There's been a cave-in."

"I know."

Something in the man's tone gave him pause.

"Have you radioed the authorities?"

"No."

"Why not?" Her voice was louder and strained. "Mack?"

"Some things are better left buried. It would've been better for you if you'd died in the explosion. I'm sorry for that."

"You're sorry? You're sorry?" Her voice rose, getting more panic-stricken with each word. A rock struck the wall and bounced off. Had she thrown it? "Then why did you bring me here? I'd never have known about this place without you."

Now that was interesting. Was this about her at all or was it about him, a trap or test?

"I had my orders."

"From whom? For God's sake, from whom?" She was panting now, close to hyperventilating.

"From God's angel. I'm sorry, but that's the way it has to be."

"Angel, what angel?" The man was obviously deranged. "Mack, don't do this." Silence greeted her. "Don't leave me here. Mack!"

His heart ached as her quiet sobs reached his sensitive ears.

"I don't understand," she whispered between sobs. "Why would he do this?"

She stumbled back into the inner chamber, the slender

light source in her hand helping her find her way. He cracked his eye enough so he could watch her. She was leaning against the wall opposite him, her hand on it for support, her gaze on the tunnel that led to the blocked entrance. Dust and grit covered her. Dirt streaked her face, marred by the tracks of the tears trailing down her cheeks.

The urge to rise, hunt down Mack, and smite him was one he could barely contain. This woman was bringing out the beast in him. That was dangerous. The dragon side of him grumbled at being denied, but the human part held him back.

She removed a pack from her back and sat on the floor with her head buried in her hands, rocking back and forth. For the longest time, all he could hear was her steady breathing.

"What are you going to do?" That gave him a jolt until he realized she was talking to herself again. "Are you going to just sit here and die? No, no you're not. Wait, my phone." She rummaged around in her pocket and produced a small rectangle. It lit up when she touched it. "Damn it." She held it up and moved it from side to side. "No signal, not in the middle of a freaking cave." It went back into her pocket.

She pulled her pack closer and opened it. "You have a sleeping bag, some food, and water. That will buy you a couple of days. You're strong. You can dig your way out." The light flickered. "Don't you dare go out." She shone it around the cavern. He closed his eye before it got to his face. It lingered there before moving on. He cracked his eye again, eager for another look.

Dirty and disheveled, she was still attractive. For the first time, he took a good look at her as a woman and not just as the person who'd disturbed his sleep. She was tall and slender with slight curves. Her hair was short and could be dark brown or black, hard to tell with so much dust covering it. The few clean spots of skin on her face appeared smooth and unblemished. Her lips were full, her nose slender, her jaw slightly pointed.

"You did not see the statue blink and look at you," she muttered. "That was exhaustion and imagination, or maybe Mack pumped some sort of gas into the air to make me hallucinate. The cave-in wasn't caused by an ancient curse, but by man."

It was fascinating the way she answered her own questions, reasoned everything out, and encouraged herself. Her courage in the face of overwhelming odds was admirable.

She took out a bottle and drank deeply before capping it. "Time to get to work." She pulled herself to her feet and disappeared. From the sound of things, she was going to try to dig her way out.

He closed his eye, ignoring the twinge of sympathy stirring with him.

Human problems weren't his concern.

Chapter Two

The jagged rock slipped from her sweaty, bloody hands. She barely yanked her foot out of the way before it smashed down on it. She hadn't been as lucky a few other times but, thankfully, hadn't broken anything. At least she didn't think she had. It was difficult to tell—she hurt everywhere.

According to her watch, she'd been digging for hours. She needed to eat and rest, even though pure terror was pushing her to claw at the rocks until she found a way out. That wasn't going to happen tonight, maybe not even tomorrow.

She swiped at the tear trailing down her cheek. She wasn't crying, not really, but every now and then a single drop rolled down her face. Crying solved nothing. Life had taught her that a long time ago. Actions mattered.

"You need to eat." And doctor her wounds. She flexed her fingers, wincing when the raw, tender skin pulled.

She swayed, caught in a dreamlike state, barely catching herself as she tilted to one side. "Definitely time for food and rest." It took every ounce of courage she possessed to walk back to the open cavern, away from possible freedom.

Nothing had changed, but the air was clearer, the dust having settled. The dragon sculpture drew her. "This is your fault." She rapped him on the side of the head. "Ouch. Crap." She shook her hand. "You've got a hard head, you know that?"

She surveyed the space, something she hadn't done up until now. The statue took up about half. That left plenty of room for her to camp. At least she had company, even if it was made of stone.

A slightly hysterical laugh rose from within her. "Why is everything so hard? No, stop that." She scrubbed at her eyes, not worrying about the dirt she was rubbing on her face. She couldn't get any worse. "No giving in to self-pity. You have so much to be grateful for. You're still alive."

Mack had meant to kill her. He'd led her here, all the while planning to trap her in the cave. Who did something like that? A shudder shook her entire body. None of this made any sense. Time enough to sort it out if—scratch that—when she escaped.

On that note, she sat down, pulled a small first-aid kit from her pack, and got to work. The antiseptic wipes made the scrapes and blisters burn. Better that than to let them get infected. The quiet was oppressive, her breathing the only sound as she affixed bandages to the worst of the wounds. What would happen when her flashlight went out, leaving her alone, buried in the dark?

"Don't think about it. You'll make it out before that happens." A clean, dry shirt was a must. She hadn't changed earlier, which was just as well, since she'd done nothing but sweat. It didn't take her long to whip off one shirt and pull on another. She didn't linger. Despite being in a cave, there was a chill. Or maybe it was exhaustion and nerves making her cold, not to mention hungry.

The chocolate granola bar she retrieved from her bag

tasted like heaven. It was tempting to eat more, but she had to conserve. Who knew how long she'd be here? "I have plenty of granola bars, trail mix, and even a few crackers and cheese." Water was the biggest problem.

Leaning against the wall, she focused on the silent giant on the other side of the room. "Don't suppose you know where I can find any water, do you?" No answer. "Didn't think so." She tilted her head back and sighed. "What I wouldn't give for a hot shower. I stink."

There was a sense of timelessness in here, as though the outside world didn't really exist. "You had to have started as one big slab of stone. Maybe whoever made you saw the stone and got inspired." It seemed not even the possibility of looming death put her curiosity on hold.

Her mouth opened on a yawn so big her jaw gave a crack. "I need to rest. I'm glad I carried my own sleeping bag." She rolled it out and crawled inside, resting her head on her pack. It was lumpy but better than the hard ground. "You look more comfortable than I do." Her hand clenched around the flashlight before she made herself flick the switch, plunging her into absolute darkness.

The pounding of her heart echoed in her ears. Her breathing grew faster. "I can do this." This wasn't the same as night in the outside world. There was starlight in the woods and ambient light in the city. Here there was only a pitch black that seemed to crouch like a monster, ready to swallow her whole.

Calm wrapped around her like a warm blanket, soothing her. "There's nothing to fear," she whispered. "Nothing at all. Good night, dragon." Exhaustion overwhelmed her, and she fell asleep between one second and the next.

• • •

Finally, he had the peace and quiet needed to think. Awake, she captured all his attention, which was why he'd sent her calming thoughts. It had nothing at all to do with wanting to ease her agitation and fear.

Disgruntled, he looked inward, searching for answers. There was no telling how long he'd been asleep. It had to be centuries. This woman was not dressed like the ones he'd last seen, and many of her belongings were strange and unfamiliar.

However much time had passed, it was long enough for his scales to be covered in a stone shell—a side effect of the Deep Sleep of his kind. It was a hibernation, of sorts. One thought to be permanent. In the thousands of years of history, he'd never heard of another drakon waking. It wasn't a step he'd taken lightly.

Only the stone around one of his eyes had cracked. He opened it and studied her, his preternatural vision cutting through the pitch black. He couldn't see her as well as he'd like, but it was enough. Her dirt-stained face was turned toward him, as if seeking comfort from his presence, even in sleep.

Warmth spread throughout his big body, driving back the chill that had permeated him after so many centuries. The steady rhythm of her heart soothed the dragon side of his nature. The human side of him was awake and had a million questions.

Who was she? Why was she here? And why had her presence awakened him? What made her different from those who had come before? They'd been nothing more than muted noise in the background, easily ignored, quickly forgotten.

His name was Lucius, that much he recalled. The Deep Sleep had dimmed his memories. The longer he was awake the more filtered back, but it was a slow process and there were thousands of years to fill in. It would take time, something he had plenty of. Raine's well-being was more precarious, as she was human and fragile.

Her breathing was deep and even, but every now and again she gasped and twitched beneath her covering. Was she having a nightmare? What thoughts haunted her sleep? He'd dreamed while he'd slept. Or maybe the images had been real-world events, memories, or simply flights of fancy. No way to know unless he rose.

No! That wasn't going to happen. His reason for embracing the Deep Sleep hadn't changed. The world wasn't friendly to his kind. Monster was the name he'd been given, and not just by humans. Images of blood and carnage flashed through his mind. Screams from the past echoed in his head. Fear of becoming what they'd called him had driven him to such drastic action. One woman's life wasn't worth the cost of what might happen if he chose to walk in the world again.

She should never have come here. That had been her choice. This was her fate. If he left the peaceful sanctuary of the cave and his rest, the entire world might burn before anyone could stop him—assuming they could.

He kept trying to access his buried memories, but the sound of her breathing was distracting. It wouldn't be long until it stopped completely. A week or two at most. Then he'd be alone again, able to rest. It's what he wanted, right? His heavy heart and churning guts said otherwise.

This was all her fault for disturbing him. Whatever connection he was experiencing with her had to be some symptom of being jolted out of his rest.

Her breathing had deepened, become slower, like his. For fuck's sake, he was breathing in sync with her. Disgruntled, he sent out a blast of anger. She jolted, bolting upright. "What? Where am I?" Fear tinged her voice as she fumbled around. A click and the light came on. "It wasn't just a bad dream."

Shame, an emotion he hadn't experienced in millennia, filled him. He estimated she'd slept only a matter of hours. Not nearly enough.

She swallowed heavily, her delicate throat rippling. "I need a bathroom." Giving a groan, she pushed to her feet. "Not exactly five-star accommodations." The light flashed over the room. "You can't pee here. Not where you're sleeping." Wrinkling her nose, she wandered deeper into the cave, disappearing around a corner.

Despite his resolve to stay detached, he inwardly smiled when he heard her singing. The woman was quiet only when she was sleeping and not even then. Her voice rose and fell, slightly off-key, but still somehow charming.

She returned and sat down on the covering she'd used. "How did you sleep?" she asked. It was getting increasingly difficult not to answer her. It had been so very long since he'd conversed with anyone. The last time had been… A flash of a big man with black hair and myriad tattoos popped into his mind and then disappeared.

"What's that? You slept better than I did? I imagine so. You're used to the cave environment." She dug out food and began to eat, taking tiny sips from a bottle between bites. "I'm worried about Penelope. She's my cat. I left her enough food and water for a couple of days. It was only supposed to be an overnight trip to confirm you existed."

Fascinated, he watched and listened. Her voice stroked over his scales like a lover's caress, warm and inviting. The fires of rage and regret that burned within him were muted by her mere presence. It had to be sorcery. There was no other logical explanation. His blood turned chilly in warning.

Maybe she'd been sent to torment him for his dark past. Most likely, like so many others, she wanted something from him. If so, she'd be disappointed. Others far more powerful had tried and failed to break him.

"What will happen to her if I don't make it home?" She swiped at a tear that trickled down her face, sniffed, and squared her shoulders. "I'll make it out of here. I have to."

Her determination thawed the cold indifference inside him. Her concern for a creature not even human warmed him, and it was genuine. The scent of her tears, smell of her fear, and tone of her voice all spoke of love for the cat.

The longer she was here, the more he itched to break free from his stone shell and speak with her. After finishing her meal, she stood, dusted off the seat of her pants, and headed toward the cave-in. "Watch my stuff while I'm gone."

The day passed slowly. Sleep eluded him, his focus entirely on Raine. She was out of sight, but he could hear her, easily imagine her actions. Tirelessly, she worked, moving stone after stone, occasionally swearing when more seemed to fall in. Worry gnawed at his gut when she didn't stop to eat. Was she drinking?

Not my problem.

Finally, her steps grew closer, her boots dragging. He lowered his eyelid, leaving it cracked enough that he could watch her. She dropped down onto the sleeping bag, turned onto her side, and pulled her legs up to her chest, radiating defeat.

He squeezed his eye shut. A tiny crack appeared at the base of his back foot. She couldn't give up. Penelope needed her.

I can help her.

No good ever came from getting involved with a human. Vivid images of bloodcurdling screams, fire, mayhem, pain, and death flashed before him, but he couldn't grasp the memories. They were foggy, as though his brain hadn't fully decided if he was waking up or not and wasn't willing to make the effort if he was going to drop back into the Deep Sleep.

Eat, he silently urged. *Drink.*

She wrapped her arms around her legs, making herself even smaller. Time passed and a shiver wracked her entire body. "Who am I kidding? I'm going to die here with a stupid stone dragon who won't even talk to me." The glare she sent him was fierce. "This is all your fault." She sniffed and pointed her finger at him.

At him. He didn't know whether to smite her or applaud her bravery.

"If you hadn't been here, I would never have come. I can't figure out Mack's angle. Why lead me all the way out here and trap me with you? The whole 'an angel told me to do it' adds another layer of weird. He could've killed me on the hike in if all he wanted was my death."

She wasn't wrong. The whole thing seemed an elaborate setup. He waited impatiently, wanting to know more.

"It must tie in somehow with the grant I got to write my book from—wait for it—the Angel Foundation. That's not a coincidence. Talk about too good to be true. I should've suspected something was up. My field of study isn't exactly one that gets a lot of funding. I love teaching, don't get me wrong, but I wanted time to write a book, maybe even two. And the grant was enough for me to take an entire year off work. Yesterday was the first day of my new adventure, and it probably marks the beginning of the end."

She lifted her sleeve and rubbed it over her face. "I'm sorry to dump all this on you, but let's face it. You're the only one here."

Giving a sigh, she leaned her head back and stared at the ceiling. "It's my own fault for believing in myths and legends. Did you know there are urban legends about werewolves and vampires in North Carolina?" She took a tiny sip of water. "But you're real. You're a freaking stone dragon."

Her insistence on referring to him as a dragon was beginning to annoy him.

"Are you based on some prehistoric flying dinosaur? Maybe they found some fossilized bones and this was their interpretation of what you might've looked like. Yeah, you're probably nothing more than a flying dinosaur."

The rumble came from deep inside him. Cracks appeared in his stone covering and traveled down to the ground beneath him.

"Holy crap." Raine jumped to her feet, her hand pressed to her chest, eyes wide.

The thick casing that had protected him for centuries crumbled. His limbs were stiff after so long, but there wasn't enough room for him to stretch, not unless he wanted to bring the ceiling down around them.

He swiveled his head in her direction. "I'm no dinosaur. I'm a drakon."

. . .

Raine would have peed her pants if she hadn't been totally dehydrated. Her heart was doing its best to thump its way out of her chest. She leaned against the wall, her legs turning to jelly.

"This isn't happening." It couldn't be. "This isn't real. You're a hallucination." She laughed when the truth sunk in. "That's it. My imagination has finally gotten the better of me. Or maybe there's some noxious gas building up. More likely I'm running out of air and my brain is playing tricks on me."

"You don't believe in me?" The voice was so deep it made her bones ache.

"Sure, I do. I believe you're a hallucination dragon."

"Not a dragon, a drakon."

Why was her hallucination arguing with her? "What's the difference, other than a k instead of a g?"

"A drakon is the son of a dragon and a human female.

Dragons came here thousands of years ago from another dimension, mated with humans, and produced sons, always sons. When our sires discovered their DNA hadn't dominated and we weren't full-blooded dragons like them, but hybrids, they left us here and returned to their own dimension."

He lowered his head, extending his long neck until his breath was a warm puff against her face. "Wow, this hallucination is realistic." She reached out and stroked the tips of her fingers over his scales. "You're warm, not cold."

"Why do you doubt your senses?"

"Because dragons, excuse me, drakons, aren't real." She spoke slowly so he'd understand. A giggle fell from her lips. She never giggled. "I'm definitely seriously food or oxygen deprived."

He blinked, as though not certain what to say or do.

She patted his long snout. The teeth he'd flashed were huge and sharp, like gleaming white daggers. But there was no need to be afraid of a figment of her imagination, right?

"Don't worry about it. Most people don't know how to take me." She leaned in. "They think I'm odd. I know, I know. It's difficult to believe, but there it is."

She was dying. There was no other explanation. Her mind had splintered, her grasp on reality slipping away. A deep sadness gripped her. "I wish my life had been different. I've never been able to connect with people, never made those lifelong, close friends that most people seem to have." Sighing, she petted his jaw while he continued to stare at her. "Maybe that's why I study creatures of myth and legend. I think I understand them. Your pink eyes are pretty. I would've thought I'd imagine them to be black or green or at least brown, but the pale pink is so cool. Like pink champagne. And your scales are gorgeous. They're gold, but not a really yellow gold." She snapped her fingers. "Rose gold. The outline at the edges matches your eyes."

The ground beneath her feet began to shake again. Her drakon tipped his head back and roared. She slammed her hands over her ears and toppled backward, landing on her butt. The air around her supercharged with heat, driving away the chill until she was sweating.

"I'm not pretty. I am fierce and deadly, feared by humans and my own kind. And you, human, are trapped in here with me."

"Holy shit! You're real!" Then her light went out.

Chapter Three

Molten fury ran though Lucius's veins. Pretty, she thought him pretty. The insult wasn't to be borne. He was a fierce drakon. And she was…terrified. Her breathing was erratic, harsh gasps tearing from her throat as she struggled to drag air into her lungs.

Turning his head to one side, he inhaled, drawing on his inner fire and releasing a tiny blast. The nearby rocks turned molten, melting beneath the tremendous heat. Some cracked and exploded, incinerated before they hit the ground. It lit the area, allowing him to better see her huddled form, but more importantly, it allowed her to see him.

Her eyes were wide, the golden brown of her irises almost swallowed by the dark pupils. Her skin was pale, her hair damp. A bead of sweat trickled down her forehead. She pressed her hand to her mouth and scooted back toward the wall, still trying to catch her breath.

He closed his mouth and the flames extinguished. "I won't hurt you." Raine had awoken him from the Deep Sleep, something that should have been impossible.

"You." She gasped for air. "You're real."

"I thought we established that." The darkness soothed him, but her heartbeat was getting faster, not slower. Frowning, he leaned forward until he was a hairbreadth from her face.

"Don't eat me," she yelled. Then she popped him in the jaw with her fist. It bounced harmlessly off his scales. She yelped again, shaking her fingers and cradling them to her chest.

Even in her fear, she fought.

"Where's my stupid flashlight?" She patted her hand on the ground beside her. He caught the edge of the light with the tip of one claw and gently rolled it toward her. "Ah-ha." She grabbed it and shook it. "There are new batteries in you. Work, damn it." She smacked the device several times against her thigh and the light reappeared.

She swiveled and shone it straight in his face. He reared back and blinked several times. "Don't like that, do you?" She continued to point it at his face. "Stay back."

Did she really think the puny light would stop him? Not wanting her to damage herself further, he settled back on his haunches. "Now what?"

"What?" His question seemed to confuse her.

"What do you plan to do now? Do you think your light will protect you?" She really was a fascinating creature. She pushed to her feet and edged toward the path leading to the entrance.

"I'm getting out of here." Her hand was shaking, the light bouncing all around the space. She grabbed her pack and sleeping bag in her free hand and inched toward her goal.

"The entrance is still blocked."

"I know that, but you can't fit through the tunnel." Her lips turned down and several lines wrinkled her forehead. "How did you get in here to begin with?"

"I walked." No reason not to be truthful.

"You walked. Of course you did." He turned slightly, angling his big body to see her better. "You probably commanded Mack to bring me here. Is he your Renfield?"

"My what?"

"Renfield, you know, Dracula's servant from the Bram Stoker book. Dracula was a vampire and was vulnerable during the day, so he had a human help him get what he wanted. Eventually drove the man crazy. Or maybe Mack is more like Harker. He was tricked into helping Dracula. I can't remember. I read the book a long time ago."

He was practically dizzy trying to keep up with her. "I'm no bloodsucker, and I don't need a Renfield." The very idea was distasteful.

"You're a stone dragon. Excuse me, drakon. Or you were. What am I supposed to be? The virgin sacrifice? According to legend, that's what they did."

She wasn't wrong. When dragons had arrived, the tribes of the earth offered up their most beautiful maidens. Only the dragons hadn't eaten them, they'd seduced and procreated with them. His heart ached at the memory of his mother who'd been one such woman.

"You've been cheated. I'm no virgin. Not that I'm super experienced or anything, but I dated a guy for a year in college and had a couple short-term relationships. So, yeah, no virgin here." She pointed at her chest, a triumphant smile on her face.

Lucius frowned and lowered his head. The idea of her having sex with another man was...distasteful. Good gods, was he jealous? Of this mouthy, dirty creature?

Yes, yes he was. He closed his eyes for a moment and prayed for deliverance. "Maybe I won't care that you're not a virgin."

Now she was frowning again. There was no guile to her,

her expression open and honest for all to see. No wonder she'd been taken advantage of and lured here. Obviously, she needed someone to look out for her. Not him, but someone.

"You can't eat me." She'd dropped her belongings and put her hands on her hips, the light now directed toward a side wall.

"Why not?" This was the most absurd conversation he'd ever had. The most interesting, too. She was a constant surprise.

"I'll give you indigestion." She punctuated it with a decisive nod. "My muscles are stringy. Not much meat. You'd likely choke on a thigh bone."

"I could roast you up and I wouldn't notice." Why was he pushing her?

She wagged her finger at him. "That's a terrible idea."

He made a playful snap toward the extended digit. Raine yelled, yanked her hand back, and scrambled for the exit. Her fear saddened him. It was also a reminder that others would see him as a monster, no matter what.

Heaving a sigh, he lay back down and rested his head on the cool ground. This was why he'd gone to sleep in the first place. There was no sound of digging, but Raine was still nearby. Where else would she be? An hour passed. Then another.

Though she tried her best to be stealthy, the slight scrunching sound of her boots, along with her breathing, alerted him to her presence. "Ah, Mr. Drakon, are you okay?"

He turned his head away. Better not to interact with her anymore. That didn't stop his ears from twitching to follow her movements as she crept closer.

Was she for real? "You need a keeper," he told her, not bothering to look at her.

"I've heard that." On a sigh, she sat down beside him. The silence lengthened. How long would she last without speaking? He counted the seconds and made it all the way to five minutes. "Thing is, I could use your help."

And there it was. "Your kind always wants something— protection in battle, power, my treasure, my very blood." And that last one was something he should have kept to himself.

"You have a treasure? That's true? Wait, forget that. It's not important. I'm not in a battle. I don't need power. And blood? I'm sorry, but no."

Unable to feign disinterest any longer, he turned toward her and opened his eyes. She wiggled her fingers at him in a wave. "If you don't want protection, power, or treasure, what do you want?"

"It occurred to me you could probably tunnel out of this place if you wanted to." Her hopeful expression made him morose. She wanted his help to leave him.

"I could."

Seconds ticked by. "Well." She waved toward the tunnel. "What are you waiting for?"

"I'm quite content here."

"How can you be happy stuck in here? And how did you become a lump of stone when you're alive? How did that happen? Is that natural? Did someone put a spell on you? Did I break it?" The hopeful tone made him want to smile. "If so, then you owe me, buddy."

"Lucius. My name is Lucius. And I chose to turn to stone."

"Why would you do that? You're a drakon. You can probably do all kinds of cool stuff."

His chest puffed out slightly. "I can."

"Then why are you in a cave in the middle of nowhere!" Her voice rose until she was yelling at the end. "Sorry." She rubbed her grubby hand over her forehead, smearing even more dirt there. "I just don't get it."

"The world is not kind to those who are different." He

clamped his mouth shut. He'd already said too much, but it was so easy to talk with her.

"No, it's not." Her voice had softened.

"Do not pity me, woman."

She snorted. "I don't pity you. You're a damn drakon, more powerful than I'll ever be. You've seen things I'll never see. How long have you been alive? How long were you locked in stone?"

His muscles were beginning to twitch with the need to move. There'd be no going back to sleep for him. Ready or not, he was back in the world of man.

"Probably none of my business," she continued. "You may not agree, but I understand you better than you think." Her fingers twined around the edge of her sweater, and she twisted it. "I know what it's like to be different."

He shook his broad head. "You think you do, but you don't. You're an attractive female human. Others will accept you."

"Fat lot you know." Turning her back on him, she walked away.

• • •

Raine bit her bottom lip when it quivered. It was stupid to be upset because some mythical creature threw her confession back in her face. She joked about being different, but the truth was, it hurt. Her entire life was one of being abandoned.

"Forget him," she muttered. The wall of rubble in front of her and the fact that someone wanted her dead were more pressing concerns. Her shoulders slumped and she sighed. She'd already moved a ton of rocks but wasn't making much headway.

Closing her eyes, she tried to remember how many steps she'd taken to get this far into the cave. A growl of frustration welled up inside her. "I have no idea how far it is to the outside."

"About eight feet."

"Ahh!" She whirled around, tripped over a rock, and slammed into the side of the wall. Lucius's huge head was peering at her. Hand on her chest, she glared at him. "Don't sneak up on me like that." And how could a creature that big be so silent?

He huffed out a breath of warm air. "I thought you'd hear me."

"I was busy thinking."

"And talking."

"Get used to it. I talk to myself a lot."

"I hadn't noticed." His deadpan delivery and the slight twitch of his lips—did drakons even have lips?—stopped her cold. He was joking with her.

The absurdity of the situation slammed into her, and she began to laugh. He tilted his big head slightly to the side, and it scraped against the walls. What started out as a giggle became a huge belly laugh. She hugged her stomach when the muscles cramped. He looked disgruntled, which set her off again. She tried to stop, really she did. Tears rolled down her cheeks. She sat on the floor to keep from toppling over.

"What's so funny?" His voice was deep, the baritone vibrating through the floor. His teeth were incredibly sharp, something she hadn't paid much attention to when she'd thought he wasn't real. Big, too. All the better to eat her with. Only if he was going to do that, he'd have already done it.

"I'm stuck in a cave, talking to a drakon who is complaining I talk too much."

"Not complaining. You're…interesting."

Her humor died as old insecurities washed over her. "Interesting is another word for odd." She pushed to her feet, rolled her shoulders, and grabbed a rock. It seemed heavier than it had earlier, even though it was the same size of many she'd moved.

I'm getting weaker. How much longer could she keep this up? "Go away. If you're not going to help, don't distract me." Probably not smart to bait the drakon, but she no longer cared.

Dead was dead. If she didn't get out of here soon, she'd eventually run out of food and water. There seemed to be plenty of air. With that realization, she dropped the rock and turned to Lucius.

His brows lowered. "What?"

As she walked toward him, he surprised her by backing out of the tunnel. "It occurred to me there may be another way into this cavern, which means there's another way out. There's plenty of air."

"There are tunnels. I never explored them."

"Oh." That was disappointing. Still, it was another option. "New plan." She rolled up her sleeping bag and tied it to her pack.

"What are you doing?"

"I'm going exploring." She groaned as she lifted her knapsack and put it on. The muscles in her shoulders and back were killing her.

"That's dangerous. No way of knowing what lies in that direction. You could end up falling into a pit or reaching a dead end."

She shrugged, even as his observations gave her the shivers. "You're right, but trying is better than dying. And it's a given if I stay here, since you won't help me."

He shuffled across the floor, moving faster than she'd thought possible, since he was hunched over. Not toward her. No, the big bastard was blocking the tunnel going inward.

"What are you doing?"

"Stopping you from doing something you'll regret."

"Regret?" Something inside her snapped. "I've got all kinds of regrets. I regret getting that grant from the Angel Foundation. I regret agreeing to meet with Mack. I regret coming into this godforsaken cave. I regret waking you. I regret you not helping me." Her voice got louder and louder until she was screaming at him. She stopped, chest heaving, heart racing.

"Are you done?"

Furious beyond caution, she grabbed a rock from the floor. Fittingly, it was one of the stones he had shed. She drew back her arm and flung it with all her might. It bounced harmlessly off his scales and right back at her, hitting her in the thigh.

"Fuck!" She fell to the floor and grabbed her leg. "See what you made me do?"

"Me? I'm trying to keep you safe."

"No, you're not. If you wanted me safe, you'd get me out of here. If you're not going to help me, then kill me. Anything is better than sitting here waiting to die."

"You'd think that." There was something in his tone—resignation, regret, a tinge of fear. Whatever. She had much bigger problems than worrying about some drakon's issues. He had options, could leave whenever he chose. She was stuck here, and all because of him.

She'd never given up, facing each challenge in her life as it arose from the time she was a kid, born into a horrible situation before being thrust into an orphanage and later foster care. Maybe there was something about her that was destined for tragedy. If so, she'd certainly found it.

Beyond tears, she shrugged out of her pack, lay down, and closed her eyes. Exhaustion tugged at her. She needed to eat and drink but couldn't work up any enthusiasm.

I'm done.

A spark inside her protested, but she squashed it. Quitting

went against her very nature. She'd fought to live from her first breath, but she was tired. Tired of always having to do everything on her own.

"Too bad you weren't a damn genie, then you'd owe me three wishes." She clamped her mouth shut. She wasn't taking to him.

Something nudged her. She squeezed her eyes shut, refusing to look. It nudged her again. "Stop that," she muttered. When it happened again, she turned, relented. One of those massive claws prodded her side. "Are you going to turn me into a human kabob?"

He pulled his arm back. Or was it a leg? Did drakons have arms or did they consider them all legs? Not important. She propped herself against her pack and wiggled around trying to get comfortable.

"I told you, I'm not going to hurt you."

"But you're not helping me and that is hurting me." She could debate with the best of them and talk rings around most. Maybe she could find a way to make him listen.

He huffed, a huge plume of smoke puffing out of his nostrils. She waved her hand in front of her, glad it wasn't fire. That had been impressive and downright scary.

"I have a life out there." She waved toward the tunnel blocked with rocks and debris. "Responsibilities. Penelope." She wouldn't lie and say she had anyone who'd miss her. Her colleagues thought she was on a year sabbatical. Maybe the people from the Angel Foundation might call—if they weren't somehow involved in this fiasco. All they wanted from her was a final report, which wasn't due for another twelve months. "And if I die here, Mack gets away with murder." As hard as it was to face, there wasn't anyone coming for her. All her bills were set up for automatic payment. With the grant money, it would be a year or more before anyone would even notice she was missing.

Talk about depressing.

Lucius stared at her, then turned his back and shuffled toward the cave entrance.

"Where are you going?"

"To get you out of here."

Chapter Four

It was stupid to feel hurt by her determination to leave. He was nothing to her but an obstacle to overcome, a creature to manipulate to her advantage. She, on the other hand, had irrevocably changed his life. He was awake in the world, something that should've been impossible.

Maybe it was fate or some dark magic that had brought her here. All he knew was the more time he spent with her, the more he didn't want to let her go. Raine was affecting his good sense. It was better if they parted ways. There was no peace for him here, not with memories of her permeating every inch of the place. He'd find another mountain somewhere and go back to sleep. They'd never see each other again.

Pain fisted his heart, squeezing it tight.

It wasn't an exaggeration to say the fate of the world was at stake. He was too unstable to be among humans, too volatile, too angry. There was no telling what he'd do if they attacked him.

Only he didn't feel that way around Raine. Amused, intrigued, and protective best described how she made him feel. He had to let her go. That could happen only if he helped her leave. Ignoring her plight or letting her die were no longer options.

His blood grew cold at the thought of her exploring the cave system on her own. It was a lie that he'd never explored it. He was an earth drakon. The first thing he'd done when he'd arrived here all those centuries ago was map out every crevice and corner of the tunnels. That's how he knew it was dangerous.

"You're really going to help?" He heard her scrambling up behind him, and then her hand pressed against his tail. The heat from her skin was slight, but it burned through him like a raging bonfire, warming his blood.

"Yes." It was a tight squeeze through the opening, but he'd fix that problem.

"Why now? Don't get me wrong, I'm happy to get out of the cave. It's a great one, as caves go, but I want to see the sky and breathe fresh air. Don't you miss that?"

"I was sleeping," he said. Time was different in the Deep Sleep. Sometimes he was almost aware of the world. Mostly there was nothing.

"Right. Sorry about that. Will you be able to get back to sleep? You broke your stone shell. Can you grow another?"

"It seems I'm done with sleep." Where he'd go, he had no idea, but that was a problem for later.

"Oh. That's my fault, isn't it?" Her shoulders drooped and then perked right back up. "If you think about it, it's really Mack's fault. If he hadn't blasted the entry shut, I would've looked at you and studied you while you were sleeping. You wouldn't have known a thing." The corners of her lips turned down. "That sounds kind of stalkerish, but it wouldn't have been that way. I didn't know you were real."

A throbbing began behind his eyes. Was he getting a headache or was it hunger? Probably the latter, but it was hard to tell. He studied the pile of rocks in front of him.

"There are a lot of rocks to be moved." She shifted her weight from one leg to the other.

"Come here."

Suspicion clouded her golden-brown eyes. "Why?"

"Do you want to get out of here or not?" Her sudden wariness baffled him. For someone who'd been in such a hurry, had been willing to risk the cave tunnels, it made no sense to waffle now.

"Yes."

"Then come here." He tapped one claw against the ground.

"There? That's really close. Why do you need me there?" Her fear was palpable. She closed her eyes and took a calming breath. "I'm sorry to doubt you. Do you call these arms or legs?" she asked as she walked around one, so she ended up between them.

"Call them whatever you want." He'd truly never thought about it.

"What do you call them?"

"Limbs."

"I like arms. You don't have paws. They're more like hands and fingers. You can move them, can't you?"

He flexed one before he thought, curling his claws toward his palm.

"There you go, they're hands." Her smile made him want to chuckle. She looked so pleased with herself.

He drew one of his arms closer, pulling her against his chest.

"What are you doing? That's awful close to your mouth. You remember I'm not very edible, right?" The slight teasing lilt to her voice caught him off guard. She bounced back and forth between fear and trust so fast it made his head spin.

"If I'm going to tunnel through the debris, I'll likely bring down the walls."

"Wait!" Before he could ask why, she scurried out from between his legs and ran back into the cavern. Not sure what the problem was now, he waited. Seconds later, she hurried back, tugging her pack on once again. "If we can't get back in after, I want my stuff." She planted her hand on top of his arm and vaulted over it, her butt skimming his scales. "I'm ready."

"You sure?"

"Do I detect sarcasm?"

Shaking his head at her banter, which was partly nerves, he urged her closer. "Stay under my jaw. That will give you protection. I'll keep you safe."

"I know you will." The solemn declaration penetrated his thick scales and made him want to stretch to his full size.

"Hold on." Moving slowly forward, he squeezed his body into the tunnel. Rock shattered, exploding upward, sending debris behind and in front of them.

"We're gonna die. We're gonna die." It was barely a whisper under her breath, but he heard it.

This was taking too long. He scooped her up and held her to his chest, careful not to hurt her with his sharp claws. With one mighty heave, he surged forward and burst out into the night. The wind brushed against him for the first time in far too long, the gentle caress as soft as a mother's kiss. The air was crisper than that inside the cave. He filled his lungs, enjoying the cold bite.

He opened his hand, and Raine tumbled to the ground at his feet, looking stunned but perfectly fine. Standing to his full height, he stretched his neck and extended his wings. A groan of satisfaction rumbled up from deep inside. Tilting back his head, he roared at the moon and stars. His tail thrashed, taking down the trees in its path. Every muscle in his body flexed. Strength surged through him. All around him, the wildlife grew quiet, acknowledging the apex predator in their midst.

"Holy crap, you're big." She shone her light on him, taking in the full breadth of his form. "You really are like something out of a legend." She rolled to her side and pushed to her feet. "Looks like Mack didn't stick around."

Mack, the man who'd lured her here, who'd trapped her in the cave, who was responsible for his waking. "I'm going to kill him."

Her jaw dropped and her eyes widened. "You can't do that."

"Why not?"

• • •

"Why not? What kind of a question is that? You can't go around randomly killing people." Everyone knew that. Although, as big as he was, who was going to stop him?

Curled up inside the cave he'd been impressive. Outside, with his massive wings extended, the rosy gold of his scales glinting in the beam of her flashlight, he truly was spectacular. And humongous. If a T-Rex happened along, it would take one look, turn tail, and run.

"Why not?" he repeated. He tilted his massive head to one side and peered at her like she was an interesting artifact, one he couldn't quite decide if he should keep or bury back in the dirt. His pale pink eyes gleamed. They should've been out of place with the rest of him, but somehow they fit. Or maybe she was getting used to them. "He was willing to kill you."

That stopped her cold for a second, but she shook her head. "It's against the law."

"Man's law."

"Woman's law too, buddy. No killing." Just the thought

of it was enough to make her queasy. Or maybe that was the lack of rest and proper food coupled with fear and more exercise than she'd had in months. The trees seemed to swirl around her, making her stomach sick. "I need to sit down." She plopped down on the hard, cold ground and lowered her head, taking slow deep breaths.

"What is wrong with you?" His voice sounded different, not quite as deep and guttural. Maybe it was the acoustics of the cave that had made it sound that way.

"I'm fine." She tilted her head back and screamed before scrambling away. A strange man was standing in front of her—a very naked and very huge one. Half his body, from neck to feet, was covered in swirling tattoos that were golden in color and outlined in the palest pink. She swallowed heavily as she looked down his broad chest, chiseled pecs, and washboard abs. The light in her hand wavered when it hit his groin. Holy shit, he was big, and half his shaft was tattooed. That had to have hurt when it was done. Since it wasn't polite to gawk, she skimmed the flashlight lower. His thighs were like tree trunks.

"Have you seen enough?"

She jerked the light back up, illuminating the random tattoos on the other side of his body. There were many, but nothing like the cohesive one on his left side. He was biker gang meets ancient god.

His jaw appeared to have been hewn from solid granite. Dark brown hair fell like silk to his wide shoulders. His cheekbones were high, his nose perfection, but it was the eyes that caught her. They were pink.

"Lucius?"

He gave a curt nod.

"How is this possible?" He'd been a huge dragon, or drakon, only moments before.

"I am the son of a dragon and human woman. Unlike my

sire, who had to work to hold a human form for any length of time, I can hold either with ease."

"You're gorgeous." The words spilled out before she could stop them. The corners of his mouth lifted, not quite a smile, but almost. Her heart went pitter-patter, her mouth was dry. A real smile would be lethal. She fought the urge to fan herself as heat washed over and through her.

Realizing she was sprawled on the ground—which seemed to happen a lot around him—she scrambled to her feet. It didn't help. He was still a giant in comparison, his sheer presence dominating the space without effort.

"You can shift." That was like something out of a science fiction book or a paranormal romance. Or a horror novel, a little voice whispered. She silenced it with a shake of her head.

Raine marched over to him and poked him in the chest. It was like hitting steel or stone—unmovable. At five ten, she was used to being eye to eye with most men. With him, she had to tilt her head back and look way up. He had to be about seven feet tall.

"Are you telling me you could have shifted at any time while we were trapped in the cave?"

"Yes." A muscle twitched in his jaw.

"Then why didn't you?"

"I didn't want to."

"Right, you were happy being a stone dragon. Excuse me, drakon." Ignoring the aches in her body and the growing headache throbbing in her temples, she oriented herself and found the path that had brought her here. It was time to leave. The flashlight, along with the stars, would be enough to guide her.

She wanted to go home, crawl into bed, pull the covers over her head, and forget any of this had ever happened. Maybe not Lucius, but everything else. As soon as she was back within cell range, she'd call the police and tell them about Mack. She'd leave Lucius out of it. They'd doubt her sanity if she started talking about drakons.

Her stomach clenched as she held out her hand. "Thank you for getting me out of there. I'm sorry you were caught in the middle of all this, whatever this is." Her hand wavered in the air a few seconds before she dropped it and rubbed it over her pant leg. "Right. I guess I'll be going." The thought of a more than four-hour trek made her want to curl up in a ball and cry.

She took the first step forward. "What will you do?" Curiosity wouldn't allow her to leave without asking. Not that he needed her or anything. He was a powerful shapeshifter.

He shrugged, seemingly unconcerned. Big and capable, he somehow seemed alone. It tugged at her heartstrings. She swung her pack down and untied her sleeping bag. "Here. You can wrap this around your waist, keep you from getting cold."

"I regulate my body temperature."

"Right." That made sense, as much as any of this did. Her ordinary, ordered life had been blown to smithereens. "But you might need it if you encounter people. A naked man strolling out of the woods is bound to attract attention."

"I'll shift and fly."

"Okay...wait, you can't do that. No flying."

"Why not?" Again, he seemed more curious than concerned.

"You don't think a drakon flying through the sky will attract attention?"

"It's remote here." He peered out into the dark woods. What did he see? How did he feel after so many years asleep?

"Um, how long have you slept?"

"What year is it?"

"Two thousand twenty-two."

"About three hundred years, give or take a few decades."

Now her head was spinning for an entirely different reason. She'd known he'd been locked in stone a long time, but it hadn't really registered until right now. "How old are you?"

The corners of his mouth twitched again. She held her breath, but he didn't smile. Probably better that way. "About four thousand years."

She staggered back a step before catching her balance. "The things you've seen." He'd lived through history while she'd only read about it. How young and silly she must appear to him.

"Much changes in the physical world, but people rarely do."

That was sad and cynical, even if it was correct. "A lot has happened while you've been sleeping." She waved at the sky. "There's radar that can track you if you fly. The military will call up fighter planes. God, you probably don't even know what that is. They're machines that can fly through the sky. They'll find you and shoot you down."

He scoffed. "They'll try, but I will crush them."

"What is it with you and killing?" Maybe it was his nature. Maybe she should shut her mouth and walk away, but she was responsible for him now, wasn't she? After all, unintentional or not, she was the one who'd woken him. "You need to come with me." Decision made, she held out the sleeping bag. "Wrap this around you."

"I'm not cold."

"Maybe not, but I don't need to see you in all your naked glory."

"Glory?" His lips twitched and his eyes danced with amusement. Good thing one of them was finding this funny.

Raine cleared her throat and plunged onward. "It's my fault you're awake. The least I can do is to help you get caught up on what's happened in the world." *And it will keep him with me longer.* She wasn't ready for their time together to end, and it wasn't only because he was a living, breathing mythical creature.

His eyes narrowed and his brows lowered. "I don't need help."

God save her from the male ego. "Maybe I need help." When his frown eased, she carried on, warming to the idea. "Mack might be out there, and who knows what else. Maybe a bear." The last thing she wanted was to run into anyone—human or animal.

"I have it on good authority that you're not good eating."

The teasing caught her off guard. Her toes curled in her boots and pleasure filled her, the warmth from it driving out the chill of the night air. "I'm really not, but a bear might not stop to listen to reason like you did." She ignored his soft snort. "It's a long walk back to my car."

"Car?"

"It's a vehicle, propelled by an engine. Mankind has made gigantic leaps forward in the past hundred and fifty years or so. We've visited the moon, sent probes into deep space, explored the oceans, and flown in the skies."

His frown was back with a vengeance.

How could she make him understand? "You try to fly out of here, they'll see you, and they'll never stop looking for you." As much as it pained her, she added, "And trying to kill you."

"Mankind never changes." The hard determination in his voice sent a shiver down her spine. Best if mankind never discovered his presence. It might not survive. This was not a man who backed down from a fight. Who knew what skills and natural weapons he possessed beyond his huge size and the fire he'd released with ease? She had the sense that was only the tip of the iceberg.

"But not everyone is like that. Some people are good and kind." She tried to believe that, even though some days it wasn't easy.

"I know." He ran his fingers down the curve of her cheek. The pads were slightly rough but his touch softer than a feather.

She swallowed heavily. "Are there any more like you out there—drakons? Maybe we could find one that might help you."

"No." The finality hit with a heavy thud. "Even among my own kind, I am considered a monster."

Chapter Five

Lucius would never admit it aloud, but all the sights and sounds were overwhelming after so many years encased in stone. It was as though he could hear the very earth speak, the insects wiggling beneath the soil, the birds nested in the trees. The stars in the sky were more brilliant, the craters of the moon visible to his naked eyes. Every sense he possessed was sharper, more powerful than it had been before he'd slept.

The loamy scent of dirt mixed with tangy pines, sweeter deciduous trees, and the freshness of the first buds of spring. The air was tainted with the faint smell of a man. He had it now and would recognize it if their paths ever crossed, but above it all was the unique scent of Raine. It was slightly spicy and sweet, below the sweat and tang of blood.

"You're no monster. Maybe a bit snarly and stubborn. And, okay, you talk about killing, more than is probably healthy. But if you were a monster, you'd have let me die."

"I almost did." He was no hero. If she saw him that way, she was doomed to disappointment.

"Almost doesn't count. When it came down to it, you did

the right thing."

He almost hadn't, and that would haunt him. His personal code of right and wrong had always guided him, kept him from straying over the line. But the line had become blurred, almost nonexistent in the years leading up to him disappearing into the cave. He'd been teetering on the edge, perilously close to becoming something he never wanted to be. *Monster.* The word echoed through the centuries.

"Are you okay?" A soft touch on his arm yanked him back to the present. Worry clouded her pretty eyes. He cursed when he noticed she was biting her bottom lip. It was wet and full and begged to be kissed. She pulled back when he swore. "I'm sorry."

He shook his head and rubbed the back of his neck. "It's nothing you did. It's me." It was always him.

Her tentative smile settled him. "Don't worry about it. Wrap the sleeping bag around you and we'll start walking. You can always fly away if you want to. Not like I can stop you."

Her kindness warmed the cold places in his soul. She had no idea how unusual her fearlessness was, or how attractive. She thought she was being clever, but he recognized her game—couching her request to make it seem as though he was the one helping her when her intention was the opposite.

Maybe we can help each other.

When was the last time anyone extended a hand of help or friendship? The dark-haired man with weapons tattooed on his body flashed into his mind once again, the memory of who he was just out of reach.

He unzipped the sleeping bag and wrapped it around his waist. It fell almost to his knees. He'd rather go naked, but if it would make her happy, he'd put up with looking ridiculous.

The urgency to leave, to find another place to sleep, was lessening the more time he spent with her. An alarm bell sounded in the back of his brain, but he ignored it. After saving her life, it would be wrong to not make sure she was safe. He owed her that much. If his logic was flawed, too damn bad.

"Come on." She held her hand out to him. This time he took it. Dirt was embedded beneath her nails. The bandages she'd put on her blisters and cuts were stained and torn, a testament to her determination.

He brought her hand to his mouth and pressed his lips against her palm. Her fingers jerked but she didn't pull away. A rosy hue spread over her cheeks, a big improvement over her earlier paleness.

With her free hand, she pulled a thin black rectangular box from her pocket.

"What's that?" It lit up when she pressed a button.

"It's a cell phone. It enables me to talk to anyone around the world." She typed in a number and then pressed another button. "And this shows me where I am in relation to my car so I can find my way out."

"All that in one tiny box?" Mankind *had* made huge advances.

"Like I said, the world is much different than it was three hundred years ago, but don't worry, I'll help you get acclimated."

An unaccountable hunger rose within him, and it wasn't for food. His cock stirred to life. A low growl vibrated through him. He licked his lips, wondering what she'd taste like. Sweet or spicy or a combination? Heat rolled over him, pouring off his skin and singeing the ground beneath his feet.

"You doing okay? You made some sort of growly sound."

"I'm fine."

She's dangerous. As much as he was drawn to her and as innocent as she seemed, he couldn't forget she'd done the impossible—awakened him and convinced him to leave the cave. He was a fierce drakon, once feared by the mightiest nations of the world, yet he was unable to walk away. A sliver of concern dimmed some of his arousal. It would be smarter to leave, but there were questions that needed answering. And, like it or not, Raine was at the center of it all.

• • •

What I wouldn't give for a cup of coffee.

Her boots now weighed fifty pounds each, and that was no exaggeration. Okay, maybe a slight one, but it could be forgiven. Every step took more effort than the last. Fatigue pressed down on her. The stump rose out of nowhere, catching her toe and sending her off balance. Too tired to correct and regain her balance, she began to fall.

Strong hands caught her. "I've got you." Lucius scooped her up like she weighed nothing. From this position, her face was right next to a wide swath of bare, warm, muscled flesh. She wanted to bury it against his broad chest and make yummy noises.

The rumble that went through him vibrated into her in the most delicious way, making her skin tingle. *He's a drakon and you're a human. Don't take advantage of him.* Some would scoff the idea was even possible. He was stronger and bigger, but he'd been asleep a long time, was disoriented after waking after so long, and only beginning to find his way.

"Thanks for the save." She patted his pectoral muscle, but come on, how could she resist? It was right there tempting her. It was as sleek and hard as it looked. "You can put me down."

"No." His jaw clenched and his lips firmed. His very kissable lips. *Don't notice that. Look away.*

"Ah, why not?" She pressed a hand against his chest, letting his warmth sink into her.

"I will carry you."

It was one thing to be independent, quite another to be stupid. "Put me down when you get tired."

The heat from his big body surrounded her and made her feel safe, a totally foreign experience. The temptation to make it into more than it was flitted through her nimble brain.

It was a pipedream, but a pleasant one. It was also pure avoidance on her part. Lucius was much more fascinating than thinking about the fact that someone had tried to kill her. Mack had led her to the cave for a reason. If he'd wanted her dead, he could've accomplished that anywhere, anytime. No matter how she looked at it, Lucius was at the center of this. Had Mack known she'd somehow be able to wake the drakon? Did he even know what Lucius was? If so, how?

Trying to figure it out only gave her a headache and made her nauseous. As soon as they were out of here, she'd pull on her big girl panties and deal with the mess her life had become.

"You're thinking loudly." His voice was different in his human form. Still deep, but not the baritone of his drakon.

"Sorry. I'm trying to process everything." Talk about an understatement. Her mind was a whirlwind of activity.

He grunted again and kept walking. His even gait, the slow rise and fall of his chest, relaxed her. *I'll close my eyes for a second. No more than that…*

She jolted when a crow cawed. The sky was much lighter than it had been. "Did I fall asleep? Why didn't you wake me?" Twisting her head from side to side, she tried to get her bearings. "You might be off course." She fumbled for her phone.

"I am going in the right direction."

She barely kept from rolling her eyes. It was official. Didn't matter the species, men wouldn't stop to ask for directions. "How do you know?" Smooth, hard skin brushed against her hand when she reached into her pocket. It took her two tries to punch in her password. The GPS came to life. She checked the reading and frowned. "You *are* going in the right direction. How is that possible?"

"I'm following my nose. In that direction, I detect things that aren't natural to the forest."

"That's some nose you've got. Oh God, put me down." She patted his chest. "Now," she added more firmly.

He stopped and lowered her legs, making sure she was steady before taking a step back. "Do you feel ill?"

"No, but I stink."

He tilted his head to one side, the pink of his eyes seeming almost lighter than they had been, glowing around the darker pupils. His nostrils flared. "I can smell sweat and the cave."

"Earth, open up and swallow me now," she muttered. On her most-embarrassing-moments scale, this one hit the top five.

"You also smell sweet and spicy." His voice dropped an octave, and he crowded against her.

"Wait. What?"

His fingers glided over her cheek. "So soft." His thumb grazed her bottom lip, sending shivers of delight rippling through her. "So alluring." Her nipples tingled and perked up, standing at attention.

Alluring? Her? "Are you sure you're not suffering from some post waking-up-from-a-long-nap thing?"

The corners of his mouth twitched. "My senses are more alive than ever."

Was that a good thing or a bad thing? It no longer mattered when he lowered his head, his breath teasing her mouth just before his lips touched hers, soft and warm and leaving her wanting more.

Fingers curling against his chest, she went up on her toes to deepen the contact. Oh, he tasted good. Like chocolate and hot male—pure heaven. When she parted her lips on a groan, he swept inside, teasing her tongue with his.

This is the best kiss ever. No, it's wrong. He thinks he's recovered from his ordeal, but he's not. I'm taking advantage of him. I'll stop. Any second now.

The world ceased to exist. The forest cocooned them. Other than his lips on hers, Lucius wasn't touching her, wasn't doing anything that might overwhelm or cause her fear. The kiss was gentle, showing great restraint, but that made it even more poignant. She ran her tongue over his full bottom lip, eliciting another of those deep groans she was coming to love.

A sound intruded her erotic bubble. She blinked and found herself staring at Lucius's broad back. The muscles in his shoulders were bunched, his head cocked to one side. Then she heard it again. "That's an engine."

His shoulders were stiff, his stony face back in place. Gone was the gentle man who'd carried her and kissed her. This man was scary. No, not a man, a male, a drakon.

Maybe he regretted kissing her. Not that it mattered. It was just a kiss. And a tsunami was just a tiny wave. Her entire body was still vibrating.

"My car is over there. Stay here while I make sure no one else is around." The last thing they needed was for someone to see and possibly record them. And it would give her a few minutes to cool down from the super-hot kiss. Her job was to help Lucius, not seduce him. If she could remember that, she'd be fine.

Chapter Six

Hours later, Lucius wheeled the vehicle into her driveway. It pained her to admit, but he was a damn good driver. A fast learner, too. Quick and competent, with sharp reflexes.

"Remind me again how you talked me into letting you get in the driver's seat?" She still wasn't quite certain how it had happened. After watching her for about an hour, he'd given her a smile that had practically blinded her. His eyes had glinted with undeniable challenge, and before she knew it, she'd stopped to switch places.

"You didn't use some drakon mind control on me, did you?" That was impossible, right?

He put the car in park and turned the key to silence the engine. "Why would I do that when reason works so well?"

"That's not an answer."

Ignoring her, Lucius shoved the door open and climbed out, stretching his arms toward the sky. The sleeping bag slipped low and then slithered down his lower half in slow motion.

Raine almost swallowed her tongue as his entire body

was put on display under the morning sun. The tattoos covering his left side seemed to glow, the gold taking on an even rosier tone. There was no pattern she could discern, but it was a series of swirls that interconnected from his neck to his ankle. The muscles in his back and shoulders bunched and flexed. The cheeks of his ass were beefy and full, his legs strong enough to withstand a hurricane.

When he turned, their eyes met. The wind playfully teased the ends of his brown hair, the silky strands sliding across his face. The pink of his eyes deepened. All the moisture in her mouth dried up, making it impossible to swallow.

She'd seen him naked, but somehow it was like seeing him anew. And he was aroused. No hiding his erection, which seemed even bigger in the light of day.

She blinked, breaking the spell. *Don't just sit here like some lovestruck idiot.* Order given, she opened her door and got out, retrieving her backpack to give him time to reposition the sleeping bag. When she deemed enough had passed, she straightened.

He was still naked.

"Put that back on." She pointed to the crumpled fabric lying on the cold ground.

"Why? This is natural."

"Maybe for you. It makes me uncomfortable." In more ways than one. "Not all of us look that good naked," she muttered.

"I heard that." His grin was fleeting, but she didn't mind if her objection amused him, since he did as she asked. When he was suitably covered, she grabbed her keys and closed the car door.

"Follow me." Her house was more than big enough for her but seemed to shrink when he entered. After dumping her gear on the floor just inside the door, she punched in the code to deactivate the security system before it alerted.

"Penelope? Come here, baby." Her pet always raced to greet her when she got home, sometimes acting more like a dog than a cat. There was no padding of feet, no happy *meow*. "Penelope?"

"She's in there." Lucius pointed toward the bedroom. "She senses me."

Raine hurried into the room, dropped to her knees, and looked under the bed. Two green eyes stared back at her. "Come here, girl." She held out her hand, letting the cat sniff it. "It's safe."

"That's a perfect picture." Lucius leaned against the doorjamb with his arms crossed, his massive biceps on display. He wasn't looking at her face but her behind, which was up in the air. She sat back on her heels and scowled.

"Stop staring at my butt."

"Why? It's a beautiful one."

Pleasure at the compliment warmed her, but she ruthlessly shoved it aside. "You don't deny it?"

"Why would I? It's the truth."

The man was as blunt as a wrecking ball. He strolled into her room, went to her dresser, and began to pick up everything on it, studying it before setting it back in place.

"Stop that."

He frowned and set a dragon statue back in place and resumed his post by the door. "You have eclectic tastes."

That was a polite way of putting it. Her bedroom wall was covered in prints of mythical creatures—fairies, dragons, werewolves, and even a phoenix. Sculptures littered her dresser and the shelf in the corner, along with chunks of amethyst, rose quartz, and other crystals. It didn't exactly scream an adult lived here. It was more adolescent fantasy nerd.

"I'm hungry." She strode toward the entry, but he didn't move. She had to turn sideways to sidle past him, sucking in a breath when their bodies slid against each other. Heat radiated from him, along with a sexual allure that was getting harder to deny.

"I'm hungry, too." His voice had deepened again, sounding more like it did when he was in dragon form. She didn't think he was talking about food.

"Look, I'm not used to being attracted to a guy I just met, especially not one who can turn into a huge dragon. Or is it drakon?" She dug her thumb into her forehead and rubbed, trying to ease the throbbing. "This entire situation is fucked up. It's not smart to bring sex into the mix. Danger and adrenaline with proximity is heightening our awareness of each other. That and the fact you haven't had sex in…God, three hundred years. You're hot and all, but I don't do one-night stands. It's all so confusing."

"It doesn't have to be."

"It really does. A couple of weeks ago, I lived a boring life. I taught classes at the university, paid my bills, bought groceries, did laundry, and had the occasional coffee with a colleague from work. Now someone's tried to kill me and I can't even call the cops because I have a drakon in my home." The laugh that escaped her lips was more than a little hysterical. "And on top of that I'm attracted to you. So yeah, it really is confusing."

She retreated to the kitchen and yanked open the refrigerator. The cold air was welcome. "I have eggs and bread." She opened the freezer. "Bacon, but it's frozen."

"Would you like me to thaw it for you?" His breath wafted over her nape, making her jump. Her head smacked against the freezer door.

"Stop sneaking up on me." She slammed the door shut and tossed the bacon into the sink.

"To answer your earlier question, I'm a drakon. I have two forms—human and dragon." Before she realized what he was about, he leaned over the sink and inhaled deeply.

"No fire!" Her homeowner's insurance wouldn't cover a blaze by a drakon.

But no flames erupted from his mouth. Only a warm blast that melted the ice crystals. He did it a second time before straightening. "That should do it."

Her hand shook as she lifted the package from the sink. Sure enough, it was perfectly thawed. "Thank you."

"No problem. Do you have a place I can clean up?"

"Of course." After taking Lucius to the main bathroom and showing him how to work the shower and toilet, she went to her bedroom and flopped onto the bed, not caring how much dirt she transferred to the fluffy green comforter that covered it.

"Meow." Penelope poked her sleek head out from beneath the bed.

"It's safe. I think." Burying her face in her hands, she rubbed her eyes. "I need to get cleaned up and cook breakfast or lunch or whatever meal it is." Everything was out of whack, including her. "Then I need to figure out what to do about this mess I'm in."

Penelope jumped onto the mattress beside her and bumped her arm with her head. "Did you miss me?" She gathered the cat into her arms and rubbed her nose over her soft fur. "I was so scared." The shaking started in her feet and worked its way up until her entire body was trembling.

Someone had really tried to kill her.

The sound of the shower reminded her she needed to get cleaned up. Pushing herself upright took Herculean effort. She gathered some clean clothes, planning on tossing out what she wore, and shut herself into the small ensuite bathroom. It didn't have a tub, only a shower, but that was just as well. As tired as she was, she'd likely fall asleep and drown.

Cranking the water on as hot as she could bear, she

stepped beneath the spray and let it fall over her. The first tear took her by surprise, but there was no stopping the flood once it started. A big sob shook her entire being. Leaning her hands against the tiled wall, she lowered her head and watched the dirty water swirl down the drain as the tears continued to fall.

. . .

She was crying.

Lucius stood outside her bedroom door, his acute hearing picking up the sobs beneath the spray of the water. He'd taken a step toward her before he stopped and clenched his hands at his sides.

He needed to maintain an emotional distance. Yes, Raine had been trapped in the cave with him. That kind of fear couldn't be faked. Her life had been in danger, but that didn't mean she hadn't agreed to the plan beforehand. Hell, maybe she was the mastermind behind it all. After all, she'd been away from the explosion when it happened. Maybe Mack had been following her instructions.

He ignored the pained howl of his dragon and locked the creature down tight when scales rippled over his arms. While all his senses screamed she was being honest, he couldn't discount the possibility the Deep Sleep might be affecting them in the same way they were his memories. The sexual attraction was also muddying the waters, making it difficult to be rational. But he wasn't an idiot. In the past, beautiful women had used subterfuge and lied to get close to him.

If she was truly innocent, she wouldn't be safe until he uncovered who was behind this and disposed of them. Those who hunted his kind were relentless.

It should have been impossible to wake him.

No human had that kind of power over a drakon, not

unless some sort of magic was involved. And, despite what most people believed, magic, real magic existed. Mages were few, but they were dedicated. There were those who pursued knowledge and others who sought power, and they would stop at nothing to get it.

There'd been rumors of dark magic being used to capture drakons. He was right to be wary. Anyone who could catch and hold one of his kind was a formidable enemy. The key to survival was knowledge. Was Raine linked to a mage or was she nothing more than a tool to be wielded. If so, why her? It always came back to her.

Mine!

The possessiveness of his dragon was worrisome. It was time to use his brain rather than allowing only instinct to rule him. What was it about Raine that made her special?

His gaze fell upon the artwork and gemstones that filled her space. He was drawn toward the fist-size chunk of rose quartz. Picking it up, he closed his eyes and absorbed the comfort it radiated. The entire world was alive, from the very rocks to the rivers and plants. Mankind rarely thought beyond itself, destroying, and taking, and exploiting. As an earth drakon, he was sensitive to the vibration of every rock and mineral.

He set the rock back and left the room, rubbing his hand over his heart. Even if she was complicit in the plot against him, he couldn't hurt her. Talk about a sobering thought. She was as effective a weapon against him as had ever been created.

A low hissing sound greeting him when he entered the kitchen. A slender gray cat arched her back and fluffed her fur. "You must be Penelope." He crouched and held out his hand. After staring at him for a long minute, she cautiously crept forward and rubbed against his fingers. A low purr vibrated from within when he scratched her head.

Straightening, he secured the towel covering his lower half. He didn't mind being naked—after hundreds of years of being cast in stone, his skin was sensitive—but, since it made Raine uncomfortable, he'd adjust.

This part of her house, along with what had to be her main living space, was more neutral. There was no hint of the woman who lived and breathed in the bedroom. Here, everything was beige and brown with green and orange accent pieces. It was comfortable but lacked the vibrancy of her other space.

Why did she hide part of herself? What was she hiding from him?

It might take time, but he'd eventually uncover all her secrets. In the meantime, he'd start preparing food. He'd learned to drive easily enough. How hard could making a meal be using modern conveniences? He could hunt and cook over an open fire with the best of them. He could handle this.

Ten minutes later, he stared at the mess on the counter. There was as much eggshell as egg in the bowl, and his big fingers were making it difficult to pick out the pieces.

"What are you doing?"

He'd heard her coming, even though she'd kept her footsteps light. "Cooking, or trying to." A whiff of vanilla preceded her. He wanted to bury his face against her shoulder and lick her skin to see if she tasted as good as she smelled.

"So I see." Head bent, she peered into the bowl. "Having a little trouble?" It was difficult to concentrate on what she was saying. Her short brown hair wasn't one uniform color but had deeper and lighter strands mixed within. The pants she wore were light blue and clung to her hips and thighs. The long-sleeved white top looked soft and hugged her breasts like a second skin. His fingers itched to stroke her.

Her feet were bare, her toenails painted a delicate pink.

Why was that so appealing?

"Lucius?" A shudder ran through him at the sound of his name on her lips. The front of his towel began to tent. He turned aside and stared out the window, hoping she wouldn't notice.

"My fingers are too large and rough for something so delicate." He held them out, studying them. They were more useful for manual labor than breaking open eggs without causing a mess or touching skin as delicate as Raine's. They were hands that had killed. Scowling, he flexed his fingers.

"It's not a big deal." She grabbed a large piece of shell and tossed it aside. "It's easy enough to fix." Her smile was soft and warm, but her eyes were red with dark circles beneath them, hinting at her exhaustion and earlier tears. "Thanks for helping."

He straightened before he realized what he was doing, her small praise making him feel as though he'd accomplished something wonderful instead of making a muck of it.

Distance, he reminded himself. He needed to leash his softer emotions and not let them blind him to the possible reality. To give himself time to rein in the uncomfortable emotions bombarding him, he walked to her small table. It had four chairs, none of which looked as though they were sturdy enough to hold his weight. Curious to know everything there was about her, he wandered into the living area. A large, thin rectangle stood on a wooden stand. "What is this?"

"Television. I can watch all sorts of entertainment and news on it." She left the kitchen and joined him, picking up a slender object from a low table. "This turns it on." With a click, a picture appeared on the screen.

"Miraculous." There'd been nothing like this when he'd gone to sleep.

"You press this button to change channels." He took the device when she handed it to him. "This is called a remote control. Or just a remote." He began to press the button, entranced, as pictures popped up. "I'll be in the kitchen." He nodded and kept going, stopping now and again.

It seemed only seconds had passed when she called out to him. "Come and eat." He set the remote down and joined her. The table was filled with a large bowl of eggs, a plate of bacon, and a stack of toasted bread.

"I should have helped."

She waved him to the chair across from hers. "It's hard to tear a man away from television once he gets the remote."

"I don't understand. I had no trouble releasing the device." He lowered himself gingerly into the chair. It groaned beneath his weight but held.

"Forget it. Bad joke." She pushed the bowl toward him. "Help yourself."

There was so much he didn't comprehend and needed to learn. What was on the table was likely a vast amount of food for her. For him, it was a barely a light snack. His stomach growled.

"You first." He would not take food before her. It pleased him to watch her fill her plate. The only thing that would make it more satisfying was if he'd provided it for her.

Fuck, he had to squash those kinds of thoughts before they took a deeper hold. It wasn't safe for either of them. "Is there a library nearby?" The faster he acclimated, the better off he'd be.

"Even better, the internet." She shoveled in a forkful of eggs and chewed. "I'll get my laptop, my computer, after we eat and get you set up. All the knowledge in the world is available at your fingertips."

"Another joke?" What she was saying wasn't possible, was it?

"No." She set her fork down and reached across the table, resting her hand on his. "It's true. It's hard to explain. Finish eating and I'll show you." He had to resist grabbing her hand when she removed it.

Gripping his utensil tighter, he made quick work of what remained in the serving dishes. His stomach was still empty when he was done.

"You were really hungry. Not surprising considering how long it's been since you ate. I'll have to go grocery shopping." She frowned and bit her bottom lip.

"What's wrong?" In a short time, he'd come to learn her emotional cues. Something was bothering her.

"It's silly." Pushing back her chair, she stood and began to gather the dishes. He stood and stopped her, taking both her hands in his. Touching her was necessary. Humans were a tactile species. It would encourage her to trust him, to let her guard down around him. It had nothing to do with how much he enjoyed it.

"If it's upsetting you, it's not nothing." His actions and words weren't duplicitous, but smart. If she had a part in this, he was protecting himself. If she didn't, no harm done.

"I was momentarily nervous about going out alone."

Every cell in his body rebelled. "You're not going out alone." He couldn't protect her if he wasn't with her. On the flipside, she could contact potential enemies if he wasn't around. Staying together was the only option.

Her eyebrows raised and her mouth firmed. "You're not going anywhere until you get clothes."

A low growl rumbled up from inside him. He didn't understand this world, but he would. Then he'd conquer a small part of it for himself.

"You know, that's a good way to show you how a computer works." She pulled on her arms until he released her. "Let me get my laptop."

Penelope was perched on a multilevel stand that stood in front of a window, staring at him, radiating distrust. He grabbed the stack of dishes and carried them to the sink.

"Thanks," Raine said as she returned with a flat rectangle. The world seemed to consist of a lot of flat rectangles—cell phone, television, remote control, and now this laptop.

She placed it on the table and opened the lid. When she pressed a button, the screen lit up. He stood behind her and studied the device. "This is like the television, but it's more interactive. See, you need new clothes." Her fingers flew over buttons with letters on them. "I typed what I was looking for here in this search bar. Press this button, and here we go." A listing of places to get men's clothing appeared. The uniform lettering made it easier for him to read and understand.

The lesson continued, and by the end she'd ordered him clothing with something called overnight shipping. The package would arrive tomorrow. It was miraculous.

Raine yawned. "Here, why don't you give it a try?" She pushed the laptop over in front of him. She'd pulled up a page that explained how computers worked. "You can press here to watch the video. It will give you a better understanding of how it works.

"When you're done, I need to dig into Mack's life. I did a basic search before I met him—social media and the like—to make sure it was safe to meet him. Obviously, there's more to him than I uncovered. I need to go deeper. The good news is he probably thinks I'm dead or at least dying. That buys us some time. If he decides to go back to check, he'll see the hole where you busted us out."

"You should rest." The dark circles beneath her eyes bothered him.

She shook her head, her mouth taking on a stubborn line. "Someone used me, was willing to sacrifice me. I can't afford to rest. The clock is ticking."

"You said it yourself. You're safe enough for now." He held up his hand when her chin went up. "You're exhausted.

You'll work better after you've slept." He played his ace in the hole. "No one can sneak up on us without me knowing." While she slept, he'd watch over her and use this computer to catch up with the rest of the world.

She stifled another yawn and rubbed her eyes. "Maybe you're right. I'm barely coherent. I'll catch a few hours. You sure you'll be okay?"

"I'll be fine."

"And you'll wake me if anyone comes?"

"I promise." To expedite matters, he helped her out of her chair and walked her to her bedroom door. In a perfect world, he'd lift her into his arms, carry her off to bed, and make love to her for hours before they finally slept.

Distance, he reminded himself. It was the smarter option but getting harder to do. Every instinct demanded he take care of her, put her needs before his. To soothe his restless dragon, he leaned down and kissed the top of her head, inhaling the vanilla scent of whatever she'd used to cleanse her hair. The beast rumbled with contentment. "Rest."

"What about you? You won't turn to stone or anything, will you?"

He heard the thread of worry. "No." At least he didn't think he would. Was that even possible? He assumed once he was awake, that was it. What if it wasn't? The food he'd eaten churned in his belly and sweat beaded on his skin. He'd be at the mercy of whoever had set this whole scenario in motion.

It would also leave Raine vulnerable. Even if she'd been an active participant in his return, mages had a reputation for tying off loose ends. If he slept, she was likely as good as dead.

"You'll be here when I wake?" She nibbled on her bottom lip. Seemed she was as unsure about him as he was about her. There were many motives—worry about her own safety, worry she'd lose him before her partners arrived, or possibly because she'd miss him. Best not to assign one particular one just yet.

"I'll be here." Giving her privacy, he returned to the table, pulled the computer in front of him, and got to work.

Chapter Seven

It was dark outside when Lucius lowered the lid of the laptop. So much knowledge and now it was his. Unlike humans, he read and learned at a rapid rate, absorbing centuries of innovation and history in a matter of hours.

He could walk out the door and not only survive but thrive. Drakons were collectors at heart—gold, jewels, art, money, property—whatever took their fancy. As an earth drakon, his affinity was with gemstones and minerals. Before he'd slept, he'd hidden his wealth deep within the bowels of the earth, in places only another drakon could reach. It would take him little time to reestablish himself. Give him another day or two and he'd understand the intricacies of the worldwide financial institutions and how best to manipulate them for his own needs.

His gaze flicked to the short hallway that led to Raine's bedroom and back to the computer. Every muscle in his body clenched. Go or stay? He was perched on a razor's edge. While many of his memories had returned, many remained beyond his grasp. He sensed they were important but trying to force them only made them retreat deeper into the recesses of his mind. No matter, they'd surface in time. He didn't need to access them to know he wasn't the type to allow anyone to get too close. It wasn't in his nature.

Distrustful. Cautious. Cynical. Those words could easily be applied to him with accuracy. He'd chosen the Deep Sleep because he was done with the world—the greed and fear and never-ending wars. Done with mankind's need to control or exploit or destroy anything or anyone different.

Being friends with me just shows what good taste you have. The smooth, cultured voice slid into his head. Lucius searched his memories for a face to put with it. A male with blond hair, brown eyes, olive-toned skin, and fangs popped into his head. Fangs? He was friends with a bloodsucker?

He shook his head. Not likely. Vampires couldn't be trusted.

The room began to close in around him. A vicious tug-of-war was being played with his soul. Pain radiated through his skull. Gripping his head, he gritted his teeth. Go or stay. He had to make a choice.

If he left now, he could bury himself so deep in the Earth's core no one, not even a mage, could reach him. But not even a mage should have been able to wake him from the Deep Sleep. And none had. It had been all Raine. Leaving would mean he'd never see her again. His dragon roared. Scales rippled over his skin. His tattoos pulsed. He clamped down on the beast. If he shifted inside, he'd destroy her home and possibly harm her.

Immediately, the creature inside him retreated. Lucius's lungs worked like a bellows as he sucked in air. *I can't leave her.* The realization struck him with the force of a meteor. Was some spell chaining him to her or was it the will of his dragon, the attraction that grew the longer he was with her? She brought light to the darkness inside him.

If she betrayed him—his heart wrenched at the idea. He clenched his jaw to keep from roaring his rage.

I need to leave. Now. Before it's too late.

A low moan had his head snapping around. He was on his feet and striding toward her before he'd made the conscious decision to do so. Raine was tucked under the covers, her head moving restlessly. Another small cry escaped her. For better or worse, he'd made his choice.

Instinct had him stretching out beside her, cramming his large body onto the small bed. The mattress dipped with his added weight, causing her to roll toward him. She snuggled her face into his shoulder and sighed, resting one hand on his chest. The anguish plaguing him receded under her gentle touch.

He ran the backs of his knuckles over her cheek. So frail, so delicate. Yet, she'd tried to dig her way out of the cave. He lifted her hand and kissed the small nicks and healing cuts.

This is where I'm meant to be.

The dragon side of him was more certain than the human part. Fate and destiny weren't things he believed in, but if he did, he'd say Raine Carson was made for him.

"You're thinking too loud." Her eyes fluttered open, all sleepy and warm.

"I didn't mean to wake you." He brushed his hand over her tousled hair, which was even shorter than his, yet somehow suited her.

"What time is it?" She yawned and rubbed her face against his arm, much like the cat had earlier.

"Not time for you to get up yet." The sun would be rising in a few hours. She hadn't wanted to sleep this long, but she needed the rest. And he'd needed the time and space to absorb all the information he required.

She made a sound of agreement and settled back down. The house gave a few creaks and groans, but the night was otherwise quiet. There was nothing keeping him here, no tethers holding him.

As if to emphasize that fact, she rolled over, giving him her back. She snuggled the covers tighter around her before going still again. He turned onto his side and hooked an arm around her. It put her back to his front, their heads sharing the same pillow.

There was no need to decide anything tonight. If there was one thing he had plenty of, it was time. Closing his eyes, he allowed himself to drop into a deep, healing sleep.

The dreams came first. Faces and places bombarded him faster than he could process. It was only when they slowed that he understood they weren't dreams but memories. As though some barrier had been lifted, his entire history slammed into his awareness. That, coupled with all the knowledge he'd absorbed earlier, threatened to overwhelm him. He clenched his jaw, riding out the pain. His dragon roared inside him, wanting to break free.

"Wake up." Raine's voice was faint, as though she was far away. "You promised me you wouldn't turn into a hunk of stone. Don't you dare shift in my bedroom."

Something or someone lightly tapped his face. "Your eyes are open and they're glowing like pink spotlights."

A drakon turned to stone only during the Deep Sleep. It was supposed to be permanent and wasn't a decision to be made lightly. For three hundred years, he'd embraced the dark silence. It would be so easy to give in. There was peace there.

"Don't do this." He barely heard her. She was slipping away from him. Was whatever spell that woke him fading or was the Deep Sleep calling him back? Could he fight it or was it inevitable?

I'm losing her.

Blinding pain coursed through him as his very lifeblood

began to solidify. His muscles hardened, his limbs refusing to move. Fear gripped his heart, not for himself, but for her.

Her face filled his fading vision. Her voice sang in his ears. He wasn't ready to leave her. Not yet. She needed him. And God help him, he just might need her.

"Lucius!"

An onslaught of primal need ignited within him. Nothing and no one was keeping him from her. With a mighty roar, he lurched upright, almost blinded by the internal fire threatening to consume him. Raine fell back onto the mattress and rolled away. Unlimited power exploded in his every cell.

If I lose control, she'll die.

Not willing to sacrifice her, he bore down, grinding his teeth, absorbing the pain that threatened to tear him apart. "Run!" The word was ripped from his throat.

She scrambled off the bed, but instead of obeying his command, she hovered beside him. "What's happening? What can I do?"

How had he ever thought her fragile? Covered only in a long shirt that fell around her thighs, her legs bare, she stood ready to fight like some avenging angel.

A shaft of pain almost split his skull in half. He knew an angel, a fallen one. And a vampire. And myriad other paranormal creatures. Their names and faces were as familiar as his own.

Sweat coated his body, the fire of his dragon crackling just beneath. His lungs heaved, unable to draw enough oxygen. His skin began to split in places, beams of light shining through. There was too much power for his body to contain. His blood pumped through his veins, healing him as fast as it could. It was a toss-up as to which would be the victor.

"Oh my God. Oh my God."

The muscles and tendons in his neck protested any

movement, but he forced them into submission and turned toward Raine. Shock and horror filled her eyes. Her mouth hung open but was partially covered with her hand. The stench of fear rolled off her.

If he didn't control what was happening, it might actually kill him. It *would* destroy her, obliterating her body so there was nothing left of her or her home.

Instead of fighting, he embraced this new energy, allowing it to flow in and around him, reforming his inner organs, strengthening his blood, making his human form and dragon stronger. It wasn't unlike the first time he'd shifted when a young male. He'd thought he'd die then, too. It wasn't about conquering but acknowledgment and integration.

The Deep Sleep had condensed what already existed inside him, multiplying and expanding it. It was his to control and use.

Yes! The light caressed his skin. It would never hurt him, only wanted acceptance. The whirlwind died down. His skin healed and his tattoos glowed golden with pink edging. He took a deep, cleansing breath and sought out Raine.

Her back was against the wall, her eyes wide, her hair tousled. "Is it over?" The hoarse whisper raised the fine hairs on the back of his neck.

"Yes."

She nodded and slowly slid to the floor, curling her arms around her legs and burying her face against her knees.

Her room was a disaster zone. All her treasures were knocked askew. Artwork had fallen from the walls, several of the frames cracked, the glass shattered. Statues were toppled over on the shelves. Chunks of rock were broken and scattered. The sheer amount of damage his change had wrought in her private space made him wince. At least her house was still standing.

Going to her side, he crouched beside her. Should he

touch her? Would she even want him to? Uncertainty was a new emotion, one he wasn't particularly fond of.

He hovered beside her, moving his hand close and then pulling it back. When she finally raised her head, her eyes appeared overly bright, the pupils almost swallowing the golden brown. Her chin quivered and then firmed. "What just happened?"

"I'm not sure. I fell asleep for the first time since I woke. The Deep Sleep tried to pull me back." He flexed his fingers, to prove to himself that he could. Terror wasn't an emotion he'd been familiar with, until now. Going under without it being his choice, his body no longer under his control? Yeah, that was pure terror.

Don't want to ever do that again.

"When I fought, it triggered a reaction in my body."

She scrambled onto her knees and began to run her hands over his chest. "Are you in pain? Your skin split." She swallowed heavily. "There was light spilling from it."

Since he wasn't quite sure what to tell her—or how much he should—he sidestepped the question. "I'm sorry it frightened you." The return of his memories he kept to himself. He doubted she was even aware it had been an issue, since he hadn't mentioned it.

She nodded, not asking any more questions. He wasn't sure if she just didn't care or was too afraid to ask. Finally, she lowered her gaze. "You're naked."

"So I am." And he was alive, his blood hot and pumping hard. Not only had Raine awakened him from an eternal sleep, but she'd also pulled him back from the brink of destruction. The compulsion to protect her—no matter the cost—had pushed him to dig deeper, try harder, to survive when every cell in his body had threatened to explode. She was both his greatest strength and biggest weakness. He had two choices—kill her or make love to her. Since the first was abhorrent to him, that left him with the second.

Cupping the back of her head with his hand, he eased her closer, giving her plenty of time to object before he pressed his lips to hers.

• • •

I thought I was dead.

Watching a blinding light spill from the pores of his body had been like something from a movie. The foundations of her house had shaken and likely had cracks. Every hair on her body stood on end. She'd expected to die. Only his determination to survive had saved them both. His hand on the back of her head steadied her as he pressed a soft kiss against her lips.

Her already racing heart kicked up another notch.

I could have died…again.

Adventure was fine in books. In reality, it was scary as hell. She didn't belong in this world of nefarious plots, deliberate cave-ins, and a real-life drakon, who'd almost exploded in her freaking bedroom. Her well-ordered life had disappeared like a puff of smoke. What she'd hoped would be the big break in her career was gone. No way could she write about any of this, not unless she wanted to land in a psych ward or endanger Lucius—neither of which were options. And whatever was going on wasn't over. Not by a long shot. She could die at any time.

Through some stroke of luck or fate, she was still alive. They both were.

Raine flung her arms around his neck and hugged him hard. He started to pull away, but she tightened her grip. There were lots of reasons why this was a bad idea, but regrets were a bitch. Trapped in the cave, she'd had a ton of them and wasn't ready to add "not making love with Lucius" to the list.

If she didn't grab this opportunity, she'd never forgive herself.

Mack Evans and the threat to her life would have to take a back seat for another hour. Maybe it was stupid. It was certainly crazy. Everything in her life had gone to crap. Surely she deserved to have this one thing.

Lucius wasn't going to stay. She wasn't sticking her head in the sand and pretending her problems didn't exist. She was human. He most definitely was not. They barely knew each other, had been tossed together in a life-and-death situation. Honestly, she was surprised he'd stuck around at all. The more time they spent together, the more she'd mourn when he was gone. It was silly to be this attached to a man she barely knew, but the heart wanted what it wanted, and no amount of reason was going to change it.

Life was tenuous. Death waited for the unsuspecting. Now was the time to celebrate being alive. She ran her tongue over his bottom lip and nipped at it. His groan vibrated all the way to her toes, making them curl.

"Are you sure?" His glowing eyes were otherworldly, but they no longer bothered her. They were part of him, the wild drakon she'd discovered.

"I've never been surer of anything in my life."

Without another word, he scooped her up and carried her to the bed, dropping them both down on top of it. The sudden weight proved too much for the metal frame. A loud groan was followed by a sharp snap. One side dropped, dumping them both off the side and onto the floor. Lucius cursed and turned so she was lying on top of him, making sure she didn't end up crushed.

After a stunned second of silence, she burst into laughter. The absurdity of the situation was too much. The vexed expression on his face, the way his thick brows lowered, only made the situation even more hilarious. Her eyes watered. She had to wrap her arms around her stomach when the muscles began to protest.

Resting her forehead against his chest, she fought to regain control. "I'm sorry, but you have to admit having the bed break is a mood killer." She swiped her hands over her eyes and huffed out a breath.

"Is it?" Big hands stroked up and down her back, pausing to squeeze her ass. He eased her upward, dragging her over his muscular body, until their mouths were almost touching.

"We're on the floor." They were wedged into the small space between the collapsed bed and the window. It was rather cozy. He made the perfect mattress.

"I slept in a cave." His fingers sifted through her hair.

"So you did." He was big and tough and hard all over. Aroused, too. That wasn't a stick poking her in the stomach. She licked her lips. "I don't usually do this."

"Do what?" His hands slid beneath the sleep shirt she'd pulled on earlier.

"Sleep with men I barely know." It was important he understood that.

He trailed his fingers over the band of her underwear before dipping beneath the elastic. "I know, but you also told me you weren't a virgin, remember?"

She lowered her head, unable to look at him. "In my defense, I thought you were going to eat me."

"Look at me, Raine." The way he said her name was like a deep purr. It was sexy as hell and dampened her panties. She raised her head. "No more talking about other men." A muscle twitched beneath one eye.

"What other men?" With him touching her, it was impossible to remember anyone else. With a grunt of satisfaction, he took her mouth, his tongue teasing inside, enticing, encouraging.

Moaning, she returned the caress, tasting the heat of him, the delicious flavor that was somewhere between wine and chocolate. Yummy.

A loud rip was followed by a light breeze on her behind. "You ripped off my underwear." Sure, it happened in romance novels, but this was real life.

"I did." The twinkle in his eye was the only hint she got that he wasn't done, before there was another tearing sound. Her sleep shirt was now a rag. Not that she was complaining. She yanked at the sleeves and tossed the fabric aside. Instead of lying back down on him, she sat on his stomach. The man didn't have a six-pack. No, he had an eight-pack. She'd never seen anyone like him, not even in magazines or on television. The colors of his tattoos seemed darker, almost alive.

Must be a trick of the light.

He slid his hand over her torso and cupped her breast. Her nipple perked up, poking his palm. His movements were slow and deliberate, his gaze watchful. "I'm not afraid of you." She grabbed his free hand and brought it to her other breast. "I won't break, either." While she appreciated his restraint, she wanted fast and hard and sweaty, needed it to forget all that waited outside the bedroom door.

"There's just one thing." He thumbed her nipples, sending a blast of heat rocketing to her core.

"What's that?" She angled her hips, pressing her wet core against him, her breath catching when she found the sweet spot.

"I do plan to eat you." Desire, not fear, flooded her when he gripped her by the hips and lifted her so she straddled his face.

She grabbed the corner of her nightstand for support, totally flustered. He was looking right at her most intimate parts, the pads of his fingers stroking over the folds of her sex. The jolt of pleasure was intense.

She bit her bottom lip and swallowed back a moan. "This is awkward." She didn't need a mirror to know her cheeks were flaming red.

"Is it?" He easily maneuvered her, holding her like she weighed nothing. His breath tickled over her sensitive skin just before his tongue flicked her clit.

"Yes!" She arched back, her eyes closed. It wasn't an answer to his question but a plea for more. And he knew it, the devilish man. He captured her clit between his lips and sucked.

"What are you doing to me?" Previous lovers had complained she talked too much during sex. Didn't seem to be bothering him. He ignored her and kept on licking and sucking until she was mindless. All thoughts of embarrassment fled in the face of her growing need. "More. Deeper."

The low purring growl was like a vibrator. "Oh God." Her head fell forward. She wanted to see him, but the angle made it impossible. Then one long finger stroked into her core.

"Lucius!" She came like a rocket, pleasure exploding inside her. Stars erupted behind her eyes. It didn't stop, because he kept on going until she couldn't take any more and started to topple forward.

He caught her and pulled her down until she was resting against him. Shivers wracked her, not because she was cold, because she was sweating. The man radiated heat better than a furnace.

"You make me hotter than drakon fire."

Didn't that make a girl feel special?

Satisfaction blanketed her, along with his arm, creating a cozy haven. He kissed her temple, the gentle action the opposite of his earlier erotic ones. Something hard prodded her in the stomach. That shook away the sensual cobwebs in a hurry. She sat up so fast she hit her head on his chin. "Ouch."

"What's wrong?"

"You didn't, you know?" She waved in the direction of his erection. "Come."

He shrugged. "You gave me a gift. Thank you." She looked him right in the eyes and saw nothing but the truth. He was serious. If she got up and walked away, he wouldn't be upset. He licked his lips. "You taste amazing."

She ignored her blazing cheeks. "Don't you want to?"

"Gods, yes." His emphatic reaction made her laugh.

"Then why don't you?" He was stronger than her, could take what he wanted. And that was her answer. It was up to her to initiate sex. He'd never take what she didn't offer freely. Without giving him time to reply, she stroked her hand over his shaft. It pulsed hot in her hand. Half of it was tattooed and the head was darker and wider and plum-shaped. He was long and hard, heat radiating from him. He was big, too. Maybe too big. She swallowed her misgivings.

He groaned and covered her hand with his. "You don't have to."

He wanted her, no doubt about it. It was a heady sensation. She'd always been plain and ordinary, more nerd than beautiful woman. But he made her feel sexy and alive in a way she never had before.

"I want to."

The glow in his eyes deepened, and he released her and lay back, stacking his hands behind his head. "Take what you want."

. . .

Lucius linked his fingers together, gripping them so hard it was a wonder the bones didn't snap. The taste of her essence lingered on his tongue, the sweet scent of her release filled his nostrils. His dragon rumbled, demanding he take her, claim her, keep her.

But he was a wily hunter. She had to come to him.

And there was the real concern he'd hurt her. It had

been centuries since he'd had a woman, and never had he desired one as much. After everything she'd been through and witnessed, it was a miracle she was still here, open and giving. She was a sensual creature, her reaction to his every touch a delight. The real Raine lived in this room with the colors and mythical creatures and crystals—many of which now lay shattered and broken. The woman she showed the rest of the world was the one who lived in the other rooms.

Her hand looked pale against his shaft, which pulsed with life and need. But she was strong, her grip sure as she pumped up and down. Her gaze flicked from his cock to his face and back again, gauging his reaction.

He clamped his lips together to keep from begging her to hurry. Sweat beaded at his temples and trickled down.

"You're so big." When she licked her lips, his hips jerked.

"Take what you want," he repeated. As much as he'd love to slam her down on top of him, she had to set the pace. He'd survive. Maybe. He'd managed to come back from the Deep Sleep—as far as he knew, first in drakon history—surely he could keep it together now.

Her lips were full and sweet and animated. She talked more than anyone he'd ever known. Rather than irritating him, it was comforting. When she started to lower her head, he stopped her. "If you do that, I'm done." There'd be no holding back if she took him in her mouth. His balls squeezed in agreement.

"Oh." Her lips turned up in a sensual smile that made his entire body shudder.

"Like that idea, do you?" It had been too long since he'd touched her, so he unlocked his hands from behind his head and ran them up her inner thighs, stopping inches from her core. A fresh blast of desire perfumed the air.

"I do." She came up on her knees and inched over him, guiding the head of his erection to her opening. "Wait, what about disease or pregnancy?"

An image of her belly swelled with his child almost made him spill his seed. "My kind doesn't carry disease. And you can get pregnant only if I allow it."

"That's not fair." When she started to move away, he gripped her hips and held her in place.

"Between two dragons, it's a mutual decision, but you're not a dragon. You can trust me." Being honest was a gamble. She could easily decide to leave him.

"I should make you wear a condom, but I don't have any, and I'm not about to wait." The head of his cock squeezed past her tight opening when she pressed down, her wet heat enveloping it. He tilted his head back, panting hard, desperately trying not to come too soon. His tattoos throbbed in time to his heartbeat.

"More." He'd promised himself he wouldn't push her, but there was a serious chance his heart might explode if she didn't keep going.

Bracing her hands on his abs, she pushed down, another few inches sliding into her warmth. The inner walls of her sex rippled, contracting and expanding to accept him.

"Fuck yes." His fingers tightened around her hips.

"You're so big. I feel so full."

The more time they spent together, the less he believed she had any willing part in his awakening.

"I can do this." She was talking more to herself than to him, but he silently urged her on. Her breasts weren't overly large, but they were perfectly shaped with rosy nipples that begged to be tasted. They lifted and fell with each deep breath she took. She was tall for a woman, her curves subtle, and her limbs long.

He was more than a foot larger than her and more than a hundred pounds heavier, but there was no fear in her eyes, only determination.

She pressed down, sliding deeper. Almost there. Something inside him broke, and he pulled her the rest of the way. Her gasp turned into a long moan of pleasure. His orgasm was ripped from the depths of his soul. He poured himself into her, wrapped his arms around her, and pulled her down so she rested over his heart.

Chapter Eight

Fuck! That was not the way it was supposed to happen.

He'd gone off faster than one of those rockets blasting into space he'd read about online. His eyes almost rolled back in his head when her inner muscles clenched around his shaft, as though trying to squeeze every drop from him.

He was still hard. No way would once satiate him, no matter how good it was. That had barely taken the edge off.

She was nestled against him, all warm and cozy, soft puffs of her breath skating over his skin. Her body was lax and still. She'd fallen asleep.

Rather than be insulted, he grinned. He'd worn her out. Maybe she wouldn't mind a repeat once she'd rested. When she shivered, he drew in a breath and released warm air, letting it circulate over her. If she got cold, she'd wake, and then she might move. He wasn't ready to let her go. Not now, maybe not ever.

He ran his hands up and down her slender spine, absorbing the feel and texture. Raine had literally exploded into his life. He'd planned to sleep forever.

His snort was loud enough that she snuffled before settling again. Fate made a joke of the best-laid plans.

I'm not sorry I'm here.

How could he be with her nestled in his arms, all warm and soft? His cock flexed, ready for round two. The musky scent of her arousal, the heat from her sex, and the weight of her lying on him were making him crazy.

If she was part of some bigger plot against him, he was falling right into their plans. Her mere presence had woken him. He'd left the safety of his stone casing—for her. How much more hold did she have over him now?

His jaw clenched, the muscle flexing hard. He was a drakon, had lived thousands of years. More than that, he was one of the most feared creatures on the planet. Whatever had happened to him while he'd slept, he was stronger, more dangerous, and powerful than he'd been before. Whoever was behind this had made a huge mistake if they thought they could manipulate and control him. If they came for him, they'd pay.

What about Raine?

His dragon roared inside him, the creature not wanting to believe she had a willing part in any of this. The human side of him wasn't so sure. People were willing to do most anything for money or power or the hope of immortality.

Just because he wanted to believe she was as innocent and kind as she appeared didn't make it the truth. He needed to be cautious. His survival depended on it. If she proved duplicitous, he could easily take to the skies and vanish. There were places in the world humans couldn't reach, no matter their technological advances. And if she was truly the beautiful spirit she presented herself to be, he'd protect her. If she was a pawn in a greater game, someone would eventually check the cave to verify she was dead. When they found it empty, they'd come for her.

She shifted position, disrupting his thoughts. Her lower half squirmed, trying to find a comfortable position. His eyes practically rolled back in his head. Gods, it was so good.

Her eyes fluttered open. "I can feel you pulsing inside me."

"Yes." He ground his hips upward and rotated, milking every sensation.

"That's good. Do it again." She undulated, rubbing against him. "Mmm. You're so deep and hard."

If she kept on talking, he'd likely come a second time.

"I'm so hot and wet."

His temple throbbed, his vision dimming.

She made a circling move, grinding her pelvis against him. "Yes. Yes." Her sex rippled as she orgasmed. Giving in to the inevitable, he came again. "How is that possible?" She went lax again, practically melting over him.

"I'm a drakon. I don't need the recovery time of a human." Honesty compelled him to add, "But this is a record even for me." Twice in a row with basically little to no foreplay. Although just being with her was foreplay.

"I came twice." Two lines formed between her brows. "Maybe it was three. I'm not sure."

"I didn't mean for it to happen so fast."

She rubbed her nose against his chest. "I'm not complaining." She yawned again and lifted her head, craning her neck around.

"What are you looking for?"

"The clock. What time is it?"

"It's late or early, depending on how you look at it." The sun would be rising soon. "You should try to get some more rest." Now that he was up to speed with computers and how things worked in the world, it was time to start getting answers. Whatever either of them might want to believe, her involvement wasn't random. It would be easier to dig into her life without her looking over his shoulder.

She shook her head and shoved a damp strand of hair off her forehead. "I'm done with sleep for now. I'm sweaty. Wet, too, from us." A slight grimace crossed her lips when she pushed upright. "Not to mention sore. I'm not used to this." A rosy hue colored her pale cheeks.

Gritting his teeth, he lifted her off him. They both groaned as their bodies separated—him because of the loss of connection, her more with discomfort. Frowning, he sat up, keeping her on his lap. "I should have stopped after the first time."

Raine placed her hand on his cheek, her smile intimate and warm. "I didn't mind. It's just you're not small, and it's been a long time. Now all I have to do is stand up."

He maneuvered in the tight space until he was upright with her in his arms.

"You're handy to have around."

Glass and tiny shards of crystals crunched under the soles of his feet, remnants from his battle against the Deep Sleep. Any cuts he got from the debris immediately healed. He'd have to clean that up before she walked on it. Not sure how far the glass had scattered, he carried her down the hall to the main bathroom. She toyed with the ends of his hair, seemingly not upset by his autocratic move.

She winced again when he lowered her legs so she was standing. "I'm stiff. It's from all the walking and digging and everything over the last couple of days."

A muscle in his jaw pulsed at the reminder of all she'd been through. He touched his lips to hers. The zing in his blood was instantaneous. He had a feeling it would be the same a thousand years from now. Only they didn't have a thousand years. She was human, and she had a life that didn't include him.

It could, his dragon whispered.

Her fingers trailed down his cheek, yanking him from his fantasy, because it was just that. Nothing would change his past—who he was or what he'd done. His presence would always put her in danger. Once he took care of whoever was a threat to her, she'd be safer without him. He jerked his head back. "I'm going to clean up the mess."

He left, part of him hoping she'd call him back, another part glad when she didn't.

The bed frame was a lost cause. He'd take it outside and reposition the mattress on the floor. Since he was naked, he had no sleeves to roll up. He got to work.

• • •

What had just happened? Raine stared at the open door, listening to the sounds coming from her bedroom. They'd gone from sharing a tender moment to him bolting from one breath to the next.

"I shouldn't care," she whispered, and then bit her lip, hoping he hadn't heard. She'd have to curb the tendency to talk to herself if she didn't want him knowing her every thought.

Penelope chose that moment to join her. The cat lithely jumped onto the closed toilet seat and stared. "Sorry your routine has been upset." The cat lifted a dainty paw and began to wash her face. At least one of them was relaxed about the situation.

Ignoring the banging and clanging coming from her bedroom, she got in the shower, letting the heat drive out the soreness from her muscles. It was only when the water began to cool she began to clean herself.

Lucius hadn't come back. Not that she was disappointed or anything.

She scrubbed her skin harder than necessary, wincing

when she hit a sore spot. There were mottled bruises on her arms and legs, a testament to her ordeal. There were also several small smudges on her hips. Those were a result of a more pleasurable experience.

Heat blasted over her skin and a throbbing began between her thighs. Really? She'd never been overly sexual, but suddenly she was craving it. *What is wrong with me?*

This was all his fault. Groaning, she closed her eyes and tilted her head back, letting the chilly water cascade over her. It did little to diminish her arousal. A low growl startled her. Her head snapped toward the door.

Surely the gods felt inadequate whenever Lucius was around. Backlit by the light from the hallway, his broad shoulders filled the entire doorway. He had to duck his head slightly whenever he entered a room. His chest and abs glistened with a light sheen of sweat. She wanted to slide her hands all over him. When her breasts began to ache, she wrapped her arms around herself, keenly aware of her nakedness. "How long have you been standing there?"

"Not long enough." His rough voice sent a blast of heat straight to her core.

She turned off the taps, the dripping sound overly loud as the silence grew. His fingers tightened around the doorframe. The color of his eyes darkened. He was fully aroused and making no effort to hide it.

An unaccountable shyness fell over her, smothering the sexy vixen from earlier. She grabbed a towel and wrapped it around herself. *Act confident.* Easier said than done with a sexy, naked hunk talking to her while she was stark naked. Talk about awkward. "What have you been doing?" He'd moved from the bedroom to outside a couple of times.

"Cleaning up the mess." He raked a hand through his hair, making his biceps ripple. "There was no saving the bed frame."

Her bank account was taking quite a hit with ordering his new clothes and now her bed. She wasn't going to think about how many of her smaller treasures hadn't survived. Some of those were irreplaceable. "It's fine." Because really, what else could she say? Not like she hadn't been a willing participant. They'd actually broken the bed. A smile twitched at the corners of her lips. They'd broken the bed. How many women could say that?

"I'm going to get cleaned up." He left as silently as he'd arrived. A few seconds later, the water began to run in the other room. She couldn't figure his moods. He turned from hot to cool faster than the water.

"He's been through a lot." And maybe she was making excuses. Their connection was tenuous. He didn't owe her anything. They'd been through a life-and-death situation—at least on her side—but they didn't really know much about each other.

"He's stealthier than you," she informed Penelope. "Considering his size, it should be impossible." But what did she know about drakons? With her towel secured, she hurried to the bedroom. It looked normal, if she ignored the fact the mattress was on the floor and several pictures on her walls had cracked frames and no glass.

The shower stopped running. She dropped the towel, grabbed a pair of underwear, and tugged them on. Then she went for a sports bra, yanking it over her head. Her skin was still wet in spots and the fabric refused to cooperate, rolling instead of smoothly settling into place.

The bathroom door opened as she was trying to untangle herself.

"Of course," she muttered, keeping her back to him. Could she be any more exposed or look more like a klutz?

"Let me." A few deft tugs and he pulled the bra into place. The calluses on his fingers stimulated the nerves in her skin, sending pulses down her spine and radiating outward to every pleasure point in her body. He skimmed them down her sides and then stepped away.

Was she disappointed or grateful?

Grateful, of course. Someone had tried to kill her. That took priority over everything else. She'd already wasted valuable time with sleep and making love. While she had no regrets, it was only a matter of time before Mack, or whoever sent him, realized she wasn't dead.

"Ah, I'm just going to finish getting dressed." Like he couldn't already see that. She resisted the urge to slap her hand against her forehead. Out of the corner of her eye, she glanced his way and sighed in relief. He was wearing a towel. That was better than him running around naked. Naked, he was distracting.

She gave a snort as she pulled a pair of jeans out of the closet and dragged them on. Fully clothed or naked, he was distracting. He was also watching her. Dressing had never been a spectator sport before. Self-conscious, she dragged a long-sleeved pink shirt off a hanger. Not that she was matching his eyes or anything. Oh God, had she unconsciously matched his eyes?

Stop it! She was being utterly ridiculous, acting more like a teenager than a grown woman with university degrees and a respectable teaching position.

"Ouch." Something dug into her foot. She was off her feet and hovering in the air in the next breath.

"You're bleeding."

"It's nothing. Put me on the bed." He hesitated, but then did as she'd asked. Bending her leg, she put her shin across her other leg and peered down at her foot. A dot of blood seeped from one spot. "It's only a tiny cut. Must have caught a sliver of glass."

"I thought I'd gotten it all." He held his hand out, showing her the little shard. He tossed it into the wastebasket in the bathroom.

The sting gone, she rubbed the blood away and went to retrieve socks. His frown deepened as she added sneakers. "What? I'm not hurt."

His nod was curt.

The day had barely started and her head was throbbing. "I need coffee." Leaving him to follow, or not, she went to the kitchen. Penelope was already atop her cat tree staring out the window. Raine made a beeline for the coffeepot. While it brewed, she leaned against the counter and crossed her arms over her chest. "So where do we begin?"

• • •

He could barely keep his gaze off her. She was wearing pink. His possessive side approved. It probably wasn't intentional, but that didn't stop his dragon from purring inside him. The soft fabric molded to her breasts, cupping them as his fingers itched to do.

He'd been so tempted to remove her bra instead of putting it on her, but they needed answers and there was only one source. "Tell me how you met Mack." He should have gone after the man as soon as he'd blown the entrance to the cave but had still been partially in the grip of the Deep Sleep. Now he'd have to hunt him down.

She shoved a damp hank of hair behind her ear. "Ah, the foundation. The one that gave me the grant to write my book."

"You mentioned that back in the cave."

"Yeah, it was a big deal for me. They put us in touch through email. Now that I think back, it was vague about why he'd contacted them about his find." She pointed her finger at him. "You were the find, the stone dragon in the cave. I assumed he was looking for money from the foundation to mount an expedition. From my application, they were aware my specialty was myth and legend. I assumed they thought we might be interested in a joint venture." She turned and poured two mugs of coffee. "God, I was so excited I ignored the little whisper of warning in the back of my brain. Told myself I was overthinking things, worrying too much."

He took the mug she handed him, hating the way her shoulders hunched and how she wouldn't meet his eyes. "They played on your passion, tapped into your hopes and dreams."

She set her mug on the counter and rubbed her hands up and down her arms. "And I was ripe for the picking. I didn't lose all common sense. When I checked out Mack online, I learned he was born and raised and lived in the area around the Smoky Mountains all his life." She frowned. "There wasn't much about his job or family. Maybe that should've been a red flag, but not everyone blasts their personal business online. I should have done more research, dug deeper."

"What about the foundation? How did you first encounter them?"

"A former colleague contacted me. Said he'd heard about the foundation and thought it might be a good fit for me. You think it was a setup, don't you?"

"I'm afraid so."

"None of it was real." Her pained whisper made him want to obliterate whoever was behind this. "All of this was one big ruse, but why? None of it makes sense."

"You're the key." As impossible as it seemed, someone had figured out Raine had the potential to wake him. How was such a thing even possible? It seemed beyond the scope of a human.

"What do you mean?"

"You were the one contacted, the one brought to the cave

and trapped inside, but this isn't about you, it's about me."

She tilted her head back and heaved a sigh. "I've figured that much out." Her smile was sad but accepting. "In the scheme of things, I'm nobody. I'm a teacher and wannabe writer who thought her life was about to change for the better. You're a freaking drakon."

"You're not nobody." Unable to bear her distress, he set his mug beside hers and drew her into his arms. She leaned against him, her arms sliding around his waist. "You did what they'd hoped. You woke the drakon."

"But Mack said, 'Some things are better left buried.' If he thought I could wake you, why put us together? That doesn't make any sense."

"It does if it was an experiment."

"What do you mean?"

"Mack is a pawn, maybe willing, maybe not. Maybe he truly believes he had to trap you in the cave to keep me from waking. I guarantee whoever is behind this was hoping for the opposite. If I remained asleep, you'd die, Mack would carry on, never breathing a word about what he'd done to anyone. If I woke, whoever masterminded this would realize their plan worked when I broke you out. I guarantee they've either sent or will send Mack or someone else back to the cave to check."

"That's wild." Her voice was a strained whisper.

"It's brilliant actually. What you need to understand is that humans have sought ways to capture, control, or kill drakons since our birth. They seek money, power, and immortality." And it wasn't only humans who'd tried to kill him. There were others, of preternatural origins.

Her mouth dropped open and she jerked out of his arms. "Immortality? You're kidding, right? You can't do that, can you?"

"They believe we can." Not a lie and not the full truth.

Drakon blood healed humans and prolonged their lives, if it didn't kill them. There was no way of truly knowing until a human consumed it.

"We need to talk to Mack." She grabbed his arm. "He has to know who's behind this. I'll get my purse and we can leave now."

"That's not necessary."

"Of course it is. We need answers. If he doesn't have them, we'll hit the Angel Foundation next." Her mouth thinned into a stubborn line. "Someone will damn well talk to us."

As he lifted her hand to his lips and kissed it, he tracked the sounds he'd been hearing for the last minute. "Oh, someone will talk, but right now there are six men outside trying to sneak up on the house."

"You're sure?"

He tapped his left ear. "Preternatural hearing."

"Right. I have a gun in my bedroom."

"You own a gun?" He'd never considered that. He'd read about them online. They were deadly, effective from a distance, and didn't take much strength to wield. Much handier than a sword or dagger, especially for a woman.

Her expression was pure exasperation. "A security system is a deterrent but not protection. I'm a single woman living alone in a rural area. There are all kinds of critters—two- and four-legged—roaming around."

Lucius stood to his full height. "Then why didn't you have it on the trip?" Not that it would have done her any good. Mack hadn't come at her head-on. He'd been sneaky, blowing up the entrance to the cave, trapping her inside. With him. Someone else was calling the shots, or else Mack could have killed her at any point and dumped her body. He needed to find out who.

"It never occurred to me I'd be in danger camping in a

national park. Oh, don't give me that look. We have bigger problems. I'm getting the gun."

He shook his head. "You don't need it. You have something better. You have a drakon." Anger pulsing through his veins, he strode to the front door and yanked it open.

Chapter Nine

His dragon rolled beneath his skin, demanding to be released. These men had come to harm Raine. Or maybe he was their target and she nothing more than collateral damage.

He shook his head, refusing to give in to mindless anger. *I need one of them alive. I need Mack alive.* He had little doubt the man was out there. *We can kill the rest.* His dragon settled, in full agreement.

Society may frown on violence, but sometimes it was the only way. Since the dawn of time, there'd been groups dedicated solely to the capture or destruction of his kind and other paranormals. He had no way of knowing if any of them were still active. That kind of information wasn't readily available. Mack might be associated with one of them.

Definitely need him alive.

He yanked the door shut behind him, ambled down the stairs, and continued to the middle of her lawn. Best to get this over with as quickly as possible. Somehow, he couldn't picture Raine waiting patiently inside while he took care of the intruders.

"I'm here. You're here. What do you want?" He didn't raise his voice. There was no need.

A shot rang out. The bullet hit him dead center in the chest. He grunted as the projectile burrowed through him, ripping through vital organs, before escaping out his back. His body immediately healed itself. That had been unexpected… and painful. Drakons healed, but they sure as hell felt the pain of every injury.

"No!" Raine's scream was followed by the sound of running feet. Shit, the situation was deteriorating faster than he'd expected. Gun in hand, she skidded to a stop beside him, her eyes wide, her breath coming in huge gulps. "You're hit." Her free hand smeared the blood over his chest, finding nothing but smooth skin. Her eyes were darker than normal against the paleness of her face. "I don't understand."

"Drakon," he said as a reminder. There was no time for a long explanation, not with guns trained on them. He locked his arm around her waist and shoved her behind him. "Stay there. I'll protect you." This would have been easier if she'd remained in the house, but there'd been nothing easy about her since she walked into his cave. "What do you want?" he called out to the waiting men.

"You have to die," someone yelled back.

"Why?" Dead silence followed.

"You were both supposed to be trapped in the cave forever. That was the plan. She'd die and you'd never have a chance to awaken and wreak havoc on the world. That was my mission. I failed, but I've been given a second chance to redeem myself."

"That's Mack," she whispered.

Lucius's gaze zeroed in on where the man was hiding. "Who gave you this mission? Who sent you to kill me?"

"An angel spoke to me. It's my holy duty to destroy you. You're a monster. That bullet should have killed you. The angel was right."

"God save me from the religious zealots." There was a tiny snicker from behind him. "I have nothing to do with your God or his angels. I'm not sure God has anything to do with his angels anymore."

"Is that true?" She kept her voice low and one hand on his back, right on the area the bullet had torn through, as though to reassure herself that he was okay. Her concern warmed his heart. And her touch had other parts of him stirring beneath the towel he wore.

"Blasphemy! You've been sent by the devil to tempt and destroy us."

"Lucifer is too smart to fuck with me. I was happy to be encased in stone and asleep. Who knew I was there?" He was talking more to himself than to the intruders. Being around Raine, he was picking up some of her habits. "Why Raine?"

"The angel told me Ms. Carson was a willing sacrifice in our holy war. Her death would save us all." Mack stepped out from behind a tree.

"That's a damn lie!"

His heart squeezed as the accusation hit home. Had she contacted these men? He wouldn't have necessarily heard her talking to anyone. There was such a thing as texting and email now. His ears began to buzz and his stomach churned. "If she was so willing, why blow the entrance of the cave and lock her inside?" Her shock and fear had been too real to be faked.

"Even the most stalwart can falter. The angel said we couldn't risk her losing her nerve and running at the critical moment. Her death had to happen at the cave, in front of the stone dragon, for it to work. I tried to time the explosion so she'd die then. That way she wouldn't be forced to starve slowly or take her own life." Like any true fanatic, he had an answer for everything. The kernel of truth in his words was troubling.

"You don't believe him, do you?" The pain in her voice tugged at him. He didn't want to, but the seed had been planted. He could have flown away, but she'd convinced him to come with her, and now these men were trying to kill him.

It was time to finish this. "Leave now and live. Stay and die." The click of a weapon reached his ears. Without conscious thought, his dragon burst from inside him. Scales slammed down on his skin as his body changed shape. The barrage of bullets fell harmlessly away, unable to penetrate the armor-like plating covering him. He spread his wings wide to protect Raine. If he hadn't shifted, she'd have been hit.

Fury whipped up inside him like a whirlwind. He threw back his head and roared. The surrounding trees bent back with the blast of force behind the sound. Reason was lost as instinct took over. *Protect!*

"Get inside," he roared. He backed up, herding her toward the steps.

"What are you going to do?" The fear in her voice made his blood boil. "We should run. Maybe we can get out the back way." She gripped an edge of his wing and tugged.

"I'm going to do what I do best. Kill." They wanted a monster, he'd damn well show them what happened when you woke the beast.

"If you don't survive, I'm going to be furious with you." With that, she released him and the door slammed. Would she welcome him once she witnessed what he was capable of? Or would she try to kill him when Mack and his friends failed?

No, the man was a liar. Her fear for him had been real. She'd run to his side, heedless of the danger, not to harm but protect. He would not let the human poison him against her.

The men spread out in the wooded area surrounding

her yard, circling him. His lip curled, exposing razor-sharp teeth. Had they learned nothing? Their puny weapons were no match for him. He moved to one side and snapped out his tail with unerring accuracy. A male scream was followed by silence. While they were stunned, he did it again. Two down, four to go.

A flurry of bullets struck from all sides. All of them deflected off his scales and hit the ground. They were using the surrounding trees for cover, but they couldn't hide from him. He tracked toward his next victim. Seeing him bearing down, the man screamed and turned to run. He brought his huge foot down on him, squashing him into the ground, his sharp claws sinking deep into the dirt.

The rest fled in terror. The sour smell of their sweat assaulted his nostrils. They thrashed through the brush, their boots pounding against the ground. They couldn't be allowed to escape. It would give them time to regroup or call in more forces if they hadn't already.

Fuck! Shifting back to his human form, he pursued his prey, his long legs eating up the distance. He grabbed one man by the back of his coat and flung him hard against a tree. A loud *snap* was followed by a low groan. The remaining two separated, going in opposite directions. He went after the unknown one, catching him a few feet from his truck. "Please don't hurt me," the man pleaded, even as he got off another shot at close range. Lucius jerked, ignoring the sting of the bullet in his shoulder as he gripped the man by the back of the neck and jerked. There was a loud *crack*, and then the man went limp.

An engine cranked and tires squealed. He was faster than any truck, even in human form. When he caught sight of the vehicle, he launched himself through the air and landed squarely in front of it. Metal crunched beneath his hands when he slammed them down on the hood. Tires spun and the scent of burnt rubber filled the air. The engine revved but the vehicle went nowhere.

Mack bailed and began to run. "God save me," he yelled.

Lucius caught him easily and dragged him into the woods. "I doubt that's who sent you." He tossed the man to the ground where he immediately rolled to his knees and began to pray. "Who contacted you?"

"An angel. His presence was mighty, the light from him blinding."

Hmm, that did sound like an angel. "And did this angel have a name?" Mack firmed his lips and shook his head. "You will tell me." One way or another, he would get answers.

"No!" Mack yanked a knife from a sheath at his waist and plunged it into his own heart. He toppled to the ground, a smile on his face.

Lucius raked his fingers through his hair and sighed. "Didn't see that one coming."

• • •

Raine paced back and forth. There'd been a shoot-out in her front yard. Her front yard!

Where was Lucius? Why hadn't he come inside when the men ran? For as long as she lived, she'd never forget watching the bullet rip through his back, the spray of blood, the terror that had clutched her heart.

"Focus, damn it." Another peek through the front window gave no clues. The clearing was empty. But beyond—

Needing to know what was happening, she used her phone to access the security cameras located on the front of her house and watched as the scene played out.

Her drakon had gone on a rampage, killing several people. Not that he'd had a choice. Those men had shot him, had hit him dead center in the chest. A normal person would have died.

He'd healed instantly.

She'd seen and felt his power, but she honestly hadn't believed even he could survive such massive damage. And where the hell was he? He'd shifted to human form and disappeared into the woods. Surely, he didn't believe the lies Mack was spewing. God, if he did, he might not come back. She might never see him again. She raised her hand to her head and almost bashed herself with the gun she still held.

Her vision began to dim. Stumbling to the nearest chair, she sat and lowered her head between her knees and stared at her hands. Her fingers were stained with blood. "Oh God." Bursting out of her seat, she hurried to the kitchen, set the gun on the counter, and cranked on the water. She washed them three times before she was satisfied no trace remained. Then she retrieved her phone from her pocket and wiped it down. There was a stain on her jeans, but it wasn't too bad.

"He's okay. You're both okay." She closed her eyes for a moment. Until she saw him, she wouldn't relax. "He'll be back." Even if only to demand answers.

The footage! She couldn't leave that on her phone. She brought it up and deleted it, thankful she'd bought and installed the cameras herself and they weren't part of her home security system. It had saved her a ton of money. She'd never been so thankful to be frugal. It would've been next to impossible to get the footage off the company's server. Maybe a hacker could do it, but those skills were beyond her.

The unmistakable sound of a vehicle coming up the driveway had her grabbing the gun and heading to the front door. "You've got to be kidding," she muttered as a familiar delivery van came into view.

She jumped when something touched her leg. "Really, Penelope. You need better timing." Totally unrepentant, the cat strolled to the living room and gracefully vaulted to the back of the chair and peered out the window.

The knock on the door made her heart race. Was this legit or was this a ploy to get her outside? She'd ordered clothing yesterday. Should she answer or not?

The pounding came again, this time louder. "Come on," she whispered. "Leave the damn package on the porch."

If the men hunting them came back, the driver might be in danger.

Raine stuffed the gun in the back of her jeans and yanked the door open. "Good morning." Her greeting was overly loud and filled with false cheer. If the delivery man noticed, it didn't show.

"Everything okay here?" Wearing only a tattered and dirty towel wrapped around his waist and a scowl, Lucius stalked toward the house.

He's okay. Her knees went weak, forcing her to grab the doorjamb for support. The driver swallowed heavily and took a step back. A huge, tattooed Lucius was an intimidating sight. She was thankful he'd managed to retrieve the towel and wasn't stark naked. That would have really freaked out the driver.

"Everything is fine," she said in a cheery voice. "The clothes I ordered arrived." The driver seemed frozen in place. "Ah, is there anything else you need?"

"No ma'am." Without another word, he dumped the package, raced to the van, jumped in, and sped down the driveway, slinging crushed stone from the driveway in his wake.

Lucius paid no heed and kept coming toward her. She bit her lip and cleared her throat. "Is...is everything okay?" Not like she was going to come right out and ask if he'd killed everyone.

"I told you to stay inside." It was either take a step back or get run over. Before she knew what was happening, she was inside, leaning against the door, with him hovering over her. His lips were flattened into a stern line. He planted one hand above her head and leaned down to glare at her.

She would not be intimidated. Okay, she would, but she wouldn't show it. He could probably tell she was sweating. Giving up, she sighed. "I was afraid the men would come back and the driver might get hurt."

"What if he'd been one of them?"

Her shoulders jerked up to her ears. "Don't yell at me. I thought of that. I had my gun." Reaching behind her back, she yanked it out to show him. "I'm not stupid."

Everything about him was hard and unforgiving, from the thick muscles in his chest and shoulders to the grim expression in his eyes. How could pink eyes look mean?

"This gun." He disarmed her in a blink and tossed it onto the sofa. It bounced once before settling without discharging.

"That was dangerous."

"Dangerous?" He gripped her shoulders and pulled her up onto her toes. "You have no idea about real danger."

It began to sink in that she might be in bigger trouble than she'd thought. "You didn't believe him, did you? I'm not part of any holy mission. I don't even go to church." She'd given up praying a long time ago, depending on her wits and strength to see her through. "You know better."

"Do I?"

Those two simple words made her flinch.

"Fuck!" He lowered his head until their foreheads touched. "I believed him for about thirty seconds."

She swallowed past the lump in her throat. "I can see why you would. I mean, you don't really know me. Well, you do in the carnal sense. Maybe I'm a femme fatale and my job is to seduce you so you'll lower your guard." She gave a snort. She was the last woman anyone would send in for seduction.

"If that was the plan, it was successful."

"Wait. What?" She shoved him back. "There's no need to mock me." Hurt bloomed, making her chest ache.

"I'm not mocking you." He cupped her face in his huge hands and lifted her chin, leaving her no choice but to look at him.

Tears of relief welled in her eyes, but she blinked them back.

He rubbed his thumbs over the curve of her cheeks. "But in the future, if I tell you to do something for your safety, you need to do it."

"I will. If I can. If you're in danger, I'm not going to stand aside and let you get hurt."

"And could you kill a man?"

She grabbed onto his wrists for support. The heat from his body warming her and the fierceness reflected in his eyes made her weak. Her stomach churned at the thought of doing violence to another. "If I had to."

He shook his head and sighed. "I don't think so."

"I know how to take care of myself. Maybe I haven't killed anyone, but I'm no stranger to a fight." Not with her upbringing.

The air in the room became charged, like before a thunderstorm. Penelope jumped off the chair and skittered into the bedroom. Raine absently wondered where the cat would hide, since she could no longer hide under the bed.

"Who hurt you?" Each word was said slowly and deliberately.

"It was a long time ago. I survived. I ended up in an orphanage at three. Did some time in a couple of foster homes but the orphanage was better."

He opened his mouth to argue, so she did the only thing she could think of to stop him from demanding names. She went up on her toes and plastered her mouth against his. His lips were warm and supple, all hot male yumminess. The muscles in his arms turned to stone. She ran her tongue across his bottom lip before slipping it inside. She was enjoying herself so much it took a second to realize he wasn't kissing her back.

The man had been in a fight for his life, was probably dealing with a lot of stuff, and what had she done? She'd all but jumped him.

"Uh, sorry about that." Her face was hot. She hoped like hell it wasn't red.

"You were trying to distract me." He sounded almost confused.

"Not distract you. I wanted to kiss you. Maybe get you off the revenge train. I fought my battles. There's no need for you to go back and fight them for me." And she didn't want anyone getting an ass-whooping on her behalf. Or worse. Armed gunmen were one thing. Idiots were another.

"Ah, you can let me go now." She'd released his wrists, but he was still cupping her face. He shuffled closer until her spine was against the door. His chest brushed against hers, making her nipples pucker. And there was no hiding his arousal behind the thin towel. "Lucius."

His big body shuddered. He lowered his head and skimmed his mouth over hers, their breath mingling. "I want you safe. I *need* you safe." He kissed her again, this time a little longer. It was slow and easy and had her breasts straining against the cups of her bra. She wanted to climb him like a tree, wrap her legs around his waist, and rub herself against his erection until she came. Probably wouldn't take long.

"If something happens to you, I won't be responsible for what I'll do. Mack was right, I am a monster. No, I'm worse than a monster, I'm the one they send to kill the monsters."

"You're not a monster." But speaking of the man, "Ah, is he still alive?"

"He killed himself rather than allow me to question him."

"That's so messed up. Wouldn't he have considered that a sin if he was so religious?"

"He'd see it as doing what needed to be done to win the fight against a demon."

"You're no demon." She smacked his shoulder and winced when her fingers stung. The man really was as hard as a rock.

"No, I am one of the Forgotten Brotherhood." He released her and took a step back. Chilled without him holding her, she crossed her arms over her chest. "We are the creatures the rest of the world, including our own kind, wants to forget. We are the bogeymen for all paranormals."

"I don't..." The words caught in her throat. She swallowed and tried again. "I don't understand."

His slight smile was cruel and edged with danger. "I am an assassin."

Chapter Ten

He should have kept his mouth shut, but he wanted Raine to know exactly who and what he was, who and what she'd invited to her bed and home.

She blinked several times and tilted her head to one side. "An assassin." Her voice was strained. She leaned against the door and stared up at him, her golden eyes filled with confusion.

"Yes."

"You kill people? For money?"

"Yes." The word tasted sour in his mouth. He wasn't ashamed of anything he'd ever done, but she might see things differently.

"Humans?"

He shook his head. "I've killed humans, but only when attacked. I primarily killed paranormals who were out of control, indiscriminately slaughtering innocents."

"And you're part of this... What did you call them? Forgotten?"

"The Forgotten Brotherhood. We are paranormals

shunned by even our own kind."

"I don't understand." She touched her hand to his chest, but quickly tugged it away, rubbing it against her leg.

He wanted to roar, to destroy the world. This was why he'd chosen to withdraw from the world. People always turned from him. It was his fault for allowing her to get too close. He straightened, crossed his arms over his chest, and hardened his heart.

"What is so difficult to understand? Among my kind, I'm bigger and stronger than most drakons. That makes me different, so they fear me. I'm even stronger now." A smile tipped up the corners of his mouth. It wasn't a pleasant one, but rather than be intimidated, she took a step toward him.

"That hardly seems fair."

"No one ever said life was fair."

She nodded and rubbed her hands over her face. "I know, but it's still not right."

Why was she not berating him or kicking him out of her home? He should already be gone, but until he was sure she'd be safe, he was sticking close, whether she liked it or not.

He'd told her he believed her innocent in any plot against him. She'd thrown herself into the path of danger when she'd thought he was hurt. She'd also had the perfect opportunity to shoot him in the back at close range.

She knows you'll heal. Maybe this had been nothing more than a test of his abilities. Maybe Mack and his cohorts were the disposable ones.

"How did those men know where to find us?" It was a question he needed answered. He had to start factoring in technology when acting or making decisions. Either she or any of the men could have texted or emailed others, and he'd be none the wiser.

She frowned, her brow furrowing. "I didn't tell them." Crossing her arms over her chest, she glared at him.

Her bravery in the face of his anger was foolish, but it lightened the heaviness pressing down on him. If there was one thing he could trust it was his senses. There was nothing to indicate she wasn't being truthful. No twitch of a muscle, no increase in heart rate, no dilation of her pupils. She looked him straight in the eyes, without subterfuge.

If she was lying, she was the best he'd ever come across. It was rare for a human to possess such control over their involuntary responses. They were usually psychopaths, emotionless and cold, neither of which described Raine. She didn't seem to fear much of anything, which was a problem. The woman needed a keeper.

I can keep her. The sly voice was a whisper in the back of his brain. He ignored it. He was a paranormal killer. She was an inquisitive, but sweet, human. She saw herself as tough, but it was a facade she wore to protect her soft and giving heart.

"Someone did. You said this foundation put him in touch with you?" They'd have her address on record.

"Yes." She gripped the door handle and turned.

"Where are you going?" He shoved his hand against the panel, keeping it closed. Had it finally sunk in what he was? Was she trying to run?

"If Mack knew where to find me, maybe other people do, too, people who would be a danger to you. We need to get out of here. And as hot as you are naked, you can't go anywhere without clothes."

He feared he could live with her a thousand years and she'd still surprise him. "I'll get the box." There was no one around he could sense, but he wasn't willing to take chances. After a quick glance, he grabbed it and shut the door.

"Let's see if any of this fits." She took the box from him and carried it toward the kitchen.

Was she in denial? She seemed much too calm considering

everything that had happened. He plucked the package from her and tossed it onto the table. Grasping her shoulders, he turned her to face him. "Look at me."

"I see you." The way she said it gave him pause. "I. See. You." She pressed her hand over his heart. "You might be an assassin, but you're no mindless killer."

"How do you know?" There were days he wasn't sure himself.

She huffed out a breath. "Face it, if you were a monster, you'd have killed me back in the cave if only to shut me up." Her self-deprecating humor thawed even more of the chill coating his soul.

"You truly believe that?" He trailed his fingers over her short hair, enjoying the slide of the silk over his skin.

"Yes." From a woman who chatted nonstop, that lone word hit with the force of a nuclear bomb.

"I have seen the seven wonders of the ancient world." He plucked her off her feet, set her on the kitchen counter, and placed his hands on either side of her, caging her in. "You are the eighth. No, you are the wonder of wonders."

"I'm no one special. I'm a normal woman who lives alone with her cat and has what most people would consider a weird job."

She truly believed that. "I have seen the best and the worst this world has to offer." He leaned down until their mouths were almost touching. "You are one of a kind." He kissed her, keeping the pressure light, fearing she'd push him away. "A treasure." And a drakon hoarded and protected his treasure.

The humming sound she made in the back of her throat had his balls clenching and his cock standing at attention. Electricity crackled in the air around them. As aroused as he was, he was content to simply kiss her. There wasn't time to make love to her the way he wanted, the way she deserved.

Not to mention she was likely sore from earlier.

For the first time in his existence, he wanted to take care of someone other than himself. She was his Achilles' heel. Tying himself to her weakened him, gave his enemies something to attack and destroy.

Never!

He'd obliterate the world before he'd allow any harm to come to her. *Yeah, then she'd know for sure I'm a monster.*

Shutting away the unsettling thoughts, he slid his tongue into her mouth, savoring the warmth and welcome he found there. Her hand slid up his forearms to his biceps. She was as vocal in her passion as she was in everyday life. Sighs and gasps and hums punctuated their embrace. She wiggled to the edge of the counter and wrapped her legs around him. They had to stop. There wasn't enough time. Danger could be closing in around them.

Digging deep, he found the Herculean effort necessary to pull away. The little sound of displeasure made him want to smile.

"Why are we stopping?"

"It's not safe." Her pouting lips were too tempting to ignore, so he kissed them.

She huffed out a breath, her cheeks still flushed. "Right. Damn it, you made me forget all about that."

Didn't that make a drakon want to puff out his chest and roar? *Focus!* Her safety came before all else. "We need to search Mack's home."

She eased off the counter and sidled away without touching him. Probably a good idea. Whenever they touched, things escalated quickly. After watching her fight with the tape on the box, he extended a claw from his forefinger and carefully sliced through the binding.

"That's handy. Let's see what they sent. Two pairs of pants, four T-shirts, and four pairs of socks. I still say you should have ordered underwear."

"No underwear." Why anyone wanted to confine themselves in that way, he didn't know.

"I hope the sneakers fit." She held up one and then looked down at his feet.

"It will be fine." He took it from her and set it with the rest. "If it doesn't, I can go barefoot."

"You'd stand out too much. And trust me, you already stand out." She nibbled on her bottom lip. It was so unconsciously sexy, he wanted to drag her to the floor and make love to her. "I don't know where Mack lives. I know the area, just not his exact…" She trailed off. "Oh crap. He came here, to my home. Either he's a hacker or someone at the Angel Foundation gave him my address."

He'd already figured that one out. "And whoever sent him here will be waiting to hear back. We need to move before we have more company. Get packed and ready to go."

"Where are you going?" She hurried after him as he went to the front door.

"I have to clean things up outside." Incinerate the bodies and the vehicles. He came to a stop. "Would Mack carry something on him or his truck that would tell where he lived?" Hadn't he read something about licenses and registration online?

She was paler than she'd been only seconds before, but she nodded. "I should've thought of that. Check his wallet for a driver's license and the glove compartment of his truck for registration. See if he has a phone on him. Do the same for the others."

He wished the violence of his life hadn't brushed up against hers, but that was his reality. As a drakon, someone was always trying to kill or control him. "I won't be long." The faster they were away from here, the better.

• • •

Raine made it as far as the bed—or rather the mattress on the floor—sat down hard, flopped backward, and stared at the ceiling. Lucius was an assassin, one of the Forgotten Brotherhood. She still wasn't quite sure what that meant or who they were, but they must be badass if he associated with them.

An assassin. It pinged around in her brain as she struggled to make sense of it. She—normal, boring, head in the clouds, Raine Carson—had made love to a mythical drakon who just happened to be an assassin.

She pinched her arm and flinched in pain, but it grounded her. It was all real. He was outside right now burying bodies. Or maybe incinerating them. His drakon fire was powerful. She swallowed hard. "I won't vomit. Breathe in through the nose, out through the mouth." After several times, the urge to, well, purge passed.

There were dead men around her home, men that had come to kill them. "I won't feel sorry for them, I won't." Only she did. Whoever had sent them on this task had known the probable outcome.

She bolted upright. They'd known the outcome. Had they wanted Lucius to kill them? Why? And how was the Angel Foundation involved in all this? Mack's crazy talk about angels, and his showing up at her home with a group of armed men, tied the two together. It was the only thing that made sense in this entire mess.

Penelope padded onto the mattress, sat, and stared. "I have to remember to ask him why someone would want him to kill." She didn't want to think about what Lucius was doing. An icy cold shudder ran through her body. That's what came from watching too many horror movies. Her imagination was powerful enough without being enhanced by Hollywood. The bodies would be incinerated immediately, not burned. The fire he'd let loose in the cave had turned solid rock molten and evaporated smaller chunks in midair.

The cat continued to stare, supremely unconcerned. "You're going to go to Mavis's house for awhile." No way was she leaving Penelope here. "I'll be back as soon as I can." She hoped. Living through this wasn't a given.

Don't think about it. If she did, the fear would paralyze her. She wasn't about to be a deadweight. Poor choice of words. She needed to act, to not depend solely on Lucius to protect her. He was here now, but that might change. Then where would she be if she let him take total control?

Rolling off the mattress, she went to the closet and pulled out a small duffel bag and began to pack, weighing what she might need against the need to travel light. All her treasures, collected over her lifetime, would remain. "If I'm dead, I won't care about them. If I live, I'll be back."

Determined to get through this, she grabbed the bag and marched to the living room. Her gun was lying on the sofa. "Never know when I might need that." After scooping it up, she stuffed it into her purse for easy access.

Where was Lucius? How long would cleanup take? As if she'd summoned him with her thoughts, he walked through the front door.

"It's done." His face was grim and a slight scent of smoke clung to his skin, along with dried blood. There was a good chance not all of it was his.

"What about the vehicles?" What would they do with them? That would be a problem.

"They're gone." He dumped several ID cards on the kitchen table.

"What do you mean gone? Did you drive them away? Stash them somewhere?"

"Drakon fire." He spread out the cards and studied them.

"They all seem to live in the same area, if I'm remembering correctly the map I studied."

"You studied a map of North Carolina?" It seemed a safer question than addressing the whole "I can incinerate a truck" thing. It really wasn't that much of a stretch, all things considered, but it was mind-blowing. The power he possessed was immeasurable.

"When I was online last night."

Why wasn't he looking at her? Was he angry he'd had to kill six men because of her? If she'd let him fly away, it wouldn't have come to that. *And I'd be dead.*

"Give me five minutes." He snagged a change of clothes and headed down the hallway.

Left alone, she studied the identification he'd brought with him. There were only four driver's licenses. Did any of the men have families who would look for them, miss them? She pressed a hand against her stomach and took a deep breath, knowing there was nothing she could do about it.

A quick check of her laptop allowed her to plot the best route. It was only two hours away. They'd be backtracking toward the park. She rolled her neck, working out the knots that had taken up permanent residence there.

"Coffee." If they were doing a road trip, there needed to be drinks and snacks. Shutting her laptop, she stored it in her bag, along with the rest of their clothes, before getting to work. The coffee was just finished brewing when he joined her.

Had she swallowed her tongue? Maybe not, but it seemed thicker or at least tangled. The jeans fit him like a second skin, the soft fabric clinging to his thick thighs. And he was commando under them. Her eyes almost bugged out of her head as she studied the impressive bulge in the front.

The black T-shirt might as well have been painted on. It was short-sleeved, leaving the bulk of his arm tattoos on display. "Holy shit." When the corners of his mouth twitched, she groaned. "Tell me I didn't say that out loud."

"I'll take that as a compliment." The chuckle was a low rumble which had all her lady parts standing up and cheering. Naked, he was unforgettable. The man had muscles on his muscles. And the tattoos only gave him an edge that made her want to jump him. The jeans and T-shirt made him look even more badass, if such a thing was possible. The swirls on the left side of his neck were barely visible above the neckline. She wanted to lick them.

"You really like these clothes, don't you?" His voice had dropped an octave and flowed through her like warm chocolate sauce through ice cream.

"They're okay." She busied herself fixing coffee in two to-go cups.

He tapped the side of his nose. "I can smell your arousal, remember."

She cleared her throat and decided to ignore his last comment. "I'm getting road snacks ready. I've mapped out the best route for us to take." Best to keep busy, otherwise she'd jump him and they'd never get out of here. "Do the sneakers fit?"

"Let's find out." He sat in the chair and tugged them on one at a time. They were simple white, nothing fancy. None of it was, but on him they looked like they cost a million bucks. "They'll work." He motioned to the bag with his head. "Is that everything?"

"I thought it best to keep things light."

"Smart."

She was trying to be, but her recent choices had imploded her life in a series of ups and downs that had left her smack-dab in the middle of this messed-up situation.

"Where's the correspondence from the people who gave you the grant? We should take that."

"The Angel Foundation? It's all email, so it's on my computer. They have to be a part of this." It made the most sense.

"At least one of the people working there is involved."

"They gave me fifty thousand dollars. That's a hell of a lot of cash to hand over, considering they don't have a chance of getting it back. Even if I'm declared missing, it would take years to settle my estate. There's a mortgage on the house, so it's not worth a whole lot. And speaking of money, we need to stop at an ATM so I can withdraw some. We don't want to leave a trail of credit and debit card purchases for someone to track."

He nodded and hefted her bag. "I'll put this in the car."

"I'll get Penelope's carrier and belongings together." In short order, she was locking the front door to her home. It was hers—and the bank's. This was her space, the one she'd carved out for herself after years of hard work. She might never see it again.

The stark reality was sobering, but she had a better chance with Lucius than going it on her own. He waited by the open passenger side of her car.

Turning her back, she walked away. Something occurred to her as she joined him. After tossing her purse into the backseat alongside the cat carrier, she leaned on the roof. "Why haven't you contacted this brotherhood you're part of for help? They're your friends, aren't they?"

His jaw tightened and his eyes began to glow. "I can't be sure they're not part of this."

Chapter Eleven

Lucius hated waiting in the car while Raine took Penelope up the walkway to her friend's home. A middle-aged woman opened the door, and after a lengthy conversation, she took the cat carrier and bags with food and toys and everything else Raine had deemed necessary. Head down, she hurried back to the car and slipped into the driver's seat.

She backed the car out of the driveway and pulled away without hesitation. "She likes Mavis's cats. She has two, Byron and Shelley. Mavis teaches literature at the college."

A muscle in his jaw flexed. That cat was her family, and she was being forced to leave her behind. "I'm sure she'll be fine. There's no reason anyone would harm her or your friend."

"Oh my God! I didn't even think about that. Should we go back and get Penelope?" The car began to slow.

"No, she's safer where she is."

"You're right." Her fingers gripped the wheel so hard her knuckles were white. "And if something happens, Mavis will keep her. She'll have a home."

Home was important to Raine. He'd figured that much out. Home was a sanctuary, a place you could be yourself without the judgment of others. A place for those you loved. He'd always lived alone, but not her. As hurt as she'd been over the course of her life, she had opened up her heart to Penelope.

And to me.

Or maybe that was only wishful thinking. Hot sex didn't mean she cared about him. She was with him now because she didn't have a choice, not until they got to the bottom of this. Even if she wanted to leave, he couldn't let her. There was still a tiny part of him that expected her to betray him. Keeping her with him was safer for them both. Once the threat was over, they'd part ways. It was better that way, for both of them.

Every single one of the thousands of years he'd lived pressed down on him. The Deep Sleep was better than being bombarded by so many volatile emotions. He absently rubbed his chest.

"What's the plan when we get to Mack's?" The car moved smoothly into another lane.

"We'll look around, see if there's any correspondence between him and this Angel Foundation or anyone else. We can't discount the idea he might have contacted them. It's a long shot, but one we have to consider."

"I hadn't thought about that." She snagged her covered cup of coffee and took a sip. "I did have a thought when I was getting ready."

Here it comes. She'd had time to consider everything he'd done. Was she about to suggest they part ways? He straightened and banged his head on the roof. Rubbing the abused area, he swore.

"Are you okay?"

"Yes," he snapped. This damn metal contraption was too

small. It was claustrophobic, and his dragon hated it every bit as much as he did.

"Anyway, I thought about things, because that's what I do. I look at information from all angles and come up with possibilities."

When she hesitated, he prompted. "And now that you've had time to think things through, you can't face what I am. Is that it?"

"What? No, that's not it at all. I thought about that, too, and I mean, if a paranormal gets out of control, who you gonna call? You're like real live Ghostbusters only for vampires and werewolves and assorted others. There are assorted others, right?"

His thoughts spun round and round as he tried to follow her. "You're not upset about what I do?"

She nibbled on her bottom lip, and his new jeans quickly became tight and uncomfortable. He barely swallowed back a heavy groan.

"It's not a career I'd choose for you, but I understand why it's necessary. It's not like the cops or FBI or anyone could handle an out-of-control werewolf. But why you? Why don't werewolves handle their own problems? Are you guys global or do you each take a country or continent? How many of you are there?"

She finally stopped to take a breath.

"Who or what are Ghostbusters?" He'd missed that in his research, spending all his time on technology, banking, military advancements, and politics—the important things.

"What?" Her laugh was breathy. "Oh, movie characters. Movies are like plays. You can watch them on television or in larger venues with a bigger screen. Anyway, they hunt ghosts because no one else can. It's like you and that Brotherhood, except it's more humorous than serious."

He made a mental note to find out more about the movie.

"Most paranormal groups handle their own problems. There's a Vampire Council."

"That's downright scary." She reached up with one hand and rubbed her face.

"And shifter alphas usually discipline or destroy any dangerous members of their packs. You have to understand that none of them want to be outed to humans."

"Because they'd be hunted."

"Yes."

"So where do you and the Forgotten Brotherhood come in?"

"We're contacted and we research the request extensively. Once we take a contract, we fulfill it. If anyone tries to hire us to kill an innocent, they're the ones who die."

Her entire body shuddered, and her fingers flexed on the wheel. "I can see where that would be an effective deterrent."

"We're contacted only in the direst of circumstances." Why was he downplaying what he and the Brotherhood did? To make it more palatable for her? "But it happens more often than you'd think." If she was going to be with him, she needed to understand and accept all of him. Every muscle in his body tensed, a low-grade anger thrummed through his veins—anger at her and the world in general. He hadn't asked to be brought back.

If I hadn't, I wouldn't have met Raine. And that would have been a tragedy.

"I get it."

There was no way she could fathom what it took out of him and the others. Some of them did it because they had no other options. They were killers and needed an outlet for their fury. But beneath it all, there was a bedrock of right and wrong. They did it because it was the right thing to do, because someone had to keep the world from running red in human blood. And they did it for acceptance. It gave them a place to belong. That might be the biggest driving force of all. They were loners, but even the most reclusive creature wanted someone to understand them, to offer a hand of friendship.

"As I said, I did some thinking. Whoever sent those men had to know you'd kill them. They sent Mack and the others to their deaths. Why would they do that?"

"You're right." As she skillfully changed lanes and picked up speed, he mulled over her revelations. "Unless another woke while I slept, I'm the first to come back from the Deep Sleep. They had no way of knowing what my mental or physical state would be if I did."

"It was a test," she whispered, sounding appalled by the very idea.

The world flashed by, but it was all a blur. The sides of the car pressed in around him. He wanted to fly with the air brushing his wings, wanted to soar high and far, leaving all this behind.

Only concern for Raine was keeping him here. "Yes. It's possible they expected me to kill you."

Her inhale was sharp and swift. "I see."

"I don't think you do. Someone purposely put you with me. How did they know you'd be the one who could wake me? You're not the first to stumble on my cave. I've sensed others before. It was more a faint buzz in the background, and I was able to tune them out. It was impossible to do that with you. Now they want to see if I'll protect you."

A sliver of lore came to him. Drakons mated for life. There would only ever be one female, one mate for him. There was not another more powerful force in existence than the call of a mate. Nothing else could have broken the grip of the Deep Sleep.

Impossible. How could anyone know who Raine was to him? Who would have access to that kind of knowledge before even he did?

Dumbfounded, he stared at the smart, mouthy, courageous woman piloting their vehicle down the highway. It was the only thing that explained the unnatural attachment he'd had for her from the beginning, the relentless need to keep her safe.

Was she experiencing anything similar? That might explain the sexual spark between them. She might be as unable to deny the pull of it as him, but it ran deeper. Being around her brought him a sense of peace and belonging that had been lacking in his entire life.

His life was forever bound with hers. He wasn't sure what that meant going forward, hadn't paid attention to the rumors of mates that had spread throughout his kind over the millennia. They were so rare as to be mythical. The irony was that a drakon mate was scarcer than a drakon.

No one special? He'd lay waste to the world to keep her safe.

"What is it? You look pale." She signaled and pulled the car onto the side of the road, the tires crunching on the roadside gravel. "What's wrong? You're scaring me." She put the vehicle in park, undid her seat belt, and leaned over, putting her hand on his face.

The concern in her eyes, the genuine caring in her voice, moved him. Something shifted deep inside him and locked into place. He finally understood and accepted what his dragon had known all along.

Mine!

• • •

He was pale as snow and seemed shaken, a far cry from the powerful male she'd known since he'd first broken out of his stone encasement. Nothing could be wrong with him. What would she do if there was? Not like she could drive him to the nearest hospital.

"Lucius?" His entire body shook, making the whole car quiver.

His eyes were glowing again, something they seemed to do when he was in the grip of strong emotions. When all he did was stare, she began to worry. They'd been driving along and talking. Granted, she'd been doing most of the talking, and he'd been avoiding answering most of her questions, but still.

What had they been discussing? "We know someone deliberately chose me to go to the cave." For the life of her, she couldn't come up with a single reason why her over someone else, unless… "Do you think it has anything to do with my career, the fact I hunt down legends? Maybe I ran across a real vampire or werewolf in my travels. I've interviewed tons of people in the past decade. To be honest, I suspected some of them might be real." And that had kept her awake too many nights to count.

A low growl filled the car, somewhere between a pissed off pit bull and a snarly T-Rex. "Ah, say something." A smart woman would run, but a smart woman would never have gotten herself caught up in this situation to begin with.

He shook his head, not in denial, more like he was trying to shake something loose. "We need to keep going." His voice was rougher than usual, like his vocal cords were strained or something. He blinked several times and the light in his eyes diminished until they were back to normal.

She nibbled on her bottom lip, concerned when he made a sound of pain in the back of his throat. Something was wrong. Whatever it was, he was hiding it from her.

He ran his thumb across her lower lip, tugging it away from her teeth. "You have to stop doing that."

"Doing what?"

"Chewing on your lip."

"Why?" What did that have to do with anything?

He took her hand and dragged it to the front of his jeans.

"You're really aroused." Duh, nothing like stating the obvious. Around Lucius, she seemed to lose access to rational thought. She curled her fingers around his hard heat. It was empowering to affect a hot guy like him so viscerally.

He gripped her wrist and pulled her hand away. "If you don't stop, I'm going to strip you bare and take you right here, right now."

A truck blew by them, horn blaring. She snatched her hand back, her palm warm from his heat. Her internal temperature had shot up so much she was starting to sweat.

She flicked the air conditioning on full and angled one vent at him and the other at her. The cold air washed over her, raising goose bumps on her arms beneath her sweater. This was not the time or place. *Men trying to kill me, remember? Places to go. Things to do.* Even that thought didn't kill her arousal as effectively as it should have.

One corner of his mouth kicked up. "Not sure that will help."

"It's better than nothing." Her hand shook as she gulped down her remaining coffee. Staring straight out the window, she took one breath in, held it, and slowly let it out. When she had herself under control, she checked her mirror and pulled the car back onto the road. "Talk to me."

"What do you want to know?" If she recorded his voice and sold copies, she'd make a mint. Instant mini orgasm. *Stop thinking about orgasms!*

"Anything. I asked you a ton of questions but got no answers." The truth might be more than she could handle, but sticking her head in the sand wouldn't change things.

He tilted his head back, his nose practically brushing the roof of the car. Poor guy really couldn't be comfortable. She checked his lap. Nope, definitely not.

"I told you werewolves and vampires are real. There is one of each in the Brotherhood, both powerful anomalies among their kind. Maybe more since I've been away. There are other kinds of shifters, mostly varieties of cats and bears. I met a phoenix once. They're scarcer than drakons."

She wanted to scream and laugh but swallowed it back. Her hands trembled. She gripped the wheel tighter. All these years she'd been right. A quick butt dance in her seat was all she could allow herself.

No one else can ever know.

Reality was a serious downer. The greatest discovery of modern times, and she could never speak of it to a single soul. Not only would it put Lucius and his kind at risk, it would endanger humanity. If paranormals were outed and hunted, they'd fight for their lives. It would make every apocalyptic movie she'd ever watched seem like a joke.

Then there was the lesser problem of losing her job if she ran around screaming they were real. Universities and other learning institutions frowned on such things. It was one thing to study myth, another to acknowledge it was real.

"There are also assorted others—demons, gods"—he paused—"and angels."

Her breath caught in her throat. Maybe this was a little too real. "Demons and gods?"

"Most of the pantheons of history have a basis in reality—Greek, Roman, Egyptian, Norse, and every native culture through the ages."

Lightheaded, she shoved a hand in the bag of snacks and yanked out a bar. Using her teeth, she ripped away the wrapper and shoved half of the chocolate treat into her mouth.

"Raine?"

Giving a shake of her head, she kept on chewing. The sugar rush helped stabilize her. When she finished the bar, she grabbed another. One was good, two had to be better, right?

He took it from her shaky hand, opened it, and broke off a piece. Instead of handing it to her, he placed it against her lips. She parted them and her tongue skimmed his fingers. God, she was a mess. Hot and cold at the same time. Aroused, excited, and scared to death.

"Do you want me to drive?"

She shook her head. Having something to focus on was better. Holding the wheel grounded her. "I'm fine."

"You're amazing. You're holding things together when most people in your situation would have fallen apart. From what I read, modern culture doesn't believe in paranormal creatures or magic."

His sincerity made her toes curl in her boots. Then she realized what he'd said. "Wait, magic is real, too?"

"I thought you believed. You mentioned me being under a spell back at the cave."

"I was joking." She huffed out a breath. "So, it's as real as the rest?"

Fury bled from his very pores, surrounding her until every inch of her skin was electrified. "Yes, and mages have used it over the years to trap and kill drakons."

"I'm so sorry." What else could she say? Mages had to wield incredible power to be able to capture or destroy a drakon. After seeing what Lucius could do, that was one hell of a scary thought.

His smile was tinged with both bitterness and satisfaction. "They learned to leave me alone."

She didn't even want to imagine how he'd accomplished that. Best not to think about it. "Tell me more about drakons, more about you."

"The more you know about my kind, the more dangerous it is if you let it slip to someone. Or do you plan to write about it? That's what you do, isn't it?"

His suspicion stabbed her in the gut. After all they'd been through, he doubted her motives. She rolled her top and bottom lips together and swallowed back the hurt. "You're right. Best not to trust me."

His hands were fisted in his lap. The tension in his voice mimicked that of his body. "It's not personal. I don't trust anyone."

"Not even your precious Brotherhood?"

"No." He stared out the window, a muscle in his jaw working.

Holy crap, he was telling the truth. "I figured you guys would be friends." How did someone live for so long unable to trust? She understood betrayal, had been victim to its vicious claws, but at least she still had hope.

I haven't lived thousands of years.

"If you were captured, and they thought you knew anything about me, they'd torture you for the truth."

"You're trying to protect me." Everything inside her settled. She reached out her hand and laid it over one clenched fist. "I'm in this with you until the end, I promise. And I've never broken a promise in my life."

He swallowed heavily and turned toward her, his face an emotionless mask. "You've never come face-to-face with an angel before. If Mack is to be believed, one is manipulating us both for some outcome. They have strict guidelines for how they interact with humans. There are consequences if they break those rules."

"A rogue angel?" She'd always bought into the image of the angel with a sword, ready to smite on command, rather than the cute cupid.

"Maybe, but it just so happens that Maccus Fury, the leader of the Brotherhood, is a fallen angel."

Chapter Twelve

"Do we go inside? Doesn't seem to be anyone around." It was the first thing Raine had said since he'd dropped his bombshell about the leader of the Brotherhood being a fallen angel.

"You haven't asked about Maccus." It was the longest stretch she'd been quiet since they'd met. Unless she was sleeping.

She shrugged and popped her door open. "You'll tell me if you want me to know." Her door slammed shut, and she stalked toward the house.

Swearing under his breath, he managed to pry himself out of the tin can he'd been riding around in and followed, his long legs eating up the distance between them. Her hand was on the doorknob when he grabbed her arm. Thankfully, Mack's house was tucked away in a rural area with no prying neighbors nearby.

"I'm trying to protect you."

"And yourself." The hurt in her eyes made his bones ache, but the understanding in them almost brought him to his knees. "I get it. You really don't know me. I could be part of this. Best to hedge your bets."

When she jerked her arm away, he released her, but only so he wouldn't accidentally harm her. "You're not part of this."

"I'm smack-dab in the middle of this whether you want me to be or not. I'm the one who was contacted, the one who was trapped on purpose with a drakon. If I hadn't woken you, I'd have died in that cave." She knocked on the door and waited.

"There's no one inside." Besides them, there were only the critters of the surrounding woods.

"Great." She tried the handle, but the door was locked. Giving a frustrated growl, she kicked it several times. He rather thought she was wishing it was his head. "We should try the back door. Or maybe there's a window that's unlocked."

Using his body to crowd her out of the way, he placed his hand on the thick panel and applied a steady pressure. The wood groaned and the metal lock squealed and cracked as it gave way. He motioned her inward with a wave of his hand.

"Or we could just do that." She stalked inside and began to look around.

He pushed the door closed before joining her. "We're looking for—"

"I know what we're looking for." Nose in the air, she walked away, leaving him staring at her back.

Ignoring her would be the best thing. They needed to stay focused. *The hell with that.* "Why are you so angry with me?"

She spun around, opened her mouth, and slowly closed it before rubbing a hand over her face. "I don't know. You don't owe me your life story or your secrets. I was the catalyst for waking you. You saved my life after I'd imploded yours."

The distance between them was growing, even though she was standing alongside him. Emotionally, she was pulling away. "I mean, we did have sex, but that's just physical—the adrenaline, drama, and forced togetherness. It was bound to happen."

Hearing her boil down what had occurred between them as nothing more than sex had his dragon roaring. A vein beneath his left eye pulsed. He clenched his jaw tight to keep from yelling.

She waited a beat. "See, you know I'm right."

"It was more than sex, damn it." He caught her chin between his thumb and forefinger. She'd been too open, her every emotion visible for him to see and enjoy. Her joy had been almost incandescent.

"I'd been in a long dry spell, and you're handsome and really good at sex." Her smile was as fake as... He wasn't sure exactly what, unable to think past the fires of fury roaring through him, but it was a far cry from the one she usually gave him.

His breathing was hard and heavy, his lungs pumping. "It. Was. More. Than. Sex." He said each word deliberately. There was no way she could misinterpret them.

"All right."

She continually baited and challenged him. In their short acquaintance, he'd experienced every emotion under the sun. It was maddening. It was invigorating. "Don't push me." Didn't she understand that he was a monster, feared by all?

She drilled her forefinger into his chest. "What are you gonna do about it?"

"Stop." His dragon wanted out, and it was taking every ounce of his control to contain the beast. Her audacity was breathtaking.

She's not afraid of me. This human woman went where angels dared not.

"Why are you smiling? This is not a laughing matter." She poked her finger against him again. Her face was flushed.

A lock of hair stuck to her cheek. He tucked it behind her ear and caressed her face. The fire in her eyes went out, replaced by confusion. "I don't understand you."

This wasn't the time or place to sort out their relationship. There were dangerous enemies stalking them, who had, so far, been one step ahead of them. Once they were dealt with, she'd be safe. But as long as she was with him, there would always be a target on her back.

He was being pulled in two directions. She was his mate, the best thing that ever happened to him, but was he the best thing for her? If he were a better male, he'd walk away to protect her. But he'd reached the point where leaving her might turn him into the monster he'd been accused of being. As long as she lived, he *had* to remain in the world. His dragon side demanded it.

Lifting her off her feet, he brought his mouth against hers. Coffee and chocolate were two flavors he now loved, even more so when mixed with her warmth and welcome. Her moan was a combination of exasperation and passion. Clasping her hands to his head, she kissed him back. Their tongues dueled for supremacy in a back-and-forth battle that had no losers.

She fit his arms perfectly, completed him in ways he couldn't yet comprehend. It might be smarter to leave. He could fly to some remote outpost of the world, but sleep would be impossible. Raine was everything he'd never known he'd wanted or needed. He'd once scoffed at the idea of fated mates, even as a burning yearning for one had filled him. His cynicism had been a protective mechanism.

How had he lived without her for so long? He tilted his head to one side, deepening the caress. His new clothing was confining. He wanted them naked, skin to skin.

A sharp ring pierced the air, shattering the moment. Dazed, she licked her swollen lips. "Ah, that's a phone."

After another ring, a machine kicked in. "This is Mack. Leave a message." The prerecorded message came from the kitchen area.

"Where the fuck are you, man? You were supposed to meet me at Joe's for a beer. Call me."

"He has a landline and an answering machine." She hurried to the kitchen and went to a machine with a blinking red light. "Not many people have these anymore. Most stick to cell phones."

She pressed a button and listened. "Message one." It was followed by silence and then abruptly ended. "Message two." The same.

"Seems like whoever Mack was supposed to meet at Joe's isn't the only one looking for him."

"Message three. This is the Angel Foundation wanting to confirm you met with Ms. Carson as planned. Please contact us when you return."

"That message doesn't tell us any more than we already knew. We need to finish our search and leave before we're discovered." She flipped through a stack of mail on the counter, looking everywhere but at him. "Mack has friends. The last thing we want is one showing up while we're here."

"I'll listen for a vehicle." He left her in the kitchen and made his way to the master bedroom. Methodically, they went through the small two-bedroom home, checking drawers and closets, under furniture, behind pictures, and any other hiding space they could think of.

"Damn it. If he had anything, he either hid it well or destroyed it. The only papers were paid bills and taxes. I thought for sure we'd find something." Raine fitted a cushion back on the couch and stood in the middle of the living room, hands on her hips. The late afternoon light beaming through the window backlit her form, making her glow.

Like an angel.

The possibility that his friend and Brother might have betrayed him was bitter on his tongue. "Where is this Angel Foundation located?" That was their next logical stop.

As she moved toward him, the light seemed to follow. "New York." There were purplish smudges beneath her eyes, and the smile she gave him was strained.

He held out his hand. "Give me the keys. I'll drive."

It was a testament to her fatigue that she handed them over without a qualm. "We'll stop and get something to eat first." He was starving, and all she'd eaten were those chocolate bars. They'd both think more clearly after a break and some food.

A thought occurred to him. "Is there a business near here named Joe's? Maybe it's a place and not a person."

"That's brilliant." She opened her phone and seconds later smiled. "There's a bar with that name not too far from here. They'll likely have food. We could kill two birds with one stone—feed ourselves and maybe dig up some information."

"Let's go."

• • •

Joe's was somewhere between a dive and a neighborhood bar whose heyday had been twenty years ago. The smell of smoke, spilled booze, and body odor slammed into her as soon as Lucius opened the door.

How much worse is it for him?

She glanced up at him and away. She owed him an apology for acting bitchy when none of this was his doing. *I could fall in love with him.* Maybe she was even halfway there. Which, of course, explained why she'd been so bitchy earlier. Better to push him away before he could leave her. It was her fallback, her fail-safe against being hurt.

I promised I wasn't going to keep doing that.

Easier said than done.

"There's an empty table in the corner." Big hand spanning her lower back, he guided her toward it. Every eye in the place was on them, some curious, others suspicious. She doubted this place saw many strangers.

Uncomfortable being the center of such scrutiny, she hurried and slid into a chair. Lucius took his time, scanning the entire room before finally sitting. The chair groaned but held.

A woman who looked to be in her early thirties with dark hair bundled up in a cascade of loose curls scurried over to the table. "My name is Sally. What can I get ya?" She cast a long look at Lucius and licked her lips. Raine wanted to smack those red painted lips.

"Do you have a menu?" Her tone was sharp.

"Nope, it's all on the board." Hip cocked and hand on her waist, she pointed to a large sign behind the bar. "Fish and chips, nachos, burgers, fries."

Ignoring the woman, Lucius leaned toward her. "What would you like?"

"Nachos and a coke."

"And what can I get you?" The waitress was either dense or not deterred by Raine's presence. "I can get you *anything*."

"I'll take two of everything. And a beer."

"Two?"

He tilted his head to one side. "Is that a problem?"

"No problem. I'll put your order in."

When they were alone, or as alone as they could get in a bar, she scooted her seat closer. "If this is the place Mack was supposed to meet his friend, how do we gather any information? It's not like we can ask, not unless we want to raise suspicions. This doesn't look like a talkative crowd."

He tapped his ear. "I listen."

Right, preternatural hearing. Toe tapping to the classic

rock song on the sound system, she rubbed her finger over a spot on the table and dug around in her purse for hand sanitizer.

Sally returned with their drinks and hovered. "Thank you." Raine gave her a pointed look, which sent her on her way. Honestly, could her interest in Lucius be any more obvious?

I'm jealous.

Propping her elbows on the table, she rested her chin on her hands and let her gaze wander over the room. Best not to think about their relationship. It could be only short-term, no matter what they wanted. She was human, and, hello, he was immortal. Or was he?

"Are you immortal?" Her life had taken a huge turn that a question like that was now normal conversation.

"Hmm, no idea. Dragons live for tens of thousands of years. We're the first and only drakons, so there's no way of knowing."

Mind-blowing. Giving her head a shake, she concentrated on the other patrons. Four tables were filled, mostly with men. Two women sat in one corner, eyeing a group of three men, who were eyeing them back.

"I think that's Mack's friend." He tilted his head to two men who were huddled over bottles of beer. "He's complaining his buddy was supposed to meet him. How Mack bragged about having a big job with plenty of money involved but wouldn't give details. His friend bailed because he didn't want to get into anything illegal."

"That saved him," she murmured. Life was odd that way. You never knew which decision might prove to be one that would change everything—for better or worse.

Just look at her.

The waitress returned with a tray loaded with plates. She slapped the nachos in front of Raine. Smiling at Lucius, she began to unload the rest. "Here you go, handsome. I'll get the second load. I love a man with a big appetite. And your eyes are amazing. Love those contacts," she added before heading back to the kitchen.

Unable to refrain this time, Raine rolled her eyes and dug into her meal.

"I know it's frustrating this was another dead end, but it was a long shot that we'd hear anything useful." He picked up a burger and took a big bite.

She took a long pull on her coke and slapped the glass onto the table. "Really? You think that's what's bothering me? Men," she muttered.

"What?" He honestly seemed perplexed.

"That waitress is all but crawling on your lap." She stuffed another nacho in her mouth to keep from blurting out anything else. They were surprisingly good, all things considered. Or maybe she was really hungry.

A slow smile curved his lips.

Don't smile. Don't smile.

He leaned toward her, a sexy gleam in his eye. "You're the only woman I want." With his hair falling around his face and the soft fabric of his shirt straining at the seams, he'd be right at home on the cover of any romance novel. He was a rogue. No, a pirate.

She sniffed. "Not my business." He was going to break her heart, no two ways about it. He wouldn't mean to, but it was inevitable. Fate—or their enemy—had thrown them together, but at the end of the day, he was a drakon and she was a human. Once he found his footing in the world, he'd say goodbye and leave her with nothing but memories.

Smile fading, he cupped her jaw. "It is very much your business." His eyes began to glow just as Sally bustled back to their table. Raine shook her head and rubbed her finger against the corner of her eye. He sat back and lowered his head.

"Can I get you anything else?" She addressed her comment to him, but Raine answered.

"Just the check." The waitress flounced away, taking her disappointment with her. Shaking off her gloomy mood, she picked at the nachos while keeping an eye on the other patrons. Best to remember why they were here in the first place.

Lucius plowed his way through six plates of food, ignoring the waitress when she slapped the check on the table. When every morsel was gone, he sat back with a sigh. "That takes the edge off."

"You really do eat a lot." Feeding him was going to take a lot more money than she had. She dug into her purse. "I think I have enough cash to pay for this."

His brow furrowed. "I will pay you back."

"Don't worry about it." He'd been sleeping for hundreds of years and literally had nothing but the clothes on his back.

He caught her hand when she pulled out her wallet. "I will repay you. I have treasure cached in remote areas all over the world. I also have money I left in trust with the Brotherhood."

Holy shit! A real drakon's treasure. It wasn't myth but reality. She swallowed back the dozen questions on the tip of her tongue. Talk about highlighting their differences. Her lifespan was a mere blip of his, while he'd had thousands of years to build enormous wealth. Then the rest of what he'd said registered.

"With the Brotherhood? The same people you don't currently trust?"

His jaw tightened. "Yes."

Talk about a dilemma. "Listen, I appreciate the thought, but I'm more concerned about figuring out who wanted you awake and why." If she survived, she'd worry about the state of her finances. She set the money on the bill, even including a tip, although it was smaller than it might have been if the woman had kept her eyes to herself.

"What's this?" He held up a napkin with a number scrawled over it and a lipstick kiss beneath it.

Gaze narrowing, she stood and zipped her purse shut. "Her phone number. I'm going to the bathroom."

"Not alone." He pushed away from the table and followed her.

"You can't go in the ladies' room with me. You should use the men's room." And she'd never be able to pee with him in there with her.

"Be sure to come back," the waitress called out.

He detoured toward her and dropped the napkin into her outstretched hand. "I won't be needing this."

She didn't exactly do a victory dance, but her steps were lighter. When she finished, Lucius was waiting for her. Taking her hand in his, they left the bar behind.

There was only one next logical step. "I guess we're heading to New York."

Chapter Thirteen

Raine sat forward, not wanting to miss anything. Everything about New York City was vibrant and alive. The buildings reached for the sky, while the people reached for the stars. She rolled down the window, letting the cold wind and raucous noise of traffic surround her.

Lucius was still driving. He was alert while she'd slept for most of the night and into the morning, waking only to visit an ATM and when they needed fuel, for themselves and the car. Probably not smart, since he didn't have a license, but he handled the vehicle like a seasoned pro, merging in and out of traffic, following the GPS directions to a moderately priced hotel she'd found online earlier.

"Have you ever been here before?" he asked.

"Once, but it's been years. I've always meant to come back but never managed to make it. Too much work, not enough money or time." And that was a crime. "There's so much to see and do, from museums to shops and restaurants and entertainment. This city has everything."

"I was here about twenty years before I headed to the

cave in North Carolina. It's nothing like when I saw it last."

She couldn't even begin to imagine how it had changed. Their lives and experiences had been so different. Shivering, she put the window up and cranked the heat. The cool air had given her a boost, but exhaustion was pulling at her. They'd agreed the best thing they could do was get some rest and have a good meal before setting out on the next part of their quest.

The chain hotel wouldn't strain her already-tight budget and put them close to where they needed to be. After parking in a nearby garage, which wasn't cheap, they collected their belongings. Lucius remained alert and allowed her to check them in, while keeping a watch on everyone and everything.

All this was new to him, but you'd never know it by the way he handled things. She envied his easy confidence. She was hanging on by the tips of her fingernails. Part of her wanted to run home, crawl under the covers, and hope that all this was nothing more than a bad dream. But that would be cowardly. This was the adventure of a lifetime. She was a real-life Indiana Jones, or better still, Lara Croft. If only she could kick ass like they could.

She really was getting loopy if she was focusing on fictional characters rather than face her own reality. On the elevator ride up to their floor, she began to weave from side to side. With his hand on her back, she managed to make it down the hallway without banging into the wall. When the door finally closed behind them, she dropped her bag and fell onto the bed with a groan, bouncing once before settling.

"You don't have to do that." Her voice was muffled by the pillow. She managed to roll to her side and watch through half-closed eyes as he removed her boots and socks.

"You need rest." He was frowning again, his lips set in a hard line.

"If you want to go to the Angel Foundation now, we can."

She might fall asleep on her feet, but she'd manage.

"No." He sat beside her and reached for the fastener of her jeans.

"What are you doing?" More bemused than concerned, she allowed him to unzip her pants and tug them off, leaving her lower half bare but for her underwear.

"Helping you get comfortable."

When he went for her sweater, she placed her hand over his. "What's wrong?" He shook his head and sighed, staring at their hands. The bleakness in his eyes when he finally looked at her shook her to her core.

"What if I discover Maccus is behind this?"

Relief flooded her. Finally, he was ready to talk, to trust her. It was a huge step forward. "You said he was the leader of the Forgotten Brotherhood. Why would he do such a thing?"

His hair swung when he shook his head again. "I don't know, but he's an angel."

"A fallen one. That's what you said." She'd studiously avoided thinking about it until now, having enough to deal with, but could put it off no longer. "Would he have given off the aura of an angel if he's fallen? Oh my God, is he like Lucifer?" If angels were real, the devil must be, too. Horrified, her entire body broke out in a cold sweat.

"No! Not many know his story, but Maccus was betrayed by an archangel, his wings stripped, and tossed into Hell. He fought for millennia until Lucifer feared him so much he kicked him out."

Surely I didn't hear that right. "You're telling me Lucifer, the devil, feared this Maccus guy so much, he threw him out of Hell? He's been kicked out of both Heaven and Hell?" Her voice rose with each word until she was practically yelling.

Just when she thought things were as bad as they could get. She hadn't really put much credence in the entire angel thing until now. Avoidance was her friend, allowing her to function in a world already gone mad. Her throat closed; breathing became difficult. Ragged gasps tore from her aching lungs. *This is not the time for a panic attack.*

"Raine." He pulled her into his arms, wrapping himself around her, his warmth seeping into her cold skin. "I'll keep you safe." He peppered her face with kisses. "I won't let anything happen to you."

Grabbing his shoulders, she held on. He was solid and strong, but would he be powerful enough to go up against such an adversary? She closed her eyes and forced herself to breathe deeply. Last thing he needed was a hysterical woman on his hands.

Several deep breaths later, she was able to continue. "So he's a fallen angel. He was your friend, right? Or was he more like a boss?" She had no idea how the whole assassin Brotherhood thing worked.

"Maccus was one of the few I trusted. He brought us together as a group, but none of us are the type to take orders."

"I can only imagine." Talk about a scary bunch of people or paranormals or whatever they called themselves. It would be so easy to bury her face in the curve of his neck and forget everything outside this room, but it would still be there waiting and eventually would come looking for them. "Why would he wake you?" That's the part that didn't make sense. "You weren't causing any problems where you were."

"I don't know. I've been away a long time."

He wasn't wrong. Things changed. People changed. "Let's take this one step at a time. We'll go to the Angel Foundation. If that's a bust, we'll find this Maccus guy. We can find him, right?"

"The Forgotten Brotherhood lives in the shadows, to protect themselves and others."

"It's not easy to hide in today's world." An idea struck her. She reached for her bag, but he kept his arms locked around her, not allowing her to leave. "I'm okay now," she assured him. "I just had a mini meltdown." Who wouldn't? Angels were real and so was Lucifer. He was someone she never wanted to come face-to-face with.

"I need to touch you." Seemed she wasn't the only one having a difficult time coming to terms with things. He was facing the possibility of a friend's betrayal.

"I'm here." She might not be a supernatural being with preternatural abilities and strength, but she could offer comfort and understanding. "We'll figure things out. How can we not with my brain and your brawn?"

That teased a smile from him.

"Or maybe it's your brain and my brawn." She flexed a bicep.

"Raine." The way he said her name had butterflies exploding in her stomach. Pink eyes glowing, he pressed his lips against hers. Sighing, she sank into the kiss, needing his touch as much as he needed hers.

• • •

Holding her made everything make sense, or at least easier to deal with. He knew better than to jump to conclusions, but there was compelling evidence.

He hadn't mentioned this to her, but Maccus had known the area he'd planned to settle in and sleep. It would be easy enough for him to find Lucius if he put his mind to it. This land had been sparsely populated at the time, with few around other than the indigenous tribes who had always given him a wide berth, sensing something different about him.

The sounds of pleasure she made as they kissed drove all thoughts of the past and future away, leaving only the now. She likely thought herself weak for having a panic attack, but courage wasn't the absence of fear. It was doing what needed to be done despite it.

His dragon shuddered when her hand stroked his face, starved for her touch, her caring. It was a strong hand with slight nicks and calluses, left over from her attempts at escaping the cave. She was slender but resilient, bending rather than breaking in the face of adversity.

He lifted her so she was sitting astride his thighs, letting her feel the hard press of his erection against her stomach. Another of those whimpers of pleasure made his scalp tingle. He slipped his hand beneath her sweater and top, finding the warm, smooth skin of her back. Her spine arched like a cat as he stroked upward.

She was wearing one of those sports bras she favored. They were utilitarian and sturdy and made his mouth water. He shoved it up and skimmed his hands around to the front to cup her breasts.

"I love your hands on me." Her nails scored his upper back and raked lightly over his biceps. "They're so big and hard."

They weren't the only big, hard thing. His cock was painfully swollen. "I want you." Never had a woman been as vital to his well-being. It made him vulnerable, gave him a soft spot his enemies could exploit, made her a liability. But the only thing that mattered right now was having her.

"Yes." She grabbed the hem of her sweater. Her elbow swung toward his nose. He jerked out of the way in time to keep from getting hit. "Sorry." It didn't stop or slow her down. Her enthusiasm was both sweet and arousing as hell.

Helping her, he dragged the tangle of bra and top up and out of the way. Her skin glowed like the finest of pearls, creamy and delicate, and marred with bruises from her ordeal.

He traced his thumb over several of the black and yellow smudges. "I'm sorry you were hurt."

"They don't matter." She planted a line of hot kisses

down the curve of his throat before nipping at his shoulder. "Get back to work."

He threw back his head and laughed. His light in the darkness, she chased away his worries. Raine was talkative and bossy and perfect at handling a drakon.

She stilled, her eyes wide and luminous.

"I'm not laughing at you."

"I don't care." Her hand stroked his chest, the muscles jumping beneath her palms. "I made you laugh." Her gentle, wistful smile brought warmth to his entire being.

All hint of laughter fled, replaced by a burning need that would never be fully quenched. He didn't kiss her as much as consume her, stealing her breath until she clung to him. But she wasn't content to be taken, not his Raine. She attacked, her tongue aggressive and demanding.

He fell back onto the mattress and rolled until she was under him. The bed was too short, his feet hanging off the end. He dragged her to the head of the bed, shoving the pillows out of the way, and ripping her underwear in his effort to get it off.

Her giggle broke through the madness tearing at him. "In a hurry, are you?" Her face was flushed, her nipples furled into tight buds.

"Yes." He dove down and captured one of those pert nipples and sucked.

"Hurrying is good." She tunneled her fingers into his hair, holding him in place. "Hurrying is an excellent idea."

Time was running out for them. His intuition screamed everything would come to a head soon. Someone would die.

It won't be Raine.

Giving a low growl, he kissed a path down her sleek stomach, nuzzling at the thatch of hair at the apex of her legs before diving deep. Her arousal was musky and spicy. She was wet and ready.

Have to taste her.

When she realized his intentions, she widened her legs, giving him space. Drunk on the scent of her, he licked her slick folds and sucked on her clit. Her thighs tightened around him, her feet thumping against his back.

The essence of his dragon rose inside him, wanting to pour into her. Something niggled at the back of his brain, something he'd read long ago.

"Now," she demanded. "I want you inside me."

Pure unadulterated need blasted through him. He surged up and over her, shoved one of her legs up and out, and notched the head of his shaft against her opening.

"Look at me." He waited until her eyes fluttered open, the golden color almost swallowed by the black of her pupils. He shoved inward, not stopping until he was buried to the hilt.

"Lucius." Her nails scored his back, sending a bolt of desire straight to his balls.

Keeping his thrusts slow and measured, he gauged her response. He needn't have worried. She was right with him, her inner muscles rippling around him, clasping him in her sweet warmth.

Supporting his weight on his forearms, he leaned down and kissed her. Their bodies were slick, gliding against each other, getting faster and more frantic. Wild, she bit his bottom lip hard enough to draw several drops of blood, which she licked away.

Her entire body stiffened as if electrified.

He reared back and stared in horror. She'd inadvertently drunk drakon's blood. A single drop would have given her a slight buzz before the Deep Sleep, now it was likely magnified tenfold, like his new powers.

Drakon blood healed. It also killed. There was no way to know for sure until a person consumed it. This was his fault.

He'd been lost in passion, not thinking or paying attention.

"You're going to think I'm crazy—or crazier than you already do—but you taste amazing. Like red wine and chocolate." Some of the glazed expression cleared away. "I'm not some vampire. I won't start craving your blood, will I?"

"How do you feel?" Her color was high, but that was likely from their lovemaking.

Her laugher was full and bright. "Like I've had at least a half dozen iced cappuccinos. Hmm, chocolate ones."

Sweat broke out all over his body as relief flooded him. *She's going to be fine.* "Don't do that again." There was no telling how a larger dose would affect her.

"I didn't mean to hurt you." Her smile fading, she rubbed her thumb over his bottom lip.

As if she could. He captured her thumb and sucked on it. His cock was hard and throbbing inside her. "You didn't hurt me, but my blood might not be safe for you." Not a lie, but not the full truth. There was so much she didn't know about him or his kind.

"I'm not going to die, am I? Although, dying while having sex isn't a bad way to go."

His lips formed a smile. Her spirit glowed so bright it was blinding. "You're not going to die. You're going to fly." He rocked against her, grinding his pelvis against her.

"We'll both fly." Her slick channel squeezed hard, legs locking around him with surprising strength.

"I'll take you really flying someday," he promised as he continued to thrust. "High in the sky with the wind whipping through your hair and caressing your skin. There's nothing like it."

"Yes. Yes." He had no idea whether her agreement was for flying in the sky or flying in bed. Not that it mattered when she tilted her head back and cried out his name. Burying his face against the mattress to muffle his roar, his entire body, no, the entire bed, shook as he came.

He collapsed, managing to do so at an angle to keep from crushing her. A sense of peace enveloped him. Raine nuzzled the arm he'd flung over her collarbone. Their skin was damp, the bed was wrecked, and he was starving.

He'd never felt better.

"I'm humming from head to toe. My skin is prickling. Almost itchy but not quite."

Concerned it had more to do with his blood than their lovemaking, he pulled away from her, even though he was still hard, and propped himself up on one arm. She'd glowed before, but now she was positively radiant. Her skin was no longer blemished, the bruises vanished.

She raised her legs in the air and curled her toes. "It's like I'm drunk, but in a good way."

"You're tired." He brushed his fingers over her face, loving the way she leaned into his touch.

"I am, but I'm not. I'm wired." Her mouth parted on a wide yawn. "Sorry about that."

He rolled onto his back and pulled her against him. "Get some rest."

"Wake me in time to get to the foundation. What time is it?"

He turned his head and found a clock radio on the nightstand. "It's not lunchtime yet. There's plenty of time." Taking him at his word, she closed her eyes and sighed.

He could leave her here and go to the Angel Foundation on his own. And she'd never forgive him. Not to mention, there was no way he'd let her out of his sight.

Mine! his dragon roared, incensed he'd even consider such a thing. The primal beast had accepted from the first what it had taken him long to acknowledge.

Raine would either be his downfall or his salvation. There was no way to know which until the end.

Chapter Fourteen

When she woke, Raine was alone in bed. Panicked, she bolted upright, slumping in relief when she heard the shower running. He hadn't left her.

Giving her head a shake, she surveyed the room. It was small and basic but clean. The bed was in shambles, the fitted sheet no longer tucked around the mattress, the blankets half on the floor. Not surprising given the intensity of their lovemaking. She gave a soft hum and wrapped her arms around herself in a quick hug. Holy smokes, but sex with Lucius was off the charts.

When he touched her, she forgot all her problems. It was a talent. He was big and sexy, the tattoos ranging over his body upping his badass factor. Someday, when she wasn't exhausted and they weren't pressed for time, she was going to map every single one of the markings with her tongue.

She swung her legs over the side of the bed. Expecting her body to protest the vigorous lovemaking combined with her residual aches and pains, she was mildly surprised when there wasn't even a twinge.

"What the heck?" Standing, she stretched her arms over her head. Nothing hurt. Frowning, she looked down at her body. "Wait, this isn't right." She ran her fingers over skin that had been marked by bruises only hours before. Now it was unblemished. Twisting to one side, she checked out her shoulder. Yup, that bruise was gone too.

The bathroom door opened, emitting a plume of steam. She hadn't even noticed the shower turning off. Lucius was framed in the doorway, a towel slung around his neck, the rest of him bare.

He was still aroused, his gaze hot and heavy as it panned over her. She swallowed heavily, her nipples perking up. "Ah." The sheet was at hand, so she yanked it around her. "Something is wrong with me."

His lips flattened. "What?" Already at her side, he yanked at the covering. Not ready to relinquish it, they ended up in a tug of war. "I've seen you naked."

"It's different when we're not making love." It seemed more brazen, more intimate. It also made no sense. Next time he pulled, she released the sheet when it started to rip. "Look at me." She pointed at her stomach.

"Believe me, I am." His voice seemed to have dropped an octave. Talk about tingling, and it wasn't just her skin.

"Don't try to distract me with sex." It would be so easy to do. "Really look at me."

He frowned, his brows furrowing. "I'm not sure what you want me to see."

"This." She pointed to her stomach. "And this." To her arm. "The bruises are gone."

He raked his fingers through his hair and huffed out a breath. "So they are."

She waited and waited, tapping her toe against the rough carpet. "You don't seem especially surprised."

"Can't you be happy about it?"

"I'm not going to complain about not hurting, but I need to know why it happened." An outrageous thought occurred. "It's not making love to you, is it? Do you have magic sperm?"

His chest began to shake, his face turning red as he manfully tried to keep from laughing in her face, which she appreciated. "No, I don't have magic sperm."

"It's not that far-fetched." He was chuckling now, not that she blamed him. When he gave her a pointed look, she dropped down onto the side of the bed, grabbed the sheet, and tucked it around herself. "Okay, maybe it's a little out there, but something happened to me."

He crouched in front of her, placing his hands on the mattress on either side of her. The scent of soap and hot male teased her. He was so close, every feature of his face seemed magnified, from his thick lashes to his perfectly straight nose and his kissable lips.

"It's nothing that will hurt you."

"Are you sure? You'd tell me if something weird was happening to me, wouldn't you? Or is this another one of those drakon secrets you can't share?"

He dropped his head and sighed. "I don't share with anyone."

A heavy weight settled on her chest. "No one?" That seemed sad. Of course, it wasn't like she had a bunch of close friends. Or anyone who'd miss her if she never went home again.

"Other drakons know about me, about what I truly am and can do. Enemies who want to either destroy or own me." When he raised his head, pain reflected back at her. "And Maccus."

The one he suspected of betraying him. "Maybe one of your enemies found out where you were." Why was she defending someone she'd never met? A fallen angel at that. "You've known Maccus a long time, right?"

"Three thousand years."

And she expected him to tell her his secrets after knowing her for a few days. Talk about naive. She had to remind herself their relationship was temporary. Once they'd destroyed the threat to them both, they'd part ways. She swallowed the lump in her throat. "That's a long time. Has he even given you reason to think he'd betray you? Betrayed any of the others in your Brotherhood?"

He shook his head. "No. He lives by the code of the Brotherhood. Kill only those that truly deserve it and let their gods sort them out. Kill them before they kill you. Never, ever, betray a fellow assassin."

A shiver ran down her spine. That was black and white. "We should try to contact him."

"How? The Brotherhood wouldn't advertise."

"Maybe they would." Her earlier idea came back to her. "If they hire out as assassins, they need a way for people to contact them. If they wanted to put some layers between themselves and others, they could have a website or something. A way for people to leave them messages."

He tilted his head to one side. "Do you think so?"

"Only one way to find out." She nudged his hand aside, slid to the end of the bed, and dug her laptop out of her bag. "Give me a second to hook into the wifi." As she powered up the machine, he dug out a change of clothes and dressed. It was slightly easier to concentrate without him walking around naked. The man oozed sex appeal.

"I'm searching for Forgotten Brotherhood." She typed it into the search bar, not surprised when a bunch of entries popped up. "This might be harder than I thought."

"There was nothing?" He sat beside her and tugged on his sneakers.

"Too much. Both words are popular with video games and fantasy role-playing groups. Give me a second." Settling in, she opened one site after another while Lucius paced. It took longer than she'd hoped, but she finally hit one that looked promising. On the surface, it seemed to be another gaming site, but there was only a homepage, no links to anything else. "I think this might be it."

"Why?" He leaned over her shoulder, so she tilted the screen so he could see it better.

"It's only a homepage, like a holding place. There's nothing else here to click on other than a contact button. Should I try?"

He pressed his fingers against the screen, rubbing the banner. A long minute passed before he finally nodded. "Do it."

Now she was the one having second thoughts. Her stomach was jumping and her fingers none too steady. "What should I say?" She clicked on the contact button and got a message screen.

"The drakon has risen."

"Drakon or dragon?" She didn't want to get this wrong.

"Drakon. If it's not Maccus, they'll likely think it a mistake."

"Got it. What now?"

"Leave your phone number. He'll call if he can."

"That's it? No personal message?" That was probably smarter now that she thought about it.

"No, we leave no identifying trace of ourselves."

"Only my phone number, which will lead anyone with even a minor amount of tech savvy straight to me. Not that it matters, since the crazies already know where I live." Her finger hovered over the send button. Once she did this, there was no going back. If it was the Brotherhood, a fallen angel would know who she was, be able to find her. Anyone who'd lived that long would have skills.

Lucius's hand covered hers. "We don't have to do this."

She clicked and the message box closed. "It's done." After closing the laptop, she took a deep breath. "As soon as I'm ready, we'll head to the Angel Foundation." As much as she wanted to hole up in the hotel with Lucius and ignore the rest of the world, that wasn't an option.

He took the laptop from her and set it aside. "It was my blood."

"What?" Had she been so lost in thought she'd missed part of the conversation?

"My blood. When you nipped my lip and licked the droplets away. That's what healed you."

"Your blood?" She touched her fingers to her lips. "It was only a couple of drops."

"Drakon blood heals or it kills. There's no in-between."

"Kills?" Her voice was a squeak. No wonder he'd been worried. She would have been, too, if she'd had any idea.

"My blood was more potent than any other drakon's before the Deep Sleep."

"But you're more powerful now." She'd watched him almost blow apart from the inside out before he'd absorbed the extra energy.

"Yes."

No wonder he was so secretive. Governments, corporations, and powerful men worldwide would hunt him to the ends of the earth if they knew about him. "Can you remove it?"

He stiffened. "There is no way to remove my blood from you. The taint is there forever."

Was he serious? She smacked him on the arm. "There's no taint in your blood. It was delicious, which is a weird thing to say but true. Not to mention, it healed me. You're incredible. I meant the memory. I won't ever tell anyone on purpose, but I've never been tortured before. I want to think I'd hold up under interrogation, but there's no telling until it's too late."

His expression was solemn, his features tight. "You'd allow me to manipulate your mind?"

"To protect you, yes. Just don't get any ideas about doing it for any other reason." Not that she could stop him if he was capable of mind control. Trust wasn't something she'd ever given easily, but Lucius had it.

"It's not something I can do." Relief flowed through her. She might have been willing but hadn't been looking forward to it. "Nor would I," he continued. He brushed his lips against hers, the action almost reverent. The passion was there but it was banked. "Get showered and dressed. We need to leave."

Shaken by the kiss, she stood on unsteady legs. "I won't be long." He was still sitting there when she closed the bathroom door behind her.

• • •

The Angel Foundation was on the sixth floor of a Manhattan midrise office building. They'd caught the subway to a stop near their destination and grabbed something to eat at a fast-food outlet before walking the rest of the way.

"This is it." Raine paused outside a door. The glass was frosted, but the name of the organization was written on it in blue.

He stepped in front of her. "Stay behind me."

"I doubt an angel would attack us in such a busy location," she muttered. He wasn't so sure and was taking no chances.

She'd been willing to let him tamper with her memories to protect him. For as long as he'd lived, he'd never met anyone like her. Protective as he'd been before, it was worse now. He'd level the city before he'd allow harm to come to her. That gave him pause. Maybe that was the entire reason behind all this. Raine made him even more dangerous than before he'd settled into the Deep Sleep. One wrong move on his part and whoever was behind this could petition the Brotherhood to have him put down. They'd have no choice but to comply.

She was the perfect weapon. She didn't have to do anything but be herself.

"What?" she whispered. "Do you hear something?"

"I had a thought. I'll tell you after." He pushed at the door, but it didn't open. "It's locked." He tried again, only adding more pressure. Metal snapped and the door swung inward.

"You're really too good at that." She slipped inside. "Hurry. There are probably cameras in the hallway. The police might already be on their way."

"I don't think so." There wasn't a soul here. The reception desk was empty—no computer or phone or even a pen. "They've pulled out."

Raine hurried down a short hallway to an office. "It's the same in here."

He looked over her shoulder into the abandoned room. Only the furniture remained. "Check the desk drawers and filing cabinets. I'll do the same out here."

"Right." She went straight to work.

The space wasn't big, but a foundation of this kind didn't need a lot. Still, it was a surprise that there was only one office, a small kitchen, conference room, bathroom, and reception area. He went through each methodically.

"Anything?" he asked when she joined him.

"Two paperclips, a quarter, and a half-filled box of tissues. You?"

"Some paper coffee cups, packets of sugar, and stir sticks."

"They took everything. They had to be in on what happened." She nibbled her bottom lip as she peered around.

"I guess our next step is to investigate the Angel Foundation. If they rented office space, someone had to sign a lease. If the organization wasn't totally bogus, there might be information about them in some records or online."

He admired the way her mind was always working, figuring out new ways to tackle the problem.

"Maybe the person behind this is a drakon hunter. Is that even a thing? There are vampire hunters. I'd think they'd need a whole team or an army to take you on."

"There've been highly organized groups dedicated to capturing or destroying us."

"Maybe one of them discovered your resting place."

"That doesn't explain why they sent you." How could they have known how she'd affect him? She'd been targeted, just as he had. More and more, he was convinced it was dark magic.

A ringing sound came from her pocket. "My phone." She dug it out and stared at it. "Unknown caller." Face pale, she looked to him for direction.

"Answer it. Put it on speaker."

"Hello?"

"Raine Carson."

It wasn't a question. The voice was very deep and authoritative. It was also very familiar. He hadn't heard it in hundreds of years, but there was no mistaking Maccus Fury.

"Yes." She shifted her weight from side to side. Lucius wrapped his arms around her from behind, silently supporting her.

"You or someone left this number."

He wished they'd gone over what she should say. He'd thought they'd have more time. Maccus was as antisocial as they came. He'd half expected the message to be ignored.

"I left it. Is this…" She huffed out a breath. "Is this Maccus?"

The silence was menacing. "What do you know about drakons, Ms. Carson?"

"More than I did a few days ago." Lucius's pride in her grew with each passing second. Not many would stand their ground with the leader of the Brotherhood.

He was about to step in when Maccus responded. "If you've hurt him in any way, I'll hunt you down and kill you. There is nowhere you can hide where I can't find you."

Relief swamped him, making his head spin. He hadn't been betrayed. "Glad that I'm not harmed then."

"Lucius? How is this possible? You went into the Deep Sleep, didn't you?" Suspicion tinged his voice.

"I did, but Raine woke me after someone worked it so she was trapped in the cave with me."

"We need to talk."

"Where are you? It might take me a while to get there, depending on what part of the world you're currently living in. I've been informed it would be dangerous for me to take to the skies." The logistics would be problematic if his friend was on another continent. Countries had identification called passports and airport screenings and more security than he'd likely had time to skim in the short bursts he'd had online.

"I had someone I trust hack Ms. Carson's phone. You're about six blocks away."

"You're here?" Mistrust reared its ugly head again. "It's a huge coincidence the same foundation that sent Raine to find me is in the same city where you reside."

He snorted. "I doubt it's a coincidence. The Brotherhood has been under attack from some powerful enemies. I thought that had been handled, but this is troublesome. Bring your Ms. Carson, or not. It's up to you."

"She goes where I go."

Maccus rattled off the address. "We'll see you in a few."

"We?"

"Don't dawdle." The phone went dead.

"Do we go or do we run?" Raine took the phone from him and tucked it back in her pocket.

It would be smarter to send her back to the hotel or to a crowded restaurant. She'd likely be safe surrounded by humans. Even as he thought it, tension bunched the muscles in his neck and shoulders and scales rippled beneath his skin. She didn't belong in his dangerous world, but his drakon would not allow them to be parted. "We go." There was no other choice if he wanted to uncover the truth. "If this is about the Brotherhood, they'll either have answers or help us find them."

"He said 'we'll see you.' Who else do you think will be there?"

He ushered her out of the office, down the elevator, and outside before replying, "Maybe another member of the Brotherhood."

"Vampires? Werewolves? Others? Help a girl out."

Taking her hand, he cleared a path down the center of the sidewalk. It was convenient that people got out of his way. Safer for them, too. "I don't know who will be there, who might have died, or if there has been any new member. I've been away a long time."

She dug in her heels, forcing him to stop. One man cursed at her until Lucius glared at him. Then he ducked his head and practically ran. "Then how can you trust Maccus? You said he's a fallen angel." The last was said in a hissed whisper. Not that anyone was listening. There were so many people all crammed into a small area, each of them rushing around. They reminded him of ants on an ant hill.

"Maccus Fury is a law unto himself." He tugged and got her moving again. It occurred to him that someone could be watching from any of the surrounding buildings. There were so many of them, offering the perfect vantage point to mount an attack with a conventional weapon. Having Raine exposed like this made her an even bigger target. Unlike him, she wouldn't survive a gunshot to the head or chest. "He also won't take kindly to being left waiting."

"We don't want to piss off a fallen angel."

"That was sarcasm, right?" He turned a corner, following the directions his friend had given. All his senses were on alert, watching and listening for anything out of the ordinary.

"You think? This is all old hat to you, but I don't know anything about these people. I hardly know anything about drakons. I know the lore and myths, but that's not reality."

She was right. She deserved the truth. Knowledge was power, and she needed all the resources she could get. It would also help deepen her trust in him if he shared. "There are four types of drakons—earth, air, fire, and water."

"Which one are you?"

"Earth."

She perked up and picked up her pace. "Don't stop now."

This was common knowledge among those who hunted his kind, but it was still harder than he'd expected to speak of it. His past had left him with emotional wounds that were still raw, and she was bearing the brunt of his mistrust. "You know how we came into being, how we procreate, and about the Deep Sleep. And you know about my blood." She knew more than she thought she did.

"How come there's never been any bones, any evidence of your kind? Or have archaeologists misclassified dinosaur bones?"

He gritted his teeth. "Once and for all, we are not dinosaurs." They'd had this discussion in the cave.

She patted his arm. "No need to be touchy. You're much sexier than a T-Rex."

If they were anywhere else, he'd show her the truth of her words, but they'd reached their destination—a tall apartment high-rise. "Dragons, and drakons, burn when they die. It destroys all evidence of their existence. Only a drakon's own fire can destroy his blood. It's an evolutionary protection so drakons can't harm other drakons with their fire."

"That is so cool. Smart, too, otherwise it wouldn't take long for the species to potentially wipe itself out. That might not be a problem, since you all live for so long." They walked back to the bank of elevators and stood there staring at it. "He didn't say what floor." The door in front of them slid open. With a shrug, she stepped forward with him close behind. "Guess we don't need to know."

There were likely cameras everywhere. This new world was fascinating, and potentially very dangerous for all paranormals. Humans had populated at an alarming rate and showed no signs of stopping. They and their technology were reaching the furthest reaches of the globe.

The doors closed and the elevator began to move.

Raine curled her fingers around his. "Looks like we're heading to the penthouse."

Chapter Fifteen

Holy lifestyles of the rich and famous. They were heading to the penthouse of a downtown Manhattan apartment building. Made sense that a fallen angel would have plenty of money. It was difficult to think in immortal terms. Most people struggled and worked their entire lives and were lucky if they could afford their own home. If you lived a long time and were smart, you'd be extremely wealthy.

A light *tapping* sound was beginning to annoy her. She looked down, only to realize it was the toe of her boot against the floor. Swearing under her breath, she made herself stop.

She tugged at the collar of her sweater. Lucius could probably tell she was sweating but was smart enough not to mention it. He'd done his best on the trip over here to take her mind off what was about to happen. While she appreciated his effort, there was no time to savor and digest all the information he'd given her. And let's face it—nothing was going to distract her from this coming meeting.

"Stay behind me."

"Why? I thought it was safe."

"I'm sure it will be. Don't worry."

Easy for him to say. She was the lone human at this meeting. The walls of the elevator closed in around her. A couple of deep breaths did nothing to calm the urge to run, not that it was even a possibility. There was nowhere to go but up.

The emergency stop button shone like a beacon of hope. She was reaching for it when the elevator slid to a halt. It chimed and the doors slid open, bringing her face-to-face with the scariest man she'd ever set eyes on. And she was on intimate terms with a drakon.

He was massive, only slightly shorter than Lucius. Dressed all in black—boots, T-shirt, and jeans. With wicked looking knives tattooed on his forearms, he was a sight to inspire nightmares. His eyes were black. Not dark brown, but pitch. Jet black hair was cut short on the sides, with the top long and pulled back into a short tail. All the fine hairs on her arms stood on end. The air snapped with tension.

He was badass biker meets mass murderer. Or fallen angel. Dread pooled in the pit of her stomach. She was so in over her head.

"Maccus." Lucius stayed in the opening of the elevator, going no farther.

"Lucius."

"This is your home."

"It is."

"The man I knew never allowed anyone into his home."

"I've evolved." The dry tone and barest hint of humor caught her off guard. There was no welcome in his eyes, no sign he was glad to see his friend.

"Either you're an imposter," Lucius continued, "or this is a sign of the end times spoken of by your holy men."

The energy in the air made her skin itch. Like watching an impending car crash, there was no way she could look away from the confrontation playing out in front of her. A nervous giggle escaped her, but neither man was paying her any attention.

They stared at each other like gunslingers in the dusty street at high noon, each waiting for the other to make the first move. At this rate, they might get around to going inside in a week or two.

"You knew where I rested." It wasn't a question. Guess they were bypassing the pleasantries and getting straight to the point.

He inclined his head. "I did. Neither of us had any idea what to expect, if you'd be vulnerable for some time."

Lucius stilled. "You watched over me."

"You're part of the Brotherhood."

Whether they acknowledged it or not, it went so much deeper than that. She might not be a powerful paranormal creature or have otherworldly abilities, but the caring between the two men was obvious, even to her. "For God's sake, hug it out. You know you want to."

Both men stared at her like she'd lost her mind.

Shut up, Raine. Nerves overriding common sense, she plowed forward. "I get that you're both badass alpha males who need to snort and stomp to try to assert dominance, but you're friends, damn it, and we don't have time to waste." When neither man made a move, she muttered, "Gods, you're all stubborn. Too bad there isn't another woman here."

"Luckily there is." With a smile on her face, a tall woman with a short cap of auburn hair and green eyes entered from a nearby hallway.

"I told you to stay in the study." Fury vibrated from Maccus. Was that how he'd gotten his name? Raine's knees turned to jelly, but the woman strode up to him and kissed his cheek. She was either brave or out of her mind or both.

"You didn't say for how long. I'm Morrigan Quill.

Welcome to our home." The welcome was heartfelt and eased some of Raine's anxiety. Not all of it. She wasn't stupid enough to believe the storm had passed. It was more the hope that the men would be less likely to come to blows in front of them.

"You have a woman. This really is a sign of the apocalypse." Lucius's surprise echoed her own. This didn't seem like a guy who'd settle down. He'd be more at home marauding and pillaging. Likely many would say the same about Lucius.

Ignoring the depression that wanted to swamp her at the reminder their time together was limited, she wiped her hand on her jeans before offering it. "Raine Carson." She started to slide around Lucius with her hand extended, but he clamped his arm around her waist and pulled her back against him. Her hand hovered in the air for a couple of seconds before she lowered it and rubbed it against her thigh.

Okay then. This wasn't going as well as it could, but they weren't trying to kill each other. That was a plus. "No niceties. Got it. How about information?"

Maccus spun around and headed toward the living area, tugging Morrigan behind him. It was as much of an invitation to enter as they were likely to get.

When Lucius hesitated, she gave him a push. It wasn't his safety he was concerned about but hers. No way would she allow herself to become a liability. They'd come too far and needed information only Maccus could provide.She knew she'd won when he gave a grunt and entered the apartment. The elevator door slid shut behind them.

The space was large and surprisingly homey. The walls were painted a warm beige and were completely empty. No artwork or photographs softened the space. Two comfy-looking sofas and a couple of oversize chairs were grouped around a round coffee table. A patterned rug of greens and browns anchored the seating area. No small, dainty furniture here.

Maccus sat in one of the chairs with Morrigan perched on the arm. Lucius chose one of the sofas, pulling her down beside him.

"Tell me everything." Maccus sat forward, his thick forearms resting on his thighs. Like magic, a dagger appeared in his hand, giving her a jolt. He began to flip it through his fingers with great skill and dexterity.

Lucius remained stubbornly silent beside her. The tension built until she couldn't stand it any longer. "I teach folklore, mostly myths and legends, at a university. Got a grant from a foundation that allowed me to take a year off from work to research and write a book."

"You didn't find that suspicious?"

Mimicking his stance, she leaned forward, resting her forearms on her jeans. "Yes, I did. I'm not stupid. I researched them. They had a good name, had been giving out grants for years according to what I uncovered. I even contacted several past recipients and asked about their experience."

"You didn't tell me that."

She glanced up at Lucius. "I told you I'd looked into them. It really did seem legitimate. After finding their offices empty, I have to believe it was nothing more than an elaborate and expensive hoax. Anyway, they put me in contact with a man who claimed to have found a dragon carved out of stone in a cave in the Smokey Mountains National Park."

"That would be you." Maccus pointed the tip of the dagger at Lucius, who only grunted.

The faster she got through this, the faster they could leave. Her heart was beating so hard her chest was aching. Sweat had her clothes sticking to her skin. No way could she hide her obvious discomfort from any of them. Their abilities were unknown to her, but she assumed her hosts had preternatural senses. Even if they didn't, it wasn't hard to tell she was uncomfortable. "When I went inside to investigate, my guide exploded the entrance, trapping me." From there, she continued recounting everything. Well, mostly everything. She skipped over the fact they'd slept together. Not that they couldn't fill in the details. "So we went to the Angel Foundation and found it empty," she concluded. "You responded to the message we left and here we are."

"Why you?" His dark eyes pierced her soul. It was as though he could read her every thought. God, she hoped he couldn't read her mind. He'd sat quietly during her explanation, asking no questions. He might be a big bruiser, but his exterior hid a keen intelligence.

"Lucius asked the same thing. I'll tell you what I told him. I don't know. I'm nobody special." Certainly not someone who belonged with this group of extraordinary people. She dropped her head back and stared at the ceiling.

"I didn't think it possible to wake a sleeping drakon." Hard to tell if it was distrust in his voice or if he was simply trying to reason things out.

Lucius stirred beside her. "I've been giving it a lot of thought. I believe there's one force strong enough to bring a drakon out of the Deep Sleep."

Curiosity had her sitting forward again. "A chatty teacher of folklore," she joked, trying to lighten the heavy mood that hung over them. Morrigan smiled, but the men remained grim.

"No, something far more elusive and unique." She cut him off with a shake of her head and rolled her eyes toward their avid listeners. Spilling drakon secrets didn't seem like the smart thing to do, especially since Morrigan was an unknown. There was no doubting she was a badass or she wouldn't be with Maccus, but she was a stranger to Lucius. Whatever he was about to reveal, it likely had something to do with her, and she could deal with only one thing at a time. Right now, surviving Maccus and getting information were the goals.

"You're a treasure, Raine, but Maccus knows all about drakons. He's far older than I am."

"He is?" That was mind-boggling but something she should have reasoned out. After all, he was an angel—a fallen one, but still—and the leader of the Brotherhood. Maccus leaned back in his chair, one hand resting on Morrigan's thigh, the other playing with a knife—a different one from earlier. *Where is he getting them?* "Just how old is he?"

"Positively ancient. I'm four thousand years old. A mere babe in comparison."

She blinked several times. He wasn't kidding. Her vision began to dim. "Excuse me." She dropped her head between her legs, closed her eyes, and tried to breathe. *Don't pass out. Don't pass out.*

"Raine." Lucius sounded far away.

"I'll be fine. Just processing." *Suck it up. Don't show weakness in front of the others.* Too late for that. Taking a deep breath, she raised her head. "Sorry about that. It's been a busy few days."

Morrigan hurried back into the room, a bottle in hand. *She must have left while I was trying not to heave.* "Here, sip some water."

Lucius helped steady her hand when it shook. The cool water soothed her dry mouth and throat. "Thank you." She took another sip.

"Don't worry about it. It's a lot to take in. I had some difficult moments when I first met Maccus, and I was a bounty hunter for Hell."

Water spurted, spraying everywhere. "What?"

Morrigan's eyes twinkled. "It's a long story. I'm not too much older than you."

This must have been what Alice felt like when she fell into Wonderland—out of her depth and totally inadequate. "Fallen angel, former bounty hunter for Hell, drakon, and human. One of these things doesn't fit with the others."

• • •

Fuck! He'd almost blurted that Raine was his mate in front of the others. It had been a primal instinct to claim, to mark her as his.

"Who would know"—Maccus hesitated for a split second—"how to wake you?"

His friend had reasoned out what Lucius hadn't said—Raine was his mate—and understood the implications. Drakon mates were likely the rarest creatures in existence. A drakon protected his treasure, no matter the cost. It placed a huge responsibility on her, whether she understood it or not. The fate of the world was literally in her hands. If she realized that, she'd likely run from him.

His friend didn't appear to be overly concerned about the implications, but looks were deceiving. The adage "still waters run deep" applied to the man. A lethal hunter—not by thought, word, or deed did he give himself away. By the time his enemies discovered he was near, it was too late.

"That's the question, isn't it?" For all his vast knowledge, he couldn't come up with an answer.

Raine rubbed her hand over her forehead. "For whatever reason I was able to wake him. I'm nothing more than bait. The non-virgin sacrifice."

Morrigan gave her a quizzical look. "I don't understand."

"Virgins were often offered up as sacrifice to appease our dragon sires when they roamed the earth," Lucius explained.

"I told him in the cave I wasn't a virgin, so it was his tough luck." Raine shot him a quick grin.

"And I said I don't want to hear about past lovers unless you want to give me their names." The thought of her with another was enough to make him crazy.

She mimed zipping her lips.

"Enemies have been trying to destroy the Brotherhood." The knife flashed as Maccus slammed it into the table, burying the blade deep. "I thought we'd dealt with that."

Raine jolted beside him. Her heartbeat skipped a beat and picked up its pace. He was worried about her. The stress couldn't be healthy. "Who?" This could be the lead they'd been hoping for.

"Gabriel tried to hire me to kill Morrigan, even though humans are off-limits to angels. That bastard's had a grudge against me since he kicked me out of Heaven. Pissed off I didn't die." He took Morrigan's hand and twined their fingers together. "Lucifer wanted her to kill me. He's still annoyed at the havoc I caused in his realm. Their plan failed, but not for lack of trying."

"And you just happened to beat both Heaven and Hell at their own game. And now you're living happily ever after with a woman of your own." Call him skeptical, but that seemed a tad too good to be true.

Maccus's lips flattened and another blade appeared in his hand. "Watch yourself. Think what you want about me, but do not disparage Morrigan." The temperature in the room was nearing a boiling point, tempers close to flaring. His dragon wanted to barbecue Maccus, which wouldn't help the already strained relations.

Releasing a growl of pure frustration, he rubbed the back of his neck. "I apologize. I'd gut anyone who spoke against Raine in that manner." Not knowing who his enemy was, having nowhere to aim his fury, was making his dragon restless and dangerous.

"We all need to calm down. No one is gutting anyone."

The slight quaver in Raine's voice shamed him. She had to be scared out of her mind. Even though she appeared calm, he could smell her fear, noted the way she was chewing her bottom lip.

He caught her hand and brought it to his lips. "I'm frustrated, but that's no excuse."

Maccus inclined his head. His friend really had changed. In the past, he would've been dodging flying blades as he shifted and attacked. Maybe the women were taming them both.

"Lucifer and Gabriel set you on each other. That's a grudge against you. What does it have to do with me or the Brotherhood? How does it all tie in?"

"When the dust cleared, I was off-limits. So was Morrigan."

"Are we talking about the Archangel Gabriel?" Her voice was steady, but he detected the slightest quiver. "Because if we are, I'm even more freaked out."

Lucius wrapped his arm around her shoulders. "Yes, that Gabriel." It was all beginning to make a sick kind of sense. "Hurt the Brotherhood. Hurt you." It was diabolical and ingenious.

"Yes." There was a wealth of pain behind that one word. His friend might seem cold and unfeeling, but he took his responsibility to the rest of them seriously. "Lucifer worked behind the scenes to put other Brothers in situations that could have turned ugly, but the threat was nullified. Or so I thought."

"If something happened to Raine, you'd attack, maybe even killing innocents." Worry clouded Morrigan's eyes.

He'd already killed to protect her, but he didn't count Mack and his armed buddies as innocent. The back of his neck prickled. "If I killed indiscriminately, Maccus would be forced to try to put me down."

"Make no mistake, it would happen." The vow slammed down between them, a dividing line. Maccus was on his feet, a deadly sword lit with blue and purple flames in his hand. A brilliant light now rimmed the black of his eyes, making them appear deep and fathomless and even more otherworldly.

Lucius slowly stood and faced his friend. "You'd try, but I'm not as I was. Before I went to sleep, I was bigger and stronger than any other drakon alive. An oddity, even among them. Something happened to me after I awakened. It almost destroyed me. I'm ten times more powerful than I was. I could blow up the Earth's core, if I chose."

"Stop it." Raine jumped to her feet. "No one's blasting anything or smiting anyone. Whoever is behind this, this is what they want. I, for one, am in no hurry to give them anything."

The flames winked out and the sword disappeared. "You're right."

Lucius's jaw dropped. "Did you just admit to being wrong?" This was a first for the ages. Maybe the apocalypse *was* upon them.

A muscle in his jaw worked. "No. I'm saying she's right."

"How *are* you doing that knife and sword thing?" Raine demanded. "They come. They go. Wait, don't tell me. I'm not sure my brain can handle much more without exploding."

The corners of Maccus's mouth twitched. A hard lump of dread loosened in his chest. He didn't want to have to fight one of the few men he called friend. "I can see why you were pulled from the Deep Sleep." High praise from his Brother.

"Hey, I talk when I'm nervous, and I've got to tell you, I've never been more nervous than I am right now. Wait, maybe when the stone cracked around Lucius and he became a real dragon, or drakon, but it's a close tie."

When she took a breath, he bent down and pressed his mouth to hers. It allowed him to silence whatever thought was about to spill out. It also gave him the touch and connection he craved. She made one of those sexy sounds in the back of her throat and flung her arms around him.

Maccus cleared his throat. "Do you want a room?"

Lucius smiled against Raine's lips and raised his head. "Did you just make a joke?"

He grunted.

"You've been good for him," he told Morrigan.

"Sorry about that." Raine straightened the hem of her sweater. "Getting back to the subject at hand, who would put Lucius and me together? There was no way to know how things would end."

Morrigan tapped a finger to her cheek. "Maybe someone was guessing you might have the ability to wake him and figured it was worth a try. It wasn't Lucifer. He knows what would happen if he poked his nose into Brotherhood business again."

"You're sure?" Lucius couldn't see Lucifer just backing down, but he had to believe there was a reason they were so certain.

"Yes." The finality to Maccus's agreement was enough for him.

"Then what about Gabriel or some other angel with a grudge? It's not by chance the Angel Foundation was behind the grant Raine received."

Maccus stared at Raine. "She's the only other new player. Are you sure she's not working with them?"

Chapter Sixteen

The shock of the accusation hit her right between the eyes. *Should have seen that one coming.* It was a perfectly reasonable question, but it hurt nonetheless. *She* was the outsider.

For once, she had nothing to say. Lucius wouldn't be swayed by Maccus's accusations. *He thought you might be guilty of working with Mack*, a voice in her head gleefully reminded her. That was before. They knew each other much better, had shared secrets, not to mention making love.

Or maybe she was grasping at straws.

Burying her hurt, she tilted her chin up and faced her accuser. "There's nothing I can do to prove my innocence. I'm done here." If the angel distrusted her, he wasn't likely to divulge any useful information while she was around. She was halfway to the elevator before Lucius caught her by the hand.

"Not without me."

Relief swamped her, making her head spin. "I would never work with anyone to hurt you." It was important he believe her. He gave a curt nod. A muscle ticked high on his cheek. "Ah, your eyes are glowing." Did he really believe her or was he just saying it?

"We're not done." Maccus was only a few steps away. "All possibilities must be considered."

She gave him props for looking out for his friend, even as she wanted to kick him where it really hurt. Not smart, considering he had a flaming sword and she had nothing more than her wits to protect her. Talk about an uneven fight.

"Raine is a victim in this."

She started to nod but shook her head instead. "I'm no victim." Anger made her voice shake as adrenaline flooded her body. She'd worked damn hard to be strong and capable, to overcome the obstacles life had thrown at her. Outmatched she might be, but she wasn't backing down. "I found myself in a situation." She nodded, liking the word. "A situation far outside the norm. I may not have superpowers like all of you, but I'm determined and I'm no quitter. Victim, my ass."

"I stand corrected." Lucius brought her hand to his lips. "You are the bravest woman I've ever known."

"If she has nothing to hide, she won't mind if we investigate."

It was official. His last name was Fury because he made people furious. Before she could think better of it, she stalked forward and poked him in the chest. "Investigate all you want. It won't change a thing."

The room grew visibly darker, shadows slithering down the walls and creeping across the floor until she and Maccus were surrounded. Sound and visibility dropped to almost nil. What she could hear was muffled.

"You touched me." His voice sounded odd, not outraged. More perplexed. She often had that effect on people.

"I didn't hurt you. Your chest is like iron." Antagonizing him wasn't going to help matters. He was Lucius's friend, not to mention he was a powerful being. She swallowed heavily as the shadows thickened. Ribbons of them wove through her legs and twined around her waist. "I shouldn't have poked you. In my defense, I was provoked." The ribbons climbed higher, encircling her neck. She coughed as one pressed against her throat.

What the hell? Shadows didn't have weight or substance, or shouldn't, yet her throat ached. Her breathing grew shallow and her limbs began to tremble. *I could die.* A fallen angel held her life in his hands. Lucius might not be able to rescue her in time. He'd blame himself for this, even though it was her impetuous behavior that put her here.

The air behind her superheated. It was like stepping out of air-conditioning into a blistering one-hundred-degree day. Despite the warmth, she shivered with a chill that went all the way to her bones.

A thunderous crack and groan split the air. The shadows retreated, allowing her to breathe more easily. They raced back to the dark corners of the room. Her ears popped and the world became audible.

Holy shit! The place was trashed. What was left of the sturdy furniture resembled a pile of matchsticks and fluff in the far corner. *That's not going to be cheap to replace.* That was the least of her worries. Lucius's huge dragon filled the entire space. His rose-gold scales reflected a brilliant light that chased the shadows until they were swallowed up. His tail whipped toward the wall. A piece of plaster crashed to the floor. Even with the high ceilings, he had to duck his huge head and fold his wings. The floor began to creak beneath him. It wasn't meant to support this kind of weight.

Wings shot out from behind Maccus. Not white, as she'd imagined an angel's would be, but black as pitch. An inner light shimmered among the feathers. They reminded her of his eyes. She would have thought fallen angels lost their wings, but here was proof to the contrary.

The flaming sword was back in his hand. His shirt was somehow gone, revealing a muscular upper body covered in tattoos of knives, throwing stars, and other sharp instruments of death, several of which eerily resembled the ones he'd been playing with earlier.

Death surrounded her. These men were immortal assassins, who wouldn't hesitate to kill if provoked, had killed many times in their long lives. Lucius had told her. She'd seen him kill to protect her. This was something more primal and dangerous.

Caught like a rabbit between two ravenous wolves, she froze in place, her legs refusing her command to run.

"Raine, come here." Lucius's deep voice made the room shake.

She wanted to, really, she did. "We should…" She cleared her throat and tried again. "We should talk about this." One wrong word and things would go nuclear.

Neither man was listening, both locked on the other. Morrigan was standing behind her man, a sword in her hand, ready to defend him. No help there. It was up to her to deescalate the situation before it got to the point of no return.

"You know, most friends who hadn't seen each other in hundreds of years would grab a beer and pizza and catch up on all the news. Not go at each other like *Clash of the Titans*."

Lucius turned his head, his big jaw dropping to expose giant teeth. At least there was no drool. That would be a huge turnoff and likely something she wouldn't be able to forget.

"I couldn't see you." Lucius's pain gave her the strength to move toward him. His tail curled around her, herding her toward his chest.

"The shadows were alive." She feared she'd dream about being trapped inside them for the rest of her life. "I'm fine. He didn't hurt me." It hadn't been a pleasant encounter, and something she could go eternity without ever experiencing again, but she was keeping that to herself. If he had any inkling of how scared she'd been, he'd attack. Then somebody would die.

"I think it's best if we leave." Before some spark lit a flame that might mean the end of the city. She patted one of his thick scales, but he remained rooted firmly in place. The floor groaned beneath his great weight. "We're going to end up in the lobby the hard way and take out the people below us. You have to shift."

His roar shook the entire building. She slammed her hands over her ears and prayed there was no lasting damage. Meteorologists would likely be checking to see if there'd been an earthquake in the area. His body shimmered. The wash of energy lifted her hair on end. Even though she closed her eyes, it was still too bright. When it died down and she opened them, he was in front of her, gloriously naked and unarmed.

"What's it going to be?" Every muscle in Lucius's back tensed as he faced his opponent. His tattoos glowed. She moved to the side, wanting to keep everyone in her line of sight.

The flames on Maccus's sword burned brighter before the weapon vanished into thin air. No warming, no fanfare. Just *poof*. He tilted his head back and stared at the hole in his ceiling. "I had to see inside her, to be sure she was telling the truth."

"You were protecting him? From me?" Incredulous, she pointed at her chest. "I'm the only human here." Morrigan didn't count, since she was a former bounty hunter for Hell.

Maccus snorted. "Humans are deadlier than many paranormals. Groups of *your kind* have dedicated their lives to harming drakons."

Letting the "your kind" comment slide, she frowned. "Why didn't you ask? I would have consented. Anything to help figure out what's going on."

"He wouldn't have allowed it. You told me I could investigate."

So she had. She'd never imagined he'd take her up on it so quickly or in such a manner.

Chin arrogantly tilted and totally unapologetic, he inclined his head toward Lucius. "I understand if you wish to leave the Brotherhood."

"No one is doing anything." The last thing she wanted was for Lucius to decide something that huge in the heat of the moment and have to live with regrets. They needed to get out of here and regroup. Myth and legend were her life's work, but she'd reached her limit. It was a hell of a lot different when it was in books, and a lot scarier in reality. "Will you call if you get any information?"

Maccus inclined his head. That was something. The trip hadn't been a total waste of time. She wished it would have ended better.

Lucius took her hand and headed toward the elevator, practically dragging her behind him. Giving a sigh, she dug in her heels. "Wait. We can't leave yet."

"Why not?"

She ran her gaze over him from head to toe. "You're naked."

• • •

White-hot anger heated his blood, making it difficult to think rationally. Maccus knew what Raine was to him. He *knew*. He might not have said it aloud, but his friend had been around long enough to understand what he meant when he'd said there was only one force powerful enough to wake him— Raine was his mate.

For a drakon, who prized treasures both large and

small, there was no greater one in this world or any other. Speculation had run rampant for millennia among his kind. They'd all wondered if there were only one mate destined for them, as was the case with dragons, or would they wander aimlessly through their lives unable to find anything but the occasional short-term relationship with a woman.

There were no longer any doubts.

And Maccus had tried to take her from him. He shook his head, fighting his dragon for control. The beast wanted to rip the male to shreds for daring such a thing.

His friend had been looking out for him, in his own way. He had no idea how close he'd come to dying. The only reason he hadn't attacked outright was out of fear of hurting Raine.

"Hold up." She tugged at his hand. "I know you're pissed, but you can't walk the streets naked."

"Maccus's clothes should fit. I'll get something for you to wear." Not waiting for an answer, Morrigan slipped down the hall.

Arms by his sides, Maccus stared at him, jaw clenched, body rigid, and eyes burning with an inner fire. It pained him to be at odds with one of the few people he'd ever called friend, but there were lines that couldn't, shouldn't be crossed.

"He was protecting you." Raine kept her voice low, even though she had to suspect everyone could hear her.

"Are you defending him after what he just did to you?" Seeing her disappear behind a wall of impenetrable shadows… Talk about a living nightmare. He'd died a thousand deaths in the seconds it had taken him to transform. She'd been alone, unable to protect herself against such a powerful foe. Although, to be honest, she looked anything but defenseless now.

Hands on her hips, she glared at him. Her hair was mussed, and the color had come back into her cheeks. He wanted to take her, claim her, mark her so the entire world would see she belonged to him.

"What did he do? Did he scare the crap out of me with that weird shadow business? You bet. But he didn't physically hurt me. And I did tell him he could investigate."

He dragged his fingers through his hair, caught the ends, and tugged so he wouldn't try to shake some sense into her. She had a way of confusing him, making him change his mind, to see things from another viewpoint. "Are you serious?"

Her expression softened, her eyes taking on a wistful look. "I always wanted a friend who would care about me so much they'd risk everything to protect me."

As much as it pained him to admit, she wasn't wrong. He slowly released the grip on his hair and rubbed the back of his neck. "What do you expect me to do?"

She placed her hand on his chest, right over his heart. "I don't *expect* you to do anything. You do whatever you think is right. But Maccus took a risk, knowing it would likely destroy your friendship." She paused and glanced around. "His home didn't fare so well, but he did it anyway. What does that tell you?"

He glanced around the room and winced at the cracks in the walls and on the ceiling, the chunks of plaster scattered about. Not to mention what remained of the living room furniture. The damage was extensive but could've been worse. At least the building was still standing.

"I think this will do." Morrigan returned with a stack of clothes. "Not sure about the sneakers." She held up a pair of plain black ones. "They're worth a try."

He was vaguely aware of Raine taking the clothes, but he had eyes only for Maccus. Now that the haze of anger had faded, and his dragon was assured the danger had passed, he was remembering details, both small and large.

"You have wings." The corners of Maccus's mouth tightened but he nodded. "How?" What else had changed while he'd been sleeping? He wasn't the only one who was stronger, had evolved.

Raine handed him a pair of jeans, which he pulled on. They fit almost perfectly. A bit short, but not uncomfortable.

"That wasn't normal?" she asked as she shook out a T-shirt and tossed it at him. "I figured a fallen angel meant no wings. I wasn't going to ask but, since you did…" She sent Maccus a quizzical look. "How did you get wings?"

"It's a long story."

Raine rolled her eyes. "You guys are not big on details, are you? Getting anything out of Lucius is like pulling hen's teeth, and FYI hens don't have teeth. Try these." She shoved the sneakers at him.

Like the rest, they fit well and were only a little snug. They'd do until he could change back at the hotel. He needed to buy more clothes. For that, he'd need money. "I need access to my account." While he had gold and gems and other priceless items cached around the globe, he'd left the fees he'd gotten from the contracts he'd taken with the Brotherhood in case any of them fell into economic hardship. Not that such a thing was likely but, since he hadn't planned to ever come back, he hadn't needed the money.

Maccus pulled out his phone. Beside him, Raine shifted her weight from one foot to the other. Two minutes passed before he slipped the device back into his pocket. "It's done. I texted the information to Raine."

This was it. Once he walked out that door, he'd never see his friend again. All these centuries, Maccus had watched out for him, guarded his money, and kept his secrets. The leader of the Brotherhood had done what he'd thought was right and would make no apology.

"You're fucking maddening, do you know that?" Hands fisted at his sides, he stalked across the room. Raine grabbed the hem of his T-shirt to try to stop him but ended up being pulled along.

"I've been told that." The damn man tilted his chin up, as if daring Lucius to take a shot. Or offering him a free one. "You'll feel better." He motioned to the clenched fist.

On a roar, he slammed his fist into Maccus's jaw. Pain radiated through his hand and up his arm, even as Maccus's head jerked back. The thing was harder than iron. Any other paranormal creature would have likely been on his ass, his face shattered, or maybe even dead. He really was stronger.

Smiling, the angel licked a drop of blood from the corner of his mouth. "That all you got?"

Shoulders loosening, he smiled back. "I'm just getting started." A fight was exactly what he needed to rid himself of all his pent-up frustrations. He raised his arm, but there was no punch thrown, no follow-through. Clinging to his biceps like a monkey, Raine hung about a foot off the floor, her short nails digging into his skin.

"You're not fighting with each other. I'm putting a stop to it."

"How are you going to do that?" Not that he would do anything, not with her stuck to him like glue, but he was curious about how she intended to stop him. He should be furious with her for putting herself between him and Maccus yet again, but could only marvel at her fearlessness.

Boosting herself up, she wrapped her entire body around him, legs around his waist and arms around his neck. "You won't risk me being hurt."

Yes, that would stop him faster than any weapon or magic incantation ever could. The fact she realized that, meant she trusted him on the deepest level.

Closing his eyes, he buried his face in the curve of her neck and breathed in her scent. It grounded him, aroused him. It was, would always be, the scent of home. "I would never risk you." It appeared she not only understood that, but also wasn't afraid to use it. Not only was she brave, she was clever.

He captured her mouth, claiming it, because he had to. And strangely enough, he trusted Maccus not to do anything that might hurt them. Damn it. He was going to have to forgive his friend.

Holding her close, he practically inhaled her, loving the way she instantly responded, her tongue stroking his. Relief flooded through him. She was safe, and they weren't in this alone. The Brotherhood would have his back. Or at least Maccus would.

He eased away and dropped several more kisses on her swollen pink lips. "You don't want me to fight."

"You're friends. Or were. Still are." Her golden eyes pleaded for understanding. When he nodded, she released him and dropped back to the floor. His lips twitched in amusement when she clasped her hand in his. She was determined to keep him from fighting.

"Feel better?" Looking no worse for wear, Maccus patiently waited.

"Yes. No." On a sigh, he kissed the top of Raine's head. "You can let go." Her fingers tightened fractionally before she released him.

Facing Maccus, he stared deep into his eyes. There was no emotion to be found, but a muscle twitched beneath his eye.

"Don't do it again." Warning given, Lucius dragged his friend into his arms. He remained stiff for several long seconds before one arm came up to wrap around him. "I'm not sorry I hit you."

When they parted, Maccus's lips twitched. "I'm not sorry for what I did either."

Good enough. "So what now?" He glanced around the penthouse and winced. "I'll pay for the damage."

Morrigan leaned against Maccus and slung an arm around his waist. "Don't worry about it. I've been meaning to redecorate."

His friend's woman was as gracious as she was beautiful. "I apologize for any upset I might have caused you." He'd been pissed about Raine being in danger, but he'd done the same thing to Morrigan.

Maccus inclined his head. It was done.

Raine eyed them both, arms crossed and foot tapping. "That's it? You guys are squared again?"

"It's what you wanted, isn't it?"

"I don't get guys. You're mortal enemies, throw a punch, and then you're friends again." She shook her head and looked to Morrigan. "Do you get them?"

"Oddly enough, I do. Friends are scarce enough, but when you're so very different, they're even harder to find."

"You're right. So we're all good again. What's the next step?" She'd taken the words right out of his mouth. It likely wouldn't be the last time, since she seemed to be in tune with what he was thinking.

"Where *do* we go for answers?"

"If angels are a problem, we go to the source." Maccus waved his hand toward the wall. Bloodred symbols appeared on the damaged plaster.

"Holy crap." Raine started forward, likely to examine them, but he hooked his arm around her and held her back.

"Wait," he cautioned. He had no idea what all the symbols were for. The ones he recognized were protective, to keep someone or something from entering.

Another wave and several of the symbols vanished. "Gabriel, get your ass down here. Don't make me have to come looking for you."

Chapter Seventeen

I've got to stop thinking things can't get crazier.

Every time she did, something else happened to prove her wrong. Raine had no idea who Maccus was calling out to, wasn't sure she really wanted to. If it took bloodred symbols on the wall to keep them out, they weren't someone to trifle with.

Her stomach turned queasy. There was a good chance that was actual blood on the walls. Many cultures used it in rituals and warding. Light shimmered in the corner of the room, growing brighter, forcing her to shield her eyes with her hand. No way was she closing them.

"Redecorating, I see." The voice was deep and melodic and tinged with humor. It was seductive, almost hypnotic.

Lowering her arm, she stared as the brilliance faded away, leaving a man in its wake. He was tall with golden hair that hung to his shoulders and eyes bluer than the ocean. He wore faded Levi's and a dress shirt so white it almost hurt to look at. He was movie star, rock star handsome.

"He has wings." Huge, pure white wings spread out

behind him, each feather soft and perfectly shaped. They were spectacular. The way he'd arrived, his sheer presence was exactly as Mack had described. He likely had been visited by an angel, and it had led to his death.

She didn't trust him. He was too pretty, too polished. There was something about him that repelled even as it attracted.

Gabriel turned his attention to her, his lips curving into a welcoming smile. "And who do we have here? Another addition to your charming group?"

"This isn't a social call," Maccus snapped.

"Then why did you call?" White wings snapped back and disappeared. "I was busy." She tried not to stare, but it was impossible not to. From the beginning, all the evidence pointed toward angels being involved, but to actually see one was making her head spin. Yes, Maccus was an angel but a fallen one. He was also Lucius's Brother. This was an actual angel from Heaven. The air snapped with energy, a powder keg just waiting to be ignited.

Maccus's lip curled. "I'm sure you were."

Beside her, Lucius stirred. "What do you know about the Angel Foundation?"

Gabriel was slightly shorter than the other men, but somehow managed to appear as though he was looking down on them. He reminded her of those stuffy academic types she ran into at faculty functions who thought they were so much better than a lowly professor of folklore.

"And who are you?" The angel ran his gaze over Lucius. "Another one of Maccus's merry band of followers, I assume."

A low growl rolled up from Lucius's throat.

"Is this one housebroken? From what I've heard, you had trouble with the werewolf. I imagine this one is a shifter of some kind." Crossing his arms over his chest, he tilted his head to one side and his eyes narrowed. "A drakon. I didn't know you had one of those. I'm impressed."

Angel or not, she wanted to kick his ass for treating Lucius like he was no more than an animal. Her muscles quivered, but she reined in the impulse. He'd smite her like she'd flick a mosquito. That would set off a chain of events that would be good for no one, least of all humanity. "What do you know about the Angel Foundation here in New York?" She was proud her voice quavered only a little. It was easy to be brave with the others around her.

"Why should I tell you?" Superiority echoed in every word. He seemed to have a dim view of humans. Or maybe it was her.

She caught a glint of metal flying through the air before a knife slammed into Gabriel's shoulder. The impact knocked him back a step. Raine jolted, swallowing heavily as blood seeped from around the wound. The casual violence made her stomach churn even worse. The others didn't even blink.

"You know you're going to tell me what I need to know, so stop provoking me." Maccus raised his hand and the knife ripped from Gabriel's shoulder and flew back to him. He flipped the blade through his fingers.

Blood stained the angel's shirt. He frowned and waved his hand, and the fabric went back to its pristine condition with no sign of blood. He didn't even think about it, didn't even strain. That kind of power was downright scary.

"We have organizations here on Earth. We're not supposed to interfere with mankind."

Maccus snorted. "That never stopped you."

"But," he continued as though he hadn't been interrupted, "we do nudge from time to time, to set someone on a certain path, encourage the dreamers, and remind people that miracles can and do happen. That job falls to lesser angels. I'm far too busy."

Yup, definitely reminded her of a puffed-up professor

she'd had once, who'd thought himself too good to actually teach the students who paid to take his course.

"You need to find out." Lucius had been quiet until now, letting his friend do most of the talking. It made sense, since it was angel to angel, even if one of them was fallen.

"I don't need to do anything. I especially don't take orders from some overgrown lizard."

It's official. I'm going to Hell because I'm going to kill an angel. No one. No one talked to her man like that. And yes, he was hers. It wasn't sensible, wasn't smart, but she didn't care.

"If you know what I am, you know what I can do."

"Of course I do. I'm an archangel."

Archangel? As in *the* Archangel Gabriel? She'd thought him a normal angel, if there was such a thing. Not a bloody archangel. Maccus had gone straight to the top for answers.

"Then why are you baiting me?" Lucius took a menacing step forward.

A slow smirk crossed his perfect face. "Because it's so much fun, and life can get tedious after so many millennia."

"I'd find ripping you to shreds and feasting on your bones fun. Life can get tedious after so many millennia," Lucius tossed his words back at him.

He wouldn't really eat the archangel, would he? His pink eyes glowed. Every muscle in his body was tense and ready for action. Pure menace oozed from him. Yup, he might do it. Normally, such a thing would appall her, but she'd make an exception in this case.

Gabriel threw back his head and laughed, seemingly unconcerned. "As amusing as this all is, I have things to do." He waved his hand, but nothing happened. He frowned and tried again.

The wards were back on the wall, vibrant and pulsing with power.

"You're not going anywhere until we get answers." Maccus was still flipping the knife through his fingers. Nothing much seemed to upset him. He *had* survived Hell. She imagined that after that, everything else was more of a petty annoyance. Fearless was the best description of all of them. She, on the other hand, was doing her best to ignore the way her legs were trembling.

"I was in the Deep Sleep of my kind." Lucius walked right up to the archangel and looked down at him. "Someone from this Angel Foundation sent Raine to me. She woke me, which should be impossible."

"Blame her for waking you. I had nothing to do with this. Why would I bother? You're nothing to me."

It rang true to her and must have to Lucius, since he took a step back.

"But he is something to me," Maccus said.

"Is this about your little Brotherhood again? Lucifer is occupied with other things these days. I heard he didn't fare so well the last time he involved you in one of his schemes. From what my spies tell me, he's been in a foul mood since." His laugh sent a cold shiver through her. No love lost there, even though Lucifer and Gabriel were brothers of a sort.

"Lucifer wasn't the only one involved in schemes to harm me." The knife disappeared and was replaced by a throwing star. She really needed to know how he was doing that.

Gabriel smiled at Morrigan and waved. "You're not still harboring hard feelings about that, are you?" He made a *tsk*ing sound. "Worked out well for the two of you in the end. You should be thanking me."

Lucius grabbed the archangel by the throat and lifted him off his feet, dangling him in the air. "If you can't help us, you're of little use."

"You. Can't. Kill. Me." Gabriel wrapped his hands around Lucius's wrist, trying to drag it away, but couldn't budge him. It was an enormous feat of strength. The angel began to glow. The light wrapped around Lucius's forearm and began to spread upward. A scream stuck in her throat.

"Stop, Gabriel."

"Stay out of this, Maccus. He thinks his puny archangel power can harm me." Red and orange flames burst from beneath Lucius's skin, burning away his shirt. They twisted around his shoulder and rushed toward the golden glow. The two energy sources slammed together in a burst that sent a shower of fire spilling into the room.

Raine stamped on several embers, as did Morrigan. A wall of heat drove the rest of them back. The fight was silent but intense, each man battling for supremacy.

"I'm an archangel." Sweat beaded on Gabriel's forehead and seeped down his temples. His golden hair was mussed, his eyes darkening with disbelief. Lucius appeared almost relaxed, like he wasn't really trying. Her drakon was special, but this display of power was unfathomable.

"I'm a drakon." Pink and rose-gold ribbons caressed his arm as they joined the flames. The angel's glow didn't get pushed back, it winked out of existence.

She blinked several times, unable to believe what she'd witnessed. Morrigan paled. Even Maccus's eyes widened. So it wasn't just her. The others were as shocked by what he'd done.

"Do I kill you or do you get us some answers?"

Gabriel stubbornly remained silent.

"Let him go." Maccus put his hand on Lucius's shoulder. "As much of a pain in the ass as he is, it would cause bigger problems if you kill him."

Lucius held steady, ignoring his friend. The last thing they needed was more trouble, and making an enemy of an archangel didn't seem like a particularly smart move. Ignoring the heat that threatened to singe off her eyebrows, she went to his side but didn't touch him. If either of them ignited their flames, she was toast. "Lucius, please." She had no idea if he'd listen to her but had to try.

Muscles in his back and arm bunched. His tattoos pulsed, brighter than normal, seeming alive. The urge to stroke them was almost too much to ignore. Her hand was halfway to his arm before she pulled back and curled her fingers inward until her nails bit into her skin.

His fingers tightened fractionally before he tossed the archangel against the wall. She winced at yet another hole. This one was man-sized or, rather, angel-sized. The repairs were really tallying up.

Gabriel rubbed his throat. "I'll see what I can find out about this Angel Foundation."

Lucius inclined his head. "Thank you."

"If I find out you had anything to do with it—"

"Stuff it, Maccus. Not everyone cares about you and your little group of friends." He motioned to the wall. "I can't do anything until you allow me to leave."

"Don't make me come looking for you," Maccus warned as he waved his hand at the wall. The symbols vanished. "I might bring Lucius with me."

Gabriel vanished between one heartbeat and the next.

"I need to sit down." Her legs were shaking, a combination of fear and adrenaline making her half sick. Only there was nowhere to sit. All the furniture was currently a pile of rubble in the corner. Left with only one option, she plopped down on the floor. "Is it just me or was that intense?"

• • •

Lucius rushed to Raine when her legs buckled, but she was on the floor before he could catch her. Worried, he settled down beside her and lifted her onto his lap. Her pupils were dilated, making her eyes appear even larger. Her skin was flushed, damp with sweat, but she didn't appear to be hurt, just dazed.

She waved away his concern. "I'm fine. Things have been off the charts since we met, but this topped everything else—getting trapped in a cave, discovering drakons are real, Mack and his buddies coming to my home to kill me, meeting a fallen angel. No offense," she told Maccus.

"None taken."

"You fought an archangel."

"It wasn't difficult." And it should have been. The changes in him went deeper than he'd thought. "It wasn't a real fight. More a testing of strength."

Maccus dragged two barstools from the kitchen area, settling Morrigan on one before taking the other for himself. "You just made a formidable enemy, my friend."

He shrugged. "Not the first time."

Raine smacked his arm and winced. "Ouch, that hurt. We don't need any more enemies. We have enough problems."

We. He'd never thought in terms of how his actions affected anyone else before, never had to. Having Raine made everything different. Shit, maybe he shouldn't have antagonized Gabriel. In his driving need to protect her, he might have made the situation worse. He brushed his fingers over her cheek, tucking an errant strand of hair behind her ear. "I won't let him hurt you." If he tried, Lucius would destroy him, which would force Maccus and the others to terminate him, putting her in danger. It went around in a never-ending circle but boiled down to the same thing. Someone was trying to stir up trouble between him and the Brotherhood with Raine as collateral damage.

"I was more worried about you." Grabbing his shoulders, she shook him. "What were you thinking, taking on a bloody archangel?" Once again, her concern was not for herself, but for him. It warmed all the cold parts of his soul. "What am I going to do with you?"

Love me. He swallowed back the plea before it escaped.

"What exactly *did* you do?" Maccus sat forward, resting his forearms on his thighs. "You didn't push his power back to him at the end."

"No, I didn't." He'd let instinct take over. "I took it."

His friend stilled, his jaw clenching. "What do you mean, you took it?"

Even now, the angel's energy pulsed inside him, mixing with his own. He'd been different his entire existence. Reviled and worshiped by turns out of fear, kept away at all costs, through battle or appeasement.

The only place he'd found acceptance was among the Brotherhood. Now that was teetering on the brink. Maccus wouldn't want him around if he thought Lucius could take his power.

He waved his hand in the air. "I'm not sure. Maybe I pushed it back. Maybe I neutralized it somehow." It was the first time he'd ever lied to his friend, and it turned his stomach sour. But he wasn't only protecting himself now, he was protecting Raine. He'd do whatever he had to, to keep her safe. Even lie to his best friend, and Maccus knew it.

"I see."

"Well, I don't." Raine leaned her head against his shoulder. "Gabriel's glow just sort of went away, like it was turned off."

"Or absorbed." Maccus held out his hand and his flaming sword appeared.

Lucius stood with Raine in his arms and then released her legs, waiting until she was steady. "We'll be going now. You can text us any new information." He needed to get her out of here before things took a bad turn.

He might not be vulnerable, but she was.

"We all change and evolve." Maccus twisted his wrist, making the sword sing as it sliced through the air. "None of us in the Brotherhood remain the same. And in the past few years, it seems we've all made a jump of some kind, our natural abilities expanding exponentially."

"I'm not sure what's happening. Could we speak in plain English and not riddles?" Raine had that adorable quizzical expression again, the one that caused two lines to form between her eyes and made him want to kiss them away. "Lucius?"

He might lie to Maccus to protect Raine, but he would not, could not, lie to her.

"I took his power." He wanted to watch her expression, to see how she was taking this new twist, but he dared not take his eyes off Maccus. "I told you the Deep Sleep changed me. There was an energy buildup inside me that almost ripped me apart." He took her hand in his and brought it to his lips. "Raine centered me, gave me a reason to fight, to survive." His gaze flickered to Morrigan. "I think you understand what I mean."

"I do."

Lucius held up his free hand and willed flames to appear. Raine jolted but didn't pull away. "It's always been easy to command fire. I may be an earth drakon, but I have a deep affinity for every element. Since waking, I have an abundance of energy. It's beyond what I had before." He twisted his hand from side to side, watching the orange and blue flames dance. He added pink ribbons, enjoying the way they threaded through the existing ones. "My first thought was to drive Gabriel's fire back into him. That wouldn't have been pleasant. But then it occurred to me that energy doesn't really change from one being to the next. If he wanted to push it on me, I'd simply take it." He closed his hand into a fist. The fire winked out, but the glow remained before slowly dissipating.

"You have angelic power in you?" Raine ran her hands over his chest. "It's not hurting you, is it?"

"No." He dropped a kiss on her forehead, touched by her concern. "It's mine now. It's drakon power." And he would use every drop to protect her.

His fate was balanced on the edge of the sword Maccus held. They might have to fight their way out of here and would forever be on the run from the Brotherhood. Was that what this entire situation was all about? Infighting among them? He wasn't sure how that could be possible, since no one could have known what would happen to him. He sure as hell hadn't.

Maccus tilted his head to one side and smiled. "That's quite a skill." He almost sounded admiring. The sword winked out of sight. "Might be useful at some point down the road. Who knows what the Brotherhood might face going forward."

The muscles in his neck unknotted, a sense of relief washing over him. It was acceptance, pure and simple. "Whatever the Brotherhood needs." And he meant it. He would lay down his life for any of the others.

"Great. We can all sing *Kumbaya* and sit around a campfire making s'mores." When they looked at Raine, she shrugged. "What, you're friends. Maccus might have been freaked out there for a second, but he's got your back. That's what friends do."

"It's what Brothers do." Maccus held out his hand. When Lucius took it, Maccus pulled him in until their chests bumped and their foreheads were almost touching. "It's what friends do."

Briefly overcome, all he could do was nod. When he stepped back, he winced at the state of the apartment. "I'm truly sorry about your home." He'd come here for help and wrecked the place.

"As I said before, don't worry about it." Morrigan offered a smile. "These things happen, especially among this crowd."

There were stories there, so many he hadn't been a part of. He didn't know where the other members of the Brotherhood were, what had happened to them while he slept. He had so many questions but swallowed them back. There'd be time to talk, catch up, when this was done and Raine was safe.

A glimmer appeared in the corner of the room, growing larger. The angel was back. Gabriel had wasted no time. His dragon rumbled in satisfaction.

"The Angel Foundation is one of ours. It was headed by an angel named Rivka. The office didn't get permission to close, and she is nowhere to be found. I'm looking into it." With that, Gabriel vanished again.

Maccus waved his hand and the warding reappeared, the symbols pulsing before fading from sight.

"Is he telling the truth?" Lucius didn't trust the archangel. Paranormal creatures were clever, and angels were no exception. Someone like Gabriel didn't attain and keep his level of power by not being able to play politics and twist the truth when it suited.

"What he said is truth. Whether there is more to it remains to be seen."

"Do you think Lucifer convinced an angel to help him? That would be one hell of a plan, pun intended." Raine sighed and straightened her clothes. "Why would an angel help him? He's the devil." Her voice was steady, but every ounce of color had left her face. The aftermath of violence surrounded them. Only days ago, she'd had no idea the world of paranormal creatures existed alongside humans. Reading and writing about it was a far cry from living it.

"Lucifer can be pleasing when he wants to be, almost seductive." Morrigan rubbed her arms. Maccus tugged her toward him until she was sheltered against him. As a former bounty hunter for Hell, she'd have intimate knowledge of such things.

He was curious how she'd ended up in such a position. That was her story to tell, if she chose to. Asking would likely bring down Maccus's wrath.

"We need to go. We have no idea who might be behind this, but there's little doubt they're likely still looking." And he'd brought enough hardship to his friend's door.

He also wanted to be alone with his mate. Was she cursing the Fates for bringing her into his life, wishing she'd never met him? His heart ached at the thought. She put on a brave face but was struggling to deal with every new revelation. The introduction she was getting to his world did little to recommend it. When this was over, would she walk away?

"You two need to go into hiding. The Brotherhood will get to the bottom of this. I'm going to call the others, see if they can dig up any information about demonic or angelic activity. In the meantime, we can't ignore other possibilities. You might want to talk to a fellow drakon and find out if any of those societies that hunt your kind are active. No low-level angel would dare disobey Heaven, but maybe they managed to use magic to control one to do their bidding. There's a number that's been circulated. I'll text it to Raine."

A drakon purposely giving out contact information—he never thought he'd live long enough to witness such a thing. Secretive and suspicious were the two words used most when referring to drakons, but it was a line to tug for information, and Maccus was right. They couldn't afford to focus solely on an angel being the mastermind. Humans had used magic to control his kind for centuries. It was possible they'd found a way to do the same to a lesser angel. If it were just himself, he wouldn't make contact, but he had Raine now. Her safety and well-being were paramount.

"Contact me if you hear anything from the others. I'll

speak to them personally when all this is over." He wasn't about to put any more of his Brothers in the crosshairs of his unknown enemy, if he could help it.

Nothing was adding up. It didn't make sense why an angel would be behind this. He'd never harmed one, not until today. And he hadn't really hurt Gabriel. Just ruffled his feathers a bit.

Whatever was going to happen, it was coming sooner rather than later. He could feel it in his bones.

• • •

Gabriel stared at the empty Manhattan office. Where was that administrative low-level angel? She'd screwed things up royally. This was a simple job. One that didn't require much intelligence.

Contrary to what some people might think, angels were like people—not all were created equal. Some got the prime jobs. Others, like this one, were office drones. In human terms, he was the CEO with the penthouse office. He planned to stay there.

He rubbed his neck, even though it didn't pain him. The insult of being held immobile by an abomination, a creature that shouldn't even exist, was too much. Not to mention he was weaker than he should be.

"You had one job." He stared out the squat window at the city skyline. "You're a paper pusher, a nobody." Why couldn't he sense her?

"I'll find you. There's nowhere you can hide from me. And when I do, you'll pay."

Leaving the empty office behind, he returned to Heaven. He needed to recharge before he began his search, but there were other things he needed to do first. This insult could not go unanswered.

Chapter Eighteen

"I need to get another phone." Her gaze darted all around.

The streets were teeming with a mass of humanity. Any of them could be working with the angel who'd targeted them. The guy buying a hot dog from the street vendor looked sketchy. Maybe the woman wearing a chili-red designer coat and carrying a white Chanel bag? Perhaps the homeless man sitting against the wall was really in disguise?

And maybe I'm losing it.

"Why?" Looking badass and sexy in his borrowed clothes—black was a good look—he seemed unconcerned, even relaxed. She could almost hate him for that. Her hair was lank and damp, her clothes wrinkled. Nerves were making her stomach jump, not to mention she was sweating despite the cool evening air. In other words, she was a mess.

"If Maccus had a guy hack into my phone, there's no reason to believe an"—she broke off, leaned closer and whispered, even though no one seemed to be listening—"angel wouldn't be able to do the same thing. Someone could be tracking us right now." It was impossible to tell if anyone was following them. There were just too many people, inhaling too much of the air until it was almost impossible to breathe. "We need to get out of the city."

"Then that's our plan. We'll get a new phone, head back to the hotel for our things, and leave." He started to put his arm around her, but she stepped aside. If he hugged her, she'd break. As it was, she was hanging on by her fingernails. He deserved a partner courageous enough to handle the danger facing them, not one who wanted to run screaming.

"Good." She nodded decisively. Having a plan took her anxiety down from the red zone to high orange. "And we need snacks." Worry always made her hungry. As did sadness, fear, and any other negative emotion. She'd always wished she was one of those women who lost their appetite at such times, but no such luck.

He slowly lowered his arm down by his side, a fierce frown on his face. "Where do we get a phone?"

She stopped on a corner and paid attention to the stores instead of the people. When she didn't see anywhere likely, she pulled out her phone and did a quick search. "Should be a convenience store two blocks down." The new text reminder stood out like a beacon. "Are we going to call that number Maccus gave us?" Would another drakon even help them?

They crossed when the light changed. Whether from fear or awe, people got out of Lucius's way, making the going easier. It also made them standout. She picked up her pace, eager to be on their way.

"I don't know." He was wearing his stony face again. She much preferred to see him happy. "They might not help us."

It couldn't be an easy decision for him. There was so much about his past that remained a mystery, but she understood how difficult it would be for him to reach out and ask for help.

The thread of pain running through his reply made her want to seek out those drakons who'd hurt him and—not much she could do to them, but she wouldn't mind giving them a piece of her mind.

Yeah, that will scare them.

They'd laugh their asses off and probably decide she'd make a decent snack. Maybe calling them wasn't such a great idea, but it was a lead, something they were short on.

"Maccus must think whoever it is will help. I can make the call. I've woken a drakon and contacted a fallen angel. I can do this." Giving into her need for contact, she slipped her hand into his much larger one and gave his fingers a squeeze.

She might be human, but she had determination on her side. And love. As crazy as it seemed, she'd lost her heart to an immortal drakon. Talk about a recipe for heartbreak. "You'd do that?" His eyes began to glow, but he blinked and they went back to normal. If having pink eyes were normal.

"Absolutely." There wasn't much she could do to protect them. That was all on Lucius. Her contribution, her specialty, was her ability to talk and ask questions. The pen might be mightier than the sword—although she doubted it applied in this situation—but getting answers was a skill she possessed. And she wasn't afraid to wield it.

"There's the store." She hurried to push the door open and get inside. Not that it was any safer. Just less exposed. In no time, she had two prepaid phones paid for with cash. Their money supply was being eaten quickly. Maybe a stop at an ATM was in order. If someone was tracking them, it wouldn't matter because they'd no longer be here in another hour.

Lucius was frowning by the time they left. "Why two?"

"We have no idea where we'll end up or who we might have to contact. As the saying goes, 'two is one and one is none.'"

"That makes no sense."

"It's a military saying, or I think it is. I read it somewhere. Or maybe saw it on a Netflix series or a movie. Could have been a documentary. Doesn't matter. It means you can't always depend on your equipment, so a backup is sensible."

With a grunt that might have been agreement, he plucked the phone from her, manifested a long claw, and tore through the packaging like it was nothing. Handy, like having a built-in box cutter. A woman passing by them stared, her eyes wide with horror.

Before she could scream, Raine smiled. "Cool special effect, right? We're making a movie." There were always movies and television shows being shot in the city.

The woman relaxed and laughed. "It's realistic."

When they'd passed by, she hissed at him. "Don't do that in public again. There are people and cameras everywhere."

He grunted—whether in agreement or to appease her, she had no idea. After handing her the phone, he took the second one and did the same thing. Raine contemplated banging her head against a nearby brick building but decided it wouldn't help. Her drakon gave "stubborn" new meaning. She took the packaging and tossed it in a nearby garbage can.

She quickly input Maccus's number into both and texted him their new numbers before tucking one of them into her pocket and offering Lucius the other. "You take the second phone."

"I don't need it."

"If I lose or break mine, you'll have one." And if something happened to her, she wanted him to be able to reach out to his friend. "Take it." When he hesitated, she gave a huff of exasperation and shoved it in the back pocket of his jeans. Maybe she copped a feel while she was at it. Probably not appropriate, given the situation, but she was only human and his ass was perfect.

"You did that on purpose," he said.

"I have no idea what you're talking about." Totally not admitting to that one. "We can catch the subway up ahead."

They'd get back to their hotel faster. Fast was the goal. She was more than ready to put the city in their rearview mirror.

He hovered behind her as they paid their fare with the MetroCards they'd purchased on their earlier trip and made their way to the platform. It was busy this time of the evening, but they found a place by the wall to wait for their train. A glance at the screen told her it would be here momentarily.

"We should call the number. Waiting doesn't make any sense. We can ditch the phone on the way to the hotel. We'll need to stop by an ATM for cash." She tapped her toe against the floor, a sense of urgency making her antsy.

His answer was a low growl. Choosing to take that as a yes instead of a no, she pulled out her phone, took a deep breath, and plugged in the number. It rang several times before it was answered by a machine. "Leave a message," an abrupt male voice ordered.

She ended the call without leaving one. "We'll try again in a few minutes." Whoever was on the other end didn't sound friendly. Were all drakons like that? Lucius was currently glaring at anyone who came within six feet of them. It was like standing in the middle of some force field that kept everyone else at bay.

The train rolled in, the doors opened, and people flooded out. "Let's go." Grabbing him by the hand, she tugged him forward. No surprise, a path cleared. She made a beeline for an empty bench seat in the far corner. As they pulled away from the station, she studied her phone, her finger hovering over the number.

"You should wait." Lucius stared at everyone around them until they all were inspired to move toward the other end of the subway car. He had her boxed in, almost squishing her against the wall, his legs extended into the aisle. The bench seats weren't built to accommodate someone of his size. His two hands were curled around the back of the seat in front of them. Metal began to bend.

She placed her free hand over his. "It's better to get it over with." Waiting wasn't going to help. "It's like pulling off a bandage. It's better to do it quick."

"I've never worn a bandage."

Of course he hadn't. He was a drakon with awesome healing powers. "I have. You'll have to trust me on this." But a glance at the phone told her they'd have to wait. "Crap, there's no service." She tapped her foot, impatient to get this over with. Finally, the train pulled into their stop. As soon as they hit the sidewalk, she pressed the number and held her breath as it rang through again. "Come on. Come on," she whispered.

"Who the fuck are you, and how did you get this number?"

Raine jostled so badly, she fumbled the phone, managing to catch it before it hit the sidewalk. "Ah." She licked her lips, her mouth gone dry. All she could hear over the line was heavy breathing. A muscle flexed in Lucius's jaw.

I can do this. I have to do this.

"Maccus Fury gave it to me."

* * *

Lucius wanted to reach through the phone and rip out the throat of the male on the other end. This whole thing was a bad idea. His kind had always shunned him.

His already bad mood had taken a nosedive when Raine had moved away from his attempt to hug her. The pain of her rejection had nearly sent him to his knees. Fire had almost burst over his skin. Hurt and angry, his drakon had wanted out. He'd wanted to roar his fury at the heavens. He feared she was having second thoughts about their relationship. His despair had lightened when she'd taken his hand, but he was under no illusions. She was his mate, but getting her to make a permanent commitment wasn't a given.

"Why would *he* give you my number?" While he disapproved of the tone, he could relate to the suspicion.

Her fingers tightened around the phone and her chin rose a notch. "He believes you have information I need."

With his keen hearing, Lucius could hear everything, including the click of computer keys in the background.

"I don't talk to just anyone, Raine Carson, professor of folklore."

She held the phone away and glanced at him. "That was fast," she mouthed. When he reached out for the phone, she yanked it back to her ear. "You know me, but I don't know you."

"And that's the way it's going to stay. Talk or I hang up."

"I have a particular problem. Or rather, a friend of mine does."

"Does that friend have a name?"

"Lucius." He spoke aloud, keeping his voice low, knowing full well if it was a drakon on the other end he'd hear him just fine.

There was more frantic clicking. "Impossible." The voice had hardened even more. "He hasn't been seen in a very long time. If you've hurt him in any way, I'll kill you."

"Glad to hear it." She looked so pleased with herself, he wanted to kiss her, but managed to control himself, unsure if she'd welcome it.

Dead silence. Lucius's lips twitched. She did have that effect on a drakon.

"You're glad?" The male asked the question slowly, as though addressing someone who might be mentally deranged.

"Absolutely. In a nutshell, I woke him up from a really, really long nap. He was cranky." She playfully nudged him with her shoulder. "After he got over wanting to kill me, he rescued me, but we ran into trouble. We're still looking into some things, but Maccus suggested we check with you to make sure there aren't any groups out there who might be searching for my friend. People with the resources to set up an elaborate operation."

When she finally took a breath, there was dead silence.

"What you're suggesting is impossible. If that is Lucius, put him on the line."

They stopped beside a parking garage, and he held out his hand. It wasn't exactly private, but there weren't too many people around. He took the phone and put it on speaker so she could hear. "This is Lucius. Who the fuck is this?" he flung the words back at the male on the other end.

Instead of hostility or anger, he got laughter. "Tarrant."

He searched his memory. "I'm not familiar with you." He'd met only a handful of his kind, all with the same result.

"If you're who you say you are, I'm very familiar with you. We need to meet in person if you want information."

His hopes plummeted. "Not going to happen." This had been a mistake.

"Wait," he said before Lucius could end the call. "Let me call and confirm. I do not want to piss off the Brotherhood. I'm enjoying the quiet life. I'll call you back if everything checks out."

When the line went dead, he handed her back the phone. "That went well." Her chipper tone made him frown. "Could've been worse," she reminded him with a pat on the arm. "There's an ATM." She pointed across the street. "I'll get some cash and we can be on our way."

They'd barely finished crossing the road when the phone rang. "That was fast. Hello, Tarrant." She continued to the bank machine, tucking the phone between her ear and shoulder as she plugged her card into the machine.

He shook his head in wonder. She never seemed to be still, had a boundless energy that drew him. Watching her lightened his heart.

She stopped and shook her head. "Here, you take it." Putting the phone back on speaker, she handed it to him and went back to getting her money.

"Maccus is a man of few words." The dry reply made his mouth twitch. "It's really you, Lucius?"

"Yes."

"I always wanted to meet you, but you were even more reclusive than I am, and that's saying something. I respected that."

Shock held him immobile. Mistrust quickly followed. Maybe this was a plan to lure him somewhere so Tarrant could try to kill him. Wouldn't be the first time a drakon had attempted such a thing. "Why?"

"Why did I want to meet you?"

"Yes." The drakons he had met had feared him.

"Knowledge is power. I wanted to learn from you. You're the best of us and we need all the skills we can get to fight our common enemy."

He'd never thought of it that way before. "Not all share your beliefs."

He gave a derisive snort. "Drakons can be idiots too. About what you asked, there was a particularly nasty group that's been around a long time. Their latest incarnation was called the Knights of the Dragon. They used magic and technology to ensnare several of us. Some have been freed, others died. The group was destroyed from the inside a few years back. All their known assets were seized or destroyed, but I wouldn't discount them. They're highly motivated."

"Understood." It was always the same, only the names of the groups changed over the millennia.

"I'll send you what I have on them."

"Do you want my email address?" She tucked the money away and zipped her purse.

"Please. I own the internet." A ding, and sure enough there was an email with an attachment.

"You're one scary dude."

Lucius frowned at the awe in her voice. He vowed to master the internet as soon as there was time for him to study it further.

"That's what my mate tells me. Call if you need assistance. We've gotten smarter and built a network."

"You have a mate?" That was unexpected. Finding one was a rare occurrence. Or it had been when he'd lived last.

"Many of us have in the past few years. We're not sure why now. I assume Raine is yours and that's why she was able to wake you."

"Thank you." He ended the call, unwilling to confirm or deny anything until he had time to check Tarrant out further.

"We didn't learn much, but if I read that guy right, he'll be digging into the matter. He's too much like me. He'll have to figure out what's going on." Her nose scrunched, making her look adorable.

She took the phone and, as he watched, forwarded Tarrant's number to her new one. "Guess we need to destroy this."

He held out his hand. Her fingers tightened around it before relinquishing it into his keeping. He took a deep breath.

Ding! An alert for a new message.

"Maybe it's from Maccus." She grabbed the device. All the color drained from her face.

He looked over her shoulder. The text was from an unknown sender. It was only one word.

Run!

Chapter Nineteen

It seemed to Raine as though she'd been on the run her entire life. She'd always thought a road trip would be fun, but she was sick to death of being in the car. The stress of waiting for the other shoe to drop was wearing on them both.

I assume Raine is yours and that's why she was able to wake you.

The words wouldn't stop running around in her brain. Rather than be put off by the idea, it made her heart sing. What exactly had Tarrant meant by that? They'd been discussing mates at the time. Lucius hadn't mentioned it. Not like she could come out and ask, "Hey, am I your mate?" Talk about putting a guy on the spot.

Yes, she'd woken him. Yes, they had amazing sexual chemistry. She knew he liked her, but that was a far cry from wanting to mate with her.

Stop thinking about it. She was making herself crazy. On the run for their lives was no time to make relationship decisions. See, she could be logical and adult. Ignoring the yearning in her soul, she turned her attention to their more pressing problems.

"Are there any more of those chips?" Lucius asked. He was driving again. The novelty of it hadn't worn off yet. As much as she hated to admit it, he had better night vision. Not to mention all the stress and lack of sleep was compounding, leaving her drained of energy. It was safer for them and the rest of the motoring public that she wasn't behind the wheel.

"We've eaten all the salt and vinegar, cheese and jalapeño, and barbecue ones." They'd gone a long way to settling her nerves. "There's only plain left." When they'd stopped to grab snacks, she'd picked up a selection, unsure what he'd enjoy. So far, he hadn't met a chip he hadn't liked. She opened the full-size bag and handed it to him. He tucked it in his lap and munched as he drove one-handed, as though he'd been doing it his entire life.

The city was far behind them and they were once again headed down the interstate. After getting that text from an unknown sender, they hadn't wasted any time grabbing their gear and hitting the road.

There was plenty of traffic, but it was dark, the lights almost hypnotic as they came toward them. Her eyes closed and her head tilted to the side, bouncing off the door window. "Ouch."

"Why don't you try to get some sleep?"

"You're not sleeping." A good thing, since he was at the wheel.

"I'm a drakon."

And she was a weak human. He didn't say it, but that's how she felt. "If I wasn't with you, you'd just head off to a cave somewhere and hunker down, wouldn't you?" Her heart skipped a beat at the thought of him flying away and never seeing him again.

He munched on the chips, swallowed, and licked his lips. She barely stifled a moan. She wanted to kiss those lips, damn it. They'd taste like hot male and salty goodness.

"At one point, I might have, but it's gone too far. Someone targeted both of us. I need to know who."

It was depressing to think that was the main reason he'd stuck around, but it was smart to be realistic. If she was his mate, surely he'd have mentioned it. Tarrant had to be wrong. Lucius cared about her, no doubt, but the obstacles between them were huge. The biggest being she was human and he was an immortal drakon. Did drakons mate with humans or other paranormals?

Needing a chip fix after that revelation, she reached over and dug into the bag, taking a handful. "If angels, some drakon hunting organization, or a combination of both, are behind this, then they're not going away." The chips she'd already eaten sat like a stone in her stomach, but she shoved more into her mouth and chewed.

"Who do you think sent that text?" Lucius had fried her old phone, breathing fire on it until it disintegrated. Whoever it was, they weren't going to track them using that device. That was cold comfort.

"I don't know."

"Maybe it was Tarrant." It was grasping at straws, but she didn't care. She needed something hopeful to hang on to.

Lucius shook his head, his hair brushing his shoulders. In the dark of the vehicle, he appeared even more menacing, his features somehow more sharply defined by the passing lights. "He doesn't have your new number."

"I forgot." Although, she'd gotten the sense that if he wanted to discover her new number, he would. Between him and Maccus, these people seemed to have no trouble hacking into her technology. New phones had been a waste of money, but it had been a proactive thing to do.

She dusted the salt from her hands and licked what remained. She really wasn't hungry. Eating was more about nervous energy and having something to do, and if she happened to put extra pressure on his lap when she scooped out the chips and noticed the bulge there...that was a bonus. Shrugging, she went back for more.

Maybe it wasn't fair to use her sexual wiles—and who knew she had them? This wasn't the time—no argument there. But Lucius was a once-in-a-lifetime lover. It went beyond him being a superhot drakon. His intensity, his protectiveness, the way he really listened to her and considered everything she said, and his innate intelligence, all drew her. The future was unknown. As a human, she was vulnerable, could die. It was becoming clearer that it was time to grab life with both hands and live it to the fullest.

He shifted in his seat when she withdrew her hand. "Anything wrong? I know it's uncomfortable." She waited a beat. "The car *is* a tight fit." A wicked imp had taken hold of her. It was more fun to tease him than to dwell on that text. There wasn't anything she could do about it, no way to track whoever had sent it. Maybe if they'd still had her phone...but keeping it hadn't been a risk worth taking.

"It's terribly uncomfortable." His voice little more than a low growl, he reached out, took her hand, and dragged it back to his lap. "And you know exactly why." The chip bag scrunched as it was pushed aside. The front of his jeans was stretched by his erection. Hot and hard, it pulsed with life. Her sex clenched and her nipples puckered beneath her shirt. The air was fraught with sensual tension.

A huge crack echoed in the small space. "You need to stop unless you want to land us in a ditch." A chunk of the plastic wheel covering fell to the floor.

Oops! She yanked her hand away and sat back, her breathing none too steady. "I'm sorry. That was uncalled for. I just wanted things to be normal. And that sounded whiny. I hate being whiny." What was wrong with her? It wasn't right to use their sexual attraction as a security blanket to ease her fear.

"I'll never be normal." If his jaw was any tighter it would snap. He was as aroused and sexually frustrated as she was.

"I didn't mean it like that." She dragged her fingers through her hair. God, she wanted eight hours of sleep in a real bed, a hot bath, and real food, not takeout. She never thought she'd live long enough to say it, but she was sick of junk food. "It's surreal that someone is manipulating us for some end we can't see. They wanted you awake. That's a given." She held up a finger to tick off her point. "They wanted me to be the one to do it but were fine if I failed in the attempt and died." She put up another. "Were they hoping or expecting you'd kill me? And if so, to what end?"

"I have no idea. You shouldn't have been able to wake me."

"So this is my fault?"

"It's a fact, not a fault."

Oh, she'd give him facts. "There must be a larger endgame here. You woke up. There had to be a reason they'd attempt such a thing. If you killed me, what would have happened?"

"I don't know."

"Speculate," she snapped. They sped through the night, just one car among many others, all heading somewhere. Probably not the smartest time to be pushing this. They were both tired, or she was, and aggravated.

"You want me to speculate?" Fury laced his words. The air became supercharged, like the sky just before a lightning strike. Her skin prickled.

"Ah, maybe not."

"Too late." A horn blared as he swerved into the outside lane and down an off-ramp. A squeak escaped her, her hand pressing against the dashboard. She had her seat belt on, but the sudden movement jerked her forward.

An all-night truck stop loomed ahead. He pointed the car to the darkest corner of the lot and pulled in. Gear jammed into park, motor still running, he released her seat belt and dragged her toward him until their noses were practically touching.

"If I killed you, the Brotherhood would have come for me. We don't have many rules, but a hard and fast one is that we don't kill innocents." His nostrils flared and his eyes were ablaze.

She'd unleashed a whirlwind. All she could do was hang on and hope for the best. "You wouldn't have hurt me."

"Before I was fully awake, I thought I'd wait you out, let you die, and go back to sleep." Couldn't get any blunter than that.

"That's understandable." It hurt, but she couldn't hold it against him. He hadn't known her then, hadn't wanted to be awakened.

"But you made it impossible for me to fall back to sleep. There's only one possible reason for that." He was breathing heavily, his chest rising and falling rapidly, stretching the seams of his T-shirt.

"You mentioned that back at Maccus's place. Is it because you're sexually attracted to me? Would any woman have had the same effect?" Talk about a lowering thought.

"I am sexually attracted to you." His voice was growing deeper by the second. She wished she could see him better, but it was dark here, the only glow from the dashboard lights and his captivating eyes. "That's part of it. But, no, any woman wouldn't do. Only you." He held her head in his hands and rubbed his thumb over her lower lip. The more intimate parts of her body began to tingle even as her heart raced. "Only a very special woman could have pulled me from the Deep Sleep."

Her stomach fluttered, and it wasn't because of the potato

chips. "Does this have something to do with what Tarrant said, when he asked if I was yours?" Now that it was out in the open, she wasn't sure she was ready for the answer.

"Maccus and Tarrant both understand." He brushed his mouth against hers. "They know what you are to me."

Breathless, she nibbled his bottom lip. "And what am I?"

"My mate."

"Your mate," she repeated. Tarrant had used that word, his tone possessive. It was more primitive than the title of wife.

He pressed his cheek against hers. It was smooth, not scratchy, even though he hadn't shaved. "My sire wasn't around when I was a boy. I was in his company only a handful of times before he left for good. One thing he did tell me was that dragons mate for life. As hybrids, we drakons had no idea if that applied to us, if we'd ever find that one woman meant for us. I'd heard rumors that one or two had, but discounted them as little more than false hope. Even if they were true, it didn't matter. The odds were astronomically against me ever finding my mate across the vast world and an ocean of time."

"That's beautiful, like something out of a storybook." It made her soul sing, made her believe in magic and possibilities.

"It's real." He drew his tongue over her bottom lip, drawing a moan. "And it's no story. You are my mate. If you accept me, I'll love you for the rest of my days. If you reject me—"

"Never."

The light slowly drained from his eyes, leaving them dull and lifeless. "I understand. You have to remain with me until the threat passes. I'll let you go when it's safe and won't bother you again."

"That's not what I meant." She grabbed his hair to keep him from turning away. "I'll never reject you, but is it fair to you? You'll love me forever." Tears pricked her eyes, and it

N.J. WALTERS   217

got more difficult to breathe. This was the kind of love she'd always longed for, always dreamed about. It was beautiful, but it also made her ache because it seemed so damn impossible. "I only have decades left while you have thousands of years." And wasn't that a kick in the pants to them both.

"A single day with you is worth everything."

A love that big was scary. It was insane to even be entertaining such an idea when they had people trying to kill them. Well, kill her. They wanted to capture him.

And what if what he thought was love was really gratitude? She'd been the one to set him free. Maybe he was still feeling the effects of the Deep Sleep he'd been locked in for centuries.

Then there were her turbulent jumble of emotions. Lucius was larger than life, a creature of myth and legend, the embodiment of her life's work. They'd been locked in one life-threatening situation after another since they'd met. Sex between them was off the charts, but that wasn't love.

And even if she believed him, how would day-to-day life work? It wasn't like he was going to hold down a nine-to-five job. What about her job? Were kids even possible? Where would they live? Would they always have enemies trying to kill them? And how on earth could they go out in public regularly?

There were so many valid reasons to take a step back and be practical. It wasn't sensible to make these kinds of life-altering decisions when everything was up in the air and there was so much at stake.

Life didn't come with guarantees, but there were defining moments. Whatever choice she made would echo through the years to come.

He was brave, laying his heart bare, while knowing she could reject him. Hurting him was the last thing she ever wanted to do. He'd already been hurt enough in his long lifetime. Taking a deep breath, she threw caution to the wind and embraced her heart. "I love you." Plastering her mouth against his, she kissed him.

. . .

I love you.

Three precious words he'd never thought to hear. He was a fierce drakon, an assassin, a feared member of the Forgotten Brotherhood, but none of those titles compared to being Raine's mate. The knowledge sank into his bones, into the very marrow of his being.

He kissed her, loving the way she clung to his hair until his scalp ached. There was no playful banter, no teasing. With a moan, he delved into her mouth. Salty and sweet combined, she gave as good as she got and demanded more.

She made him hotter than the lava pools deep in the heart of the Earth, but he was a drakon. Not only could he withstand her fire, he craved it. He'd been cold for so long. That's why he'd gone into the Deep Sleep. His internal flames had no longer been enough to spark life. All he'd seen before him were endless and empty centuries and death.

He peppered her face with kisses. "I can't get enough of you." He wanted to inhale her, to keep her next to him every second from now until eternity. "Never leave me." Vulnerable in a way he'd never been before, he gave his heart into her keeping.

"I won't. Not on purpose." He leaned into her touch, letting her soothe the uneasiness welling inside him. "I'll grow old, but for whatever time I have, I'll never stop loving you." Her smile was tremulous, her eyes dark with concern.

Damn it, he was being an ass, pushing her for a commitment when she was dependent on him for protection. It wasn't right, but he couldn't stop himself. After thousands of years of stark loneliness, he understood the gift, the value of a mate. A creature of instinct, every cell in his body screamed for him to snatch her up and take her somewhere safe.

But until they found their enemy, there was nowhere safe. Whoever had masterminded this plan had supernatural power, most likely an angel. An ability that went beyond human meddling and even magic.

"I can extend your life." It was too soon to broach this, but he wanted her with him forever. It was also time to show her there were benefits to being with him. So far, all she'd experienced were the darker, deadly aspects.

Her eyes widened and she slapped her palm over his forehead. "You're feeling warm. Do you have a fever?"

Her reactions were a constant source of surprise and pleasure. On a laugh, he captured her hand and kissed the center of her palm, licking the sensitive spot before releasing her. "I'm not out of my mind. I'm a drakon."

"I know." She drew the words out. "But in this case, what exactly does that mean?"

It wasn't a comfortable place to have this discussion. They were jammed into a tin can with no room to maneuver. He couldn't even hold her properly in his arms, not unless he punched a hole through the roof and the door, which she wouldn't appreciate. "We can talk at our destination." And it would give him a reprieve in case she objected to his proposal.

"Oh no. You can't drop a bomb like that and expect me to leave it. We're so doing this now." She shook her finger at him, her lips turning down in a frown. "I'm not sure what it means to be a mate, but if we're in a committed relationship, you need to level with me. I need to understand what I'm getting myself into." Her stubborn chin was tilted up. She wasn't going to let this go. If he didn't tell her, she'd keep talking until he did.

"My blood."

When he added nothing else, she frowned. "What about it?" She tilted her head to one side. He could practically hear the wheels in her brain turning. Her golden eyes widened, and the lines in her forehead smoothed as the perplexed expression gave way to one of wonder. "It's healing, but it's more than that, isn't it?"

"We know it won't kill you." As terrifying as it had been at the time, it was good to have that worry gone. "If you ingest a small amount on a regular basis, it will heal any physical problems with your human body and prolong your life." Would she tie herself to him indefinitely? It was a lot to ask.

"You would do that?" When he went to speak, she pressed her fingers against his lips. "Really think about this. What happens if after seventy-five or a hundred years you change your mind?" She rubbed her forehead. "That's a very long time."

His heart shrank and his body grew heavier, weighed down by regret. It was enough that she'd told him she loved him. It would have been smarter to broach the subject in a decade or two. Give her time to get used to being with him, to show her how good their life together would be.

What she'd experienced so far did nothing to recommend it. They'd had unknown people trying to kill them. All the money they'd spent had been hers. He'd destroyed her bed and some of her treasures. She'd been forced to leave behind her beloved cat. Hell, he'd threatened to kill her. Not exactly prime mate material.

She loves me.

He could work with that. Disappointment dissolved beneath his new resolve. He'd shower her in jewels, only she didn't seem the type who enjoyed jewelry. Tiny silver hoops adorned her ears. Other than an inexpensive watch, she wore nothing else. Come to think of it, back at her home he had noticed only some stretchy bangles made from semiprecious stones. He could provide her with beautiful houses, but she already had a home that she loved. She made her own money, had a career.

There had to be something she desired. All he had to do was discover it.

In the meantime, he could slip some of his blood into her food or drink. He discarded the idea as quickly as it formed. If she ever discovered he'd deceived her in such a fashion, she'd never forgive him. And she was his mate. She deserved his total honesty.

And she'd certainly notice if she didn't age.

"I understand and will take whatever years you want to give me." His spine was stiff, or as straight as it could be in this cramped vehicle. The urge to break out, to fly, beat at him. His dragon was not happy with him.

"You're doing it again." She caught his face in her hand, her grip surprisingly strong. "Assuming the worst. I. Want. To. Be. With. You. You get that. I want you to be sure you're ready to commit to me. I have it on good authority I'm a handful."

Laughter rumbled from him. "I've heard that." Pressing his forehead against hers, he inhaled her unique scent. It was buried beneath the flavors of the chips they'd eaten, but it was there, along with the delicious perfume of her arousal.

His cock jumped to life, ready to seal their commitment. "We need to get out of here." There was no way he could make love to her in this small space. He glanced toward the wooded area but discounted it. She deserved better than a tumble in the trees.

I have a mate. One who wants me. Deep within him something snapped into place. Raine belonged to him. The certainty sizzled in his blood, solidified into his bones.

"I will take care of you." This was his reason for waking, the purpose that had been missing. He wanted to build a life with her, to wake in the morning by her side and go to bed alongside her each night. "I will raze the earth to the ground if I have to in order to keep you safe."

Her eyes were damp. She swiped at them, even as she gave a ragged laugh. "A girl can't ask more than that, but let's forego the razing. I'm not sure if you're exaggerating or telling the truth, and I don't want to take chances."

"I make no promises."

Chapter Twenty

"Are you sure this is a good idea?" The yard appeared empty, but Raine searched the wooded area, certain each shadow was someone waiting to pounce.

Anyone could be lurking there. The trees seemed to lean forward, their presence ominous rather than comforting.The sky was growing lighter, but the clouds blocked the rising sun, adding to the oppressive atmosphere.

Or maybe it was just her mood. Now that she'd admitted her love for Lucius, she was waiting for the other shoe to drop. As much as she wanted to scream in delight, to sing and dance at the idea that she was the mate of this wonderful man, a skeptical voice in the back of her head whispered that it was all too easy. She almost snorted at that. Nothing had been easy since she'd laid eyes on him.

"If anyone is searching for us, they'll have already checked here. They'll assume we fled and won't expect us to double back." Lucius turned off the engine, deepening the silence.

She prayed he was right. A sense of desolation and

abandonment had settled over the place, even though they hadn't been gone that long. Or maybe it was her that had changed. The house she'd loved no longer seemed safe, was no longer her refuge, her haven from the world. It appeared it belonged to another person, another lifetime.

"Wait here." He opened the car door, gripped the outside edge, and pulled himself up and out. An owl hooted, and the breeze teased the bare limbs of the trees, making them sway.

She fumbled with the lock and got out. Cool air seeped down the collar of her coat. Shivering, she went up the short walkway.

"I told you to wait." Looming behind her, heat and impatience rolled off his big body.

"If there'd been anyone around, you would've told me. You have super hearing and smell." After only two tries, she got the key in the lock. The scent of disuse clung to the place. Or maybe it was her imagination. She felt around until she found the switch and turned on the lamp in the foyer to drive back the gloom.

He put his hand over hers and turned it off.

"The car is parked out front," she reminded him. "Anyone looking is going to notice. A light won't matter."

"I'm going to hide it down the road."

"There's a shed around back. The roof leaks but the walls are sound. It's mostly empty. There's enough room for it there." And it would be closer if they had to flee.

"I won't be long." His lips grazed the back of her neck. Then he was gone. She half-turned to call him back but pressed her lips together. This was her home, a place she'd spent many, many hours on her own and loved every moment.

Besides, she needed a few minutes to herself. The emotional rollercoaster she'd been on was making her queasy. They hadn't talked about the whole "mate" thing during the rest of the drive, tacitly agreeing to table the discussion until a better time.

It wasn't that she was having second thoughts. It was just a lot to process in such a short period. Was there some kind of ceremony or were they already considered mates since they'd both declared themselves? Wasn't like there was a handbook—*How to Date and Mate Your Drakon.* Her laugh sounded a little wild.

"Focus," she muttered. There'd be time to iron out the details when the threat was dealt with. Otherwise, none of it would matter a damn because she'd be dead.

Hand on the wall for support, she crept down the hallway toward her bedroom. It was strange not to have Penelope run out to meet her. As much as she missed the cat, it was safer for her to be away from this madness.

The mattress lay on the floor, a stark reminder of what had occurred last time they were here. Cheeks flushed, she turned away and headed toward the kitchen. A snack might not help, but it couldn't hurt. The light from the refrigerator made her squint as she perused the contents. There wasn't much. Lucius had cleaned her out. His appetite was huge.

When the front door opened, she jerked back, heart pounding. Her gun was in her purse, which she'd stupidly left in the car.

"It's done." He shoved the door closed and dropped their bags on the floor. He dominated the small space as he walked toward her and tossed the keys on the counter. "Are you hungry?"

She closed the refrigerator and leaned against it in relief. "I don't know."

"You need to rest."

"I'm too wound up." Her body hummed with a low-level anxiety that wouldn't stop. "I need to take my mind off things."

A low growl had the fine hairs on her body standing on

end. "I can think of a way to do that."

She just bet he could. The man was walking, talking sex. Her breasts swelled and her sex began to throb. Her body was on board. Her brain, however, had other concerns. "It's not smart. Maybe I should meditate." Not that she'd ever been able to quiet her mind before, but it was worth a shot.

He nuzzled her neck, his breath warm against her ear. "Why not?" His teeth nipped her earlobe. It was impossible to think as he slid her coat down her arms and tossed it aside.

"Ah. Um. What was the question?" Tilting her head to one side, she gave him better access, shivering when he traced the tip of his tongue over the swirls of her ear.

"Why shouldn't we make love?"

No good reason she could think of. It was a splendid idea. No, wait. She shook her head, trying to clear the sensual haze. "Making love when we're being hunted isn't smart. In the romance books I've read and movies I've seen, whenever the hero and heroine make love when it's dangerous, something always goes wrong." She didn't want to be TSTL, or in layman's terms, too stupid to live. "We need to be on our guard." It pained her to say it, but it was the truth.

He caught her chin between a thumb and forefinger. "Do you think anyone could sneak up on me?"

"Yes. No. Maybe." She clasped his thick wrist. "An angel could pop in unannounced." Gabriel had appeared out of nowhere when summoned. Maybe it was an archangel skill, but it made sense that all angels would have that ability. And there was another thing. "When you think about it, it's kind of insulting to me if you don't lose control and forget your surroundings when we're making love."

His chuckle was low and deep. "Only you." His lips pressed the spot between her brows.

What did he mean by that?

"Those worry lines are back. I promise, I'll get carried

away, but my dragon will alert me if anyone comes close."

Her resolve weakened. Damn it, she was tired of worrying about everything. She ached to have his arms around her. Leaning against him, she let her breasts rub against the hard planes of his chest. Her heart pounded, her blood flowed through her veins like thick honey, warm and sweet. She slipped her hands around his neck and went up on her toes. "If you're sure."

"Very." On a groan, he lifted her off her feet and kissed her. One hand cupped her bottom, the other spread across her back. Holding her easily, he took her mouth again and again, tongue delving deep.

It was different this time. They'd had sex before. Stupendous, earth-moving sex, to be sure, but they hadn't known each other that well. Now they'd made a commitment. Each stroke of his fingers heightened her senses, the nerve endings in her skin alive with sensation.

"Take me to bed." She was more than ready to get naked. Maybe it was stupid, considering angelic forces might be searching for them, but if not now, then when? There might never be a better opportunity. If that made her TSTL, then so be it.

She wanted to make love to the man, the male, the drakon she loved. As much faith as she had in him and his friends, there was a chance she might not survive. Being human, she was the weak link. This might be her last opportunity to be with him.

When he began to walk, her lower body pressed tighter to his. She wound her legs around his waist, grinding against the hard bulge behind the zipper of his jeans. Groaning, he pushed her against the wall, his kisses ravenous and hot. He didn't just kiss her, he consumed her. And she loved it.

Desperate to touch him, she yanked at his shirt. "Take it off."

He reared back and tore it over his head, dropping it to the floor. Licking her lips, she ran her fingers over the heavy, defined muscles, teasing his hard nipples. It was such a pleasure to touch him.

A deep rumble emanated from him. Not a groan. More like a low purr of pleasure. *Rip!* Cool air washed over her torso as her sweater and shirt were reduced to rags. "Can't get enough." Lifting her, he buried his face between her breasts. A quick tug and her bra was gone.

When he touched her, there was no room for thoughts of death. Only life. Her nipples were tight nubs, begging for attention, and he provided it, licking and sucking one and then the other. Panting, she raked her fingernails over his broad shoulders, marking him as hers. "More," she demanded, almost breathless with desire. "Bedroom. Now."

For a big guy, he could move fast and had her on the mattress in a flash. Supporting himself on his forearms, with the weight of his lower body pressed against hers, he brushed his lips over hers. She bowed up, stimulating her clit through their clothing. Delicious, but not nearly enough.

"Get naked," she ordered, as she toed off her boots and reached for the button of her pants.

He pushed her hands aside and peeled her jeans away, taking her panties and socks with them, leaving her naked. He licked his lips. "Mine."

The declaration wasn't exactly politically correct, but she didn't care. It made her heart sing and filled the emptiness inside her. Their connection was special.

Her breath caught in her throat when he shucked his jeans. His cock sprang free, hard and ready. Keeping their gazes locked, he tugged the drapes together, shutting out the light, leaving them cocooned inside. "I won't let anything harm you."

It was a promise he might not be able to keep. Not with

such powerful forces after them. That he wanted to meant everything to her.

She flung her hand toward the night-light in the nearest outlet. It wasn't something she needed, but she enjoyed the way the delicate glass fairy glowed when it was on. Now it would give her enough light to see him while, hopefully, not giving them away to anyone who might care to look at the house.

A quiet *snick* was followed by a low glow. Green, blue, red, and yellow patterns splashed across the wall and over his face. Fierce was the only word that fit. With his strong jaw, straight nose, and high cheekbones, he was too rugged to be classically handsome. Lucius was a force of nature, bold and powerful and compelling.

"Lie down."

Arching a dark, questioning brow, he rolled, landing on his back, nostrils flaring when she threw one leg over him and settled on the top of his thighs. His chest rose and fell. The veins in his shaft pulsed with life.

The tattoos on his body began to glow. Starting at his neck, she traced them with the tips of her fingers. "They're so beautiful. Do they have a meaning?"

"Birthmark."

"The color is the same as your dragon form." She skimmed the edgings. "The pink outline matches your eyes." Having this much strong, hot male at her disposal amped up the heat. Her sex aching, she rubbed it against his muscled thigh, spreading her juices over him.

His hands fisted at his sides, his biceps bulging as he struggled for control. It gave her a heady sense of feminine power, tempered by a deep, abiding love.

"What about the other ones? These are regular tattoos, right?" Some looked vaguely familiar, variations of stars and other religious symbols. Some were totally foreign.

"Protective symbols."

Protection from what? She'd ask when she wasn't so busy. Continuing her journey downward, she scooted back to give herself a better vantage point to explore. The meager light gave her a perfect view of his cock. Lowering her head, she ran her tongue over the swirls that covered half of it.

"Raine." His fingers tangled in her hair, but he didn't pull her away or force her to take him.

"I'm busy." Wrapping her hand around the lower half, she held him steady. His lips were curled back, his face a mask of pain and primal longing. The pink of his irises had spread to the entirety of his eyes. His breathing was ragged. Sweat covered his chest.

His moan broke the spell. Licking her lips, she took the plum-shaped, velvety tip into her mouth. His roar shook the room.

So much for being stealthy. If anyone was outside, there'd be no doubt they were inside.

His hips bucked, pushing him deeper. Liquid seeped from the tip. She flicked it with her tongue, capturing more. It was salty with a slight hint of spice. Using her hand to guide him, she began to glide up and down, hollowing her cheeks and sucking.

"Ride me. I want to be inside you when I come." He tugged on her hair until she released him with a gentle *pop*.

"Yes." That's what she wanted, too. Clumsily, she scrambled into position, poised over him. Taking him in hand, she lowered herself, biting her lip to keep from screaming. Her inner walls rippled as he forged deeper. Gasping, she shoved down until he was fully seated.

Connected, her sex pulsed in time to the throbbing of his cock. He skimmed his hands up her torso, briefly cupping her breasts before continuing down her arms. When their hands met, he turned his so their fingers clasped.

"Mine."

She licked her lips and nodded. "And you're mine." Then she began to ride.

• • •

Like a pagan goddess, Raine rose above him, her skin bathed in colored lights. She needed no jewels to adorn her, but he longed to drape her in gold and diamonds. No, rubies or sapphires. Maybe emeralds. None of them were worthy of her.

His brethren would laugh if they could see him. The mighty drakon brought to heel by a human woman. They might laugh, but they would envy him. No drakon ever had a mate as worthy as Raine.

Her body glowed like a candle. The gold in her eyes deepened until it almost matched his tattoos. *Mine!* His dragon insisted, trying to push to the fore.

Not now. His dragon could take her flying through the sky later. Now he wanted to make her fly with passion.

Her hands clung to his with surprising strength. She was slender, but there were supple muscles beneath. She bit her bottom lip, her head thrown back, exposing her vulnerable throat. He wanted to mark her in some way so the world would know who she belonged to, who protected her.

His dragon shoved again, making his tattoos glow brighter. Gritting his teeth, he asserted control. "Come for me." Holding back from shifting was becoming more difficult by the second.

Releasing her hands, he gripped her waist and rolled until she was on her back. Shoving one hand under her ass, he lifted, stimulating her clit with each thrust. He loved the way she clutched his biceps, the sounds of pleasure that fell from her lips.

Resting his forearm on the mattress for support, he captured her lips in a scorching kiss. Hips pumping, the strokes grew faster and harder. Her nails dug into his skin. "Yes!" she cried. Her heels thumped against the backs of his thighs.

She threw back her head, neck arching, eyes blind with pleasure, and came. Her sex rippled around his cock, bathing it in her heat. Her name spilled from his lips as he found his own release. Stars exploded behind his eyes. His skin grew hot, his birthmark itching.

Blind to all else but Raine, he kept thrusting until she went limp in his arms. Spent, he collapsed alongside her, dragging her into his arms. She snuggled close and moaned. "Amazing."

He'd reduced her to one word, but she could still talk. He grinned, looking forward to loving her into silence. How fragile she seemed in comparison to him. He loved the contradictions about her. Pagan warrior one moment and delicate fairy the next.

As he ran his fingers up and down her back, her eyelids fluttered open, filled with a sleepy satisfaction. "Are you tired?" He shouldn't even be asking. She needed to rest.

"A little. Not too much." The invitation in her eyes made his cock twitch.

"Maybe I can do something about that." He'd never played with a woman before. Sex had been sensual at times, blunt at others, but he'd never relaxed his guard enough to banter.

"Mmm, maybe you can." She ran her index finger down his chest.

His dragon stilled. The atmosphere outside the house became charged. Lucius rolled to his feet. "We have company."

"Crap, I knew this would happen. Would've been worse

if it'd happened a few minutes ago." Scrambling, she grabbed clean clothes from the dresser and closet and yanked them on. Her nose wrinkled. "I smell like sex."

Yes, yes, she did. Despite the danger lurking, he was hard as a rock and ready to kill whoever dared to disturb them. He headed down the hallway with her hot on his heels.

"Aren't you going to get dressed?"

"No." Whoever was outside, there was no discernable heartbeat. It was a life-force, for lack of a better word, that he detected. He should've taken her to the far-reaching ends of the Earth, but she couldn't survive in the harsher climates. Not for long, anyway. His flaw was wanting her to be comfortable, to feel some sense of normalcy. He prayed it wouldn't prove to be a fatal error. If something happened to her… "Stay inside."

Determined to end this once and for all, he disabled the locks and went out the door to the center of the yard. "I know you're there. Show yourself." He cast his senses all around, zeroing in on a stand of tall pines on the right.

A brilliant light shimmered. Like a curtain being lifted, a woman was revealed. She was short and slight with flaming red hair. Silver wire-rimmed glasses perched on her nose, giving her a scholarly air. The loose white dress she wore seemed about two sizes too big, and her feet were bare. The silver wings protruding from her back were the dead giveaway.

"Angel." His dragon was crouched inside him, ready to spring if necessary.

She inclined her head. "I'm here to warn you."

The back of his neck itched. The scent of sex followed. "I told you to stay inside," he muttered. Having to worry about Raine would hamper him if he had to fight. He wasn't foolish enough to underestimate his opponent because she was female.

"Who are you?" Raine asked.

"Rivka. My name is Rivka." She kept her voice low, but it carried easily.

"You signed the papers from the Angel Foundation. I remember your name from the grant check I received. It's unusual and pretty."

He'd heard enough. It was the name Gabriel had given them, and she'd confirmed she was part of this. Drawing in a breath, he released a blast of drakon fire.

"No!" Raine yelled as the angel vanished. "Did you kill her?" She spun in a circle, searching.

"No." He could still sense her presence.

"Let's not do that again. There's no time." Rivka appeared off to the left, glancing nervously about. "My foundation was used to hurt you." Her eyes grew luminous. "All I ever wanted to do was help. I was told to give you the grant."

"Who told you?" Raine took a step toward her, but he dragged her back. They were going to have a long discussion about her penchant to disregard his orders about her safety.

"I'm not sure. It was a directive from up the food chain. I'm a low-level angel."

He shook his head. "I don't think so. You have power." The ability to cloak her presence would hide her from most creatures. This woman had secrets.

"That doesn't change my designation." She tapped one small foot against the ground. "Look, I'm risking my life to warn you, but it's only fair. I'm not sure what's going on, but I want no part of it."

"How did you find us?" They hadn't been followed from New York. He would've known.

"I had a hunch you might come back. Drakons are territorial."

"You know what I am?"

"Yes, but I have no idea why you're involved or what this mess is all about."

"So you say." It didn't add up.

Her entire body stiffened and her gaze darted around. "They're coming."

"Who is coming?" There was a faint whirring sound in the air, a whisper from afar getting louder and closer each passing second.

She swallowed heavily. "I've done what I can. Use what you are to save her." With those cryptic words, she disappeared from sight.

Hurricane winds howled across the yard. He caught Raine before she was carried off, dragging her toward the porch. The stars in the sky were shrouded. The moon disappeared. A veil of darkness fell around them. Pressure built until it threatened to crush them.

Light exploded as Lucius's dragon sprang forth with a roar, ready to rain death on whoever threatened them.

Chapter Twenty-One

Crouched on the steps, she gripped the railing so hard splinters pierced her skin. Jagged flashes of lightning revealed Lucius in all his deadly beauty. His huge head was tilted back, fire spewed from his mouth. Like a prehistoric giant, he stretched at least twenty-five feet in length, not including his tail.

He was an awesome and terrifying sight.

The wind battered them. Trees cracked like toothpicks and crashed to the ground. Her Adirondack chairs skated across the porch and smashed into the railing. The house groaned. Fear clutched her heart. It wasn't safe to stay here, but there was nowhere else to seek shelter.

"Show yourselves, you cowards," Lucius roared to the heavens.

The wind ceased and the air grew still. It was like being in the eye of a hurricane. Or the calm before the storm. She gasped, her breathing ragged.

Six spotlights beamed on Lucius, coming from all directions. Arm up to shield her face, she tried to see who or what was behind the lights but couldn't. They were far too bright.

Turning in a semicircle, he sent drakon fire around the space. Better than a flamethrower. The fire slammed against the lights. Sparks flew, neither giving ground as they battled for supremacy.

The spotlights winked out, exposing six tall, well-built men in formfitting white pants and shirts. They all had huge wings flared out behind them with varying shades of cream, white, and light gray.

They all had weapons.

Her fingers dug into the rail. "Holy crap, a horde of angels." Technically, they were probably considered a host, but she'd always pictured a host of angels as, well, angelic. These were badass warriors with very big, very sharp swords.

"You must die, abomination," the tallest one proclaimed.

"Why?" Lucius's voice was deeper now that he was shifted. "What have I done to be sanctioned by Heaven? I don't answer to you."

She bit her lip so hard she drew blood. Interrupting wouldn't help. Splitting Lucius's attention could result in his death.

"We do not judge. We are sent to carry out the sentence."

"Mindless idiots." He gave a quick nod. "Got it."

"Blasphemy." One of them sent a bolt of lightning toward him. Even as she screamed, the bolt struck one of his beautiful scales. It began to glow, the pink outline becoming even brighter. "What is this sorcery?" the same angel demanded.

The leader peered beyond Lucius, homing in on her. "You have involved yourself in angelic business."

She was getting damn tired of being blamed for something that wasn't her fault. "Listen, buddy." Righteous anger got her upright and carried her down the steps. "I was minding my own business when I got a grant from the Angel Foundation. I was guided to a cave where I found him." She pointed at

Lucius. "He was sleeping, minding his own business."

"You woke him, you admit it."

"It wasn't a conscious choice, but it happened. Someone set us up so it would happen. All the evidence points to some high-ranking angel. You're angels. You're supposed to be the good guys." Praying seemed appropriate, so she silently muttered a few.

"You have been judged." the angel repeated.

"I figured angels would prefer to fly under the radar. You're making a huge spectacle." It was a good thing her house was in a remote area, especially now that she had a paranormal showdown of epic proportions unfolding in her front yard. The brilliant lights and sudden storm over her home should've prompted some response, but it was eerily quiet. Not even an insect or animal stirred.

"There is a dome of silence around us. None will see your deaths or stop us in our mission."

This guy was over-the-top with the doom and gloom. His jaw was taut, grim determination on his face. They were so screwed.

"Enough!" Lucius positioned himself in front of her. "I'm more than a drakon. I'm one of the Forgotten Brotherhood. Do you really want to start a war with us?"

A ripple of unease ran through the group. Note to self, her man and his friends were even more badass than she'd thought.

"Who sent you?" he asked again. They had to get to the person behind this.

She peeked over his tail. The angelic leader frowned but raised his sword. It might be her imagination, but he didn't seem nearly as sure about this as he'd been. He silenced that hope with his next words.

"It matters not. Sentence has been given."

Talk about blindly following the chain of command.

Never in her wildest imagination had she thought Heaven would work that way. Her view of everything was being shattered and rewritten.

A battle roar ripped through the air and the angels attacked en masse. Lucius's tail snapped out. The tip sheared one angel in half. Talk about slicing and dicing like a Ginsu knife. That thing was sharp. She caught a glimpse of surprise on the male's face before a light flared and he winked out of sight.

The mighty tail swung at another target who managed to jump back in time to keep from meeting the same fate as his friend. Sparks flew as their swords struck drakon scales with little effect.

"Go for the neck and eyes," the leader yelled.

To hell with this. Raine stumbled up the steps, ran inside the house, and went straight to her bag, digging down to the bottom. Her hand hit metal. Grimly determined, she gripped the 9mm and ran back outside.

The battle hadn't abated. The air rang with curses—not very angelic on their part—and flashes of lightning lit the night sky. That had to be some protective dome around them to keep the neighbors from seeing or hearing the battle. But it was working, as the night remained eerily quiet beyond the fighters.

The remaining five warriors spread out around Lucius, trying to hit his vulnerable spots. He held them off, but for how long? He needed help.

I'm all he's got.

Her arms shook as she raised the gun and took aim at the one nearest her. *I'm going to shoot an angel.* Heaven was going to be out for her if she didn't live through this. Firming her jaw, she took a deep breath and released half of it. Lucius was worth it.

She pulled the trigger.

The angel jerked back a step. Light poured from the hole instead of blood. Her mouth fell open when the wound began to close immediately and was sealed within seconds. Crap, should have seen that coming. His head snapped toward her and the gun in her hand.

Sweat beaded her brow. Her palms grew damp. *I'm in huge trouble.*

The angel rushed toward her, sword swinging. She threw herself to the side. The lightning blast that erupted from the tip of the blade exploded her front door. Glass shattered. Heat singed her face. Ignoring the throbbing in her hip and leg, she rolled up onto her knees and fired, emptying the clip into his chest.

The angel staggered, the wound closing more slowly as energy bled from him. He was like the frigging Terminator. He just wouldn't go down or die.

Lucius spun around, leaving his back vulnerable. "No!" she yelled.

Four angels soared through the air, their weapons all trained on his neck and head. Her attacker staggered closer, sword aimed. She rolled but came up solid against the house.

I'm so screwed.

It was her last thought before excruciating pain exploded in her chest. Her hand went numb. The gun slipped from her fingers.

I can't feel my legs.

The world around her dimmed. Tears leaked from the corners of her eyes and trickled down her temples. She didn't want to leave Lucius. Not yet. They hadn't had nearly enough time.

"Love—" A cough wracked her body and she tasted blood. She wanted him to know he wasn't alone. Even when she died, her love would remain. Praying he could hear her, she fought the oncoming darkness. "Love you."

Brilliant lights filled the sky above her. *So pretty.* The air released from her lungs one final time. Darkness took her.

Lucius's roar of pain followed her into death.

• • •

"No!" Lucius whipped his tail around but wasn't fast enough to stop the killing blow. It deflected it, but enough of it caught Raine.

She can't die.

Only she could. She was human, not drakon, not paranormal. A roar of pure agony ripped out of him, sending a shockwave blast in its wake. The angels flipped in midair and were slammed into the surrounding trees.

"Love you." Her last words seared his heart as her breathing stopped.

The one who'd killed her dared to smile in satisfaction. Raine, who was all that was good in this world, had been destroyed by this male who called himself an angel.

Maybe I can save her.

His blood might be able to bring her back. His gaze narrowed on the enemy in his way. Charging, he released fire hotter and deeper than he'd ever produced. The angel had no time to teleport. It incinerated him, leaving nothing, not even ash.

Shifting, he bolted onto the porch. Her body was lifeless, her head turned away from him. The gun she'd used to try to protect him lay beside her outstretched hand.

"It's time for you to join her," the leader proclaimed.

He'd had it with these self-righteous types who followed orders without question. "You murdered an innocent woman, a human."

"Humans fall under our domain." His voice was flat, emotionless. He could have been discussing the weather.

Ignoring them, he manifested a claw and scored his wrist. He used his free hand to support her head and held the cut to her mouth. "Drink." Blood smeared against her lips, but none of it seemed to be getting down her throat.

The four angels stood in a semicircle around them, swords pointed. "Sentence has been decided." Four bolts speared toward them.

Lucius grabbed his mate and shifted, his huge dragon form wrapping around her. The porch collapsed under his weight and the front corner of the roof partially caved in. He took the hits, accepting the pain, greedily taking the power.

If she was lost to him, Heaven would pay.

"Aim for his vulnerable parts," the leader directed.

He could wait them out indefinitely, but the clock was ticking. If he didn't do something soon, it would be too late for Raine.

"I love you." He inhaled her scent and nuzzled her. "Don't leave me."

"Again," came the command. His scales were superheating. Her body couldn't take the rising temperature. If he didn't release her, she might burn up.

A battle cry ripped through the air, followed by the sound of metal hitting metal.

"Leave off, Viking."

Lucius knew only one Viking. He raised his head, expecting to see Bjorn Knutson, another member of the Brotherhood. This male was the same height and build as his friend, but this wasn't Bjorn. This stranger was wrapped in an aura of power and wielded a battle-axe as though it was an extension of his hand.

He had no idea who the man was but, since he was targeting the angels, Lucius would count him as a friend until proven otherwise.

Taking the reprieve, he shifted back to his human form,

carefully laid Raine on the ground, and opened a vein with a sharp claw. Tilting her head back, he let the drops fall down her throat.

"You leave off, angel. Maccus Fury sent me to inform you that you have no authority here." The stranger even sounded vaguely like Bjorn. "He's currently up in Heaven getting to the bottom of this. The Forgotten Brotherhood is off-limits."

Ignoring the drama unfolding behind him, he focused his attention on Raine. "You must drink. You must live." The cut closed and he opened it again and again. He'd bleed himself dry if necessary. Without her, he had no life.

Two booted feet came into view. "They're gone," the newcomer told him. "At least for now."

Lucius kissed her, breathing into her lungs. "Please, little one. Try for me."

"I'm sorry. I'll keep watch until you're ready to leave."

Ignoring the stranger, he lifted her into his arms, rocking back and forth. The Fates could not be so cruel, to give him his heart's desire for such a short time. He, a drakon, whose blood had been sought for millennia for its healing properties, could not save the only person who'd ever mattered.

A cloak of numbness settled over and around him. This was all his fault. He'd broken his promise, hadn't protected her.

Use what you are to save her. Rivka's parting words echoed in his head. He had, but his blood hadn't worked. His breathing deepened as he searched his memories for answers in something he'd read a long time ago.

Heart thundering, he jumped to his feet with her in his arms. There was no door and a corner of the living room ceiling was gone, but the other side of the house was intact. He carried her into her bedroom and kicked the door shut.

This was probably crazy, but he was out of options.

A papyrus scroll he'd read centuries ago had suggested

that a drakon might share his life-force with his mate. Sex was supposed to be part of the deal, but that wasn't possible.

"This has to work." The alternative was unthinkable. He had no idea what the results would be, how it might change her, or if she'd even still be human. She loved him, but she hadn't agreed to eternity. He was effectively taking the choice out of her hands. If she lived, she might end up hating him.

He clenched his jaw, ignoring the doubts beating at him. So be it. The alternative was to let her die, something he wasn't willing to do, not without exhausting every possibility.

He put her on the bed and stripped away her clothes. Bruises mottled her skin, an abomination. The colorful light spilling over her from the night-light mocked him. They'd been so happy here such a short time ago.

"Don't leave me," he begged. "What would I do without your chatter and laughter? There's no one else to help me find goodness and magic in this world." There was only Raine.

Unsure how to go about this, he stretched out beside her and pulled her against him so her head rested on his chest. Her skin was cool, but retained some warmth. There was still time. There had to be.

Closing his eyes, he called on his dragon, who was unusually silent. "Share what I am with her. I don't care if it diminishes me. Give her what she needs." The swirls of his tattoos rippled beneath his skin. A light emanated from them, changing color rapidly, going from rose gold and pink to a shimmering rainbow.

Blood was next. He manifested a claw and drew it across his chest over his heart. "Drink." He needed her to take him inside her. His blood. His energy. His very essence. He'd already given her his blood, but wasn't taking any chances, trying to follow the ritual as closely as possible. He pressed her mouth against the wound, praying some of it was getting past her lips.

His tattoos seemed to rise from his skin. It wasn't painful, more a tingling. Pink and gold tendrils of energy spread from him to her, lovingly wrapping around her. Closing his eyes, he willed it to continue.

"Whatever she needs." He'd give the last breath in his body if that's what it took for her to live.

Heat surrounded them. The rainbow of light bathed them. Holding his breath, he waited, listening intently for a heartbeat, a breath. Any sign to let him know his desperate plan was working.

Nothing.

He rolled so she was on her back and brushed away the damp hair that clung to her forehead. She was so pale, so still, when she was always so animated, so alive.

His vision blurred. He tried to swallow but couldn't get past the lump. "I'll turn to stone again," he threatened, trying to get a rise out of her. But it was the truth. He couldn't be in this world without her.

The taste of defeat was bitter. He'd failed the only person he'd ever loved. The only one who'd ever loved him. He pressed his lips to hers in one final kiss.

A tear rolled down his cheek and landed on her face. She twitched.

Lungs seizing, he yanked her upright in bed. "Raine?" Had he imagined it? Seen what he'd wanted to?

She rolled her lips together, her tongue flicking over the bottom one. "Tired."

His heart was thundering so loud he wouldn't hear a host of angels if they stomped into the room. "Open your eyes." He tapped her cheeks lightly. "Look at me."

Her eyelids fluttered before finally parting the smallest amount. A frown turned down the corners of her mouth. "Don't cry." Raising a shaky hand, she swiped at a tear. It changed as soon as she touched it. She blinked several times, looking from the gemstone in her hand to him. "I…" She trailed off and licked her lips again. "I don't understand."

A rare pink diamond shone in her palm as more fell around her.

"It's a drakon tear."

"Why are you crying?" She dropped the diamond onto the mattress and cupped his face. "Oh crap." She clutched her chest, her entire body bowing back. "What's wrong with me?"

Catching her so she didn't accidentally harm herself, he held her tight. "You were…" He swallowed heavily. "You were dead. I brought you back."

"The angels?" She tried to get up again, but he kept her wrapped in his arms. He wasn't sure he'd ever be able to let her go again.

"They're gone. Two of them were destroyed."

She cried out and clawed at her chest, leaving long red marks on her skin. "Too hot." Her breathing came so hard and fast she was almost hyperventilating.

Fuck, had he given her more of his blood than she could handle? Too late to worry now. "I had to take drastic measures." Her whole body shook, her teeth chattered. If he hadn't been holding her, she would be thrashing around the bed.

"Blood?" Her lips were pale, her skin flushed, feverish. Her golden-brown eyes were even brighter, the color becoming more gold with each passing second.

"And more." He rocked her, trying to soothe them both. "I couldn't let you go."

"What did you do?" It was almost impossible to understand her, she was shaking so hard.

"I gave you some of my essence." He pressed frantic kisses to her forehead and face. "Breathe through it. I'm here with you. I'll never leave you."

"Love you." She gasped, as though not getting enough air. He sat upright, putting his back to the wall with her securely perched on his lap.

"I love you. Now breathe." Orders of any kind always got her back up. It scared him senseless when she nodded and tried to do as he'd asked instead of arguing. Wheezing, she took a few shallow breaths.

Had he brought her back only to kill her again?

"Burning." Sweat beaded her entire body.

"I'm so sorry. There was no other way." Closing his eyes, he concentrated on drawing the intense fever from her skin. There was resistance, but he was relentless. If there was one thing he could handle, it was heat.

"Ah." Her sigh of ease was all the reassurance he needed that it was working. He swallowed heavily and kissed her damp temple. Relief flooded him.

Her entire body went rigid and she cried out.

Chapter Twenty-Two

All her inner organs were on fire. Pain enveloped her. She couldn't think, could barely breathe. Every inch of her hurt, inside and out.

I'm in Hell. She *had* shot an angel. It was self-defense, but she doubted that mattered to the powers that be. That wasn't fair, but no one could ever claim that life was.

Lucius! She had to get to him, protect him. Had she talked to him or was that wishful thinking? Tears rolled down her cheeks at the thought of him being alone.

"I've got you."

His voice sounded so near.

"Breathe through the pain. Fight for us."

That was definitely her bossy drakon.

Her reply was lost in the low cry that ripped from her. Panting, she clung to him. It was his powerful arms around her, his thick thighs under her, his chest supporting her.

The left side of her chest began to sizzle. It didn't burn, but something was happening. Head lolling to one side, she blinked, unable to believe what she was seeing. Deep rose gold swirls pushed upward from beneath her skin. They continued down her left arm, stopping at the elbow.

So pretty. Just like her drakon's markings.

That snapped her back to reality in a heartbeat. "Lucius."

"I'm here. I've got you." His voice was hoarse. She got the sense he'd been talking for a long time, but she'd been locked in pain, unable to hear him.

"What did you do?" Had he already told her? She rubbed her forehead, wishing she could order her thoughts.

He kissed her temple and the top of her head. "What I had to."

Blood. His essence. "Stop it."

"I can't." His anguish made her want to soothe him, but she had to be firm.

"Don't hurt yourself." If he gave her essence, he'd weaken himself.

His laugh was ragged. "Always worried about me. I'm fine."

She wasn't so sure, but whatever he'd done, there was no going back. The pain lessened. A cooling balm washed over her, bringing blessed release. Breathing became easier, her head cleared. With it came awareness.

"I'm naked." It was more an observation than a concern. After all she'd been through, that was the least of her worries.

He shifted her in his arms so she was lying across him. His skin was pale, his cheeks almost sunken, as though he'd lost weight, but his eyes burned with love.

Concerned, she touched her hand to his face. "What happened?" He looked positively drained.

"What do you remember?"

Frowning, she concentrated. "We fought. The angels—"

"Are gone."

That didn't seem right. "They were so intent on carrying out orders."

One corner of Lucius's mouth kicked up. "Seems Maccus went to Heaven on our behalf."

"He can do that?"

"Apparently. He also sent someone to help."

"Who?"

"I have no idea, and, right now, I don't care." His arms tightened around her, and he buried his face against the curve of her throat. "Don't ever do that again."

"Die?" She shuddered. "Believe me, I plan on holding that off as long as possible." The lightning bolt from the angel's sword had hit her in the chest. The pain had been unbearable. She should have broken bones, massive bleeding, at the very least a scar. She touched the area with wonder. There was only smooth, healthy skin...and a tattoo. She traced one of the swirls. "This is pretty, but why do I have a tattoo like yours?"

A muscle in his jaw flexed. "You have part of my drakon inside you."

She tapped her hands against her ears. "A part of your drakon?" *Don't freak out. Don't freak out.* Surely, she'd misunderstood.

"Yes."

Her breathing quickened and the world began to dim. "Raine, take a breath." If his jaw got any tighter, a bone was going to snap. "There was no time, no way to ask your permission. I couldn't let you die. I apologize for making the choice for you, but I'm not sorry, and I'd do it again in a heartbeat."

His eyes were glowing and scales rippled beneath his skin. He seemed to be waiting for her to pronounce some kind of judgment. She licked her dry lips. "I can't say I'm happy you had to make a unilateral decision." There was no denying it, he was tied to her permanently now, whether he wanted to be or not.

He flinched and lowered his gaze, but she caught his jaw in her hand and applied pressure until he looked at her. "But I understand why you did. I'm glad to be alive, to be with you." It sure as heck beat the alternative. The battle with the angels would cause nightmares for years to come, but at least she had those years, thanks to her drakon. "Thank you. I owe you my life."

He shook his head and growled. "You owe me nothing. You are my mate." The possessive way he said it sent a sensual shiver down her spine.

A random thought occurred to her. "Does this mean I can shift?" That would be cool.

He shook his head, his gaze softening. "No." He smoothed her hair away from her face. "I'm not sure what any of this means, beyond that it brought you back to me. I read a scroll a very long time ago that suggested a drakon could share his essence with his mate so she'd live as long as he did. I'd forgotten about it until now."

Holy crap, he'd done more than simply bring her back to life. It was one thing to think in terms of drinking his blood to live longer, but this took their relationship to a whole other level. They hadn't known each other for that long and forever was…well, forever. Okay, maybe not quite that long, since he wasn't immortal. But he'd likely live for thousands of years. *And now so will I.* Talk about life taking another crazy turn.

"Is that what you want?" Her head was spinning again, her stomach a little sick. She wanted to be more than a responsibility, didn't want him to feel trapped.

"Yes." That was it. No words of love, no poetry or fancy explanation, but he'd done better. He'd risked everything to bring her back to life.

I was dead.

There was nothing she could say to adequately express her gratitude. Or maybe there was. "I love you."

"I made the choice for you. I have no regrets." So fierce, her drakon.

"I have none either," she assured him. "I'm right where I want to be."

Releasing a sigh, he brushed his lips over hers. "I was so scared."

Those simple words shook her to her core. He was the fiercest creature, the most amazing man she'd ever met. For him to admit being afraid was something she'd never expected. Warmth filled her chest, her heart aching with love for him.

"I'm here with you. Whatever the future holds, however long that may be, we're together. Whatever that means going forward, we'll figure it out."

"I could almost forgive the person behind all this." He brushed a damp lock of hair off her cheek. "Whoever they are, they gave me my greatest desire." He kissed her temple. "You." Then his expression hardened. "But they put you in danger. That is unforgiveable."

A chill wafted over her, causing her to shiver. Someone had made a very dangerous enemy in Lucius. And speaking of enemies... Time waited for no one, not even magical drakons. "I need to get cleaned up before we figure out our next course of action."

She was about to move off his lap when a pink glimmer caught her attention. Reaching out, she plucked the large gemstone off the mattress. Something about it called to her soul. She wanted to clasp it to her chest and hold it against her heart.

"This is stunning." Over the course of her career, she'd visited a ton of museums and viewed private collections, but she'd never seen anything quite like this. As she turned it in her hand, admiring the way the facets caught the light, a memory intruded. Lucius had cried, for her. His tear had turned from liquid to this pink stone. What had he called it? "A drakon tear." She looked to him for confirmation.

He gave a curt nod. "It's a pink diamond."

"Holy shit!" It was one more impossible thing in a long list of them. The huge stone had to be worth a small fortune, but it had come from his tears. That made it priceless to her. She closed her fist around it.

"Drakon tears are rare." He cupped her cheek and lowered his head. "A drakon cries for only one reason." His breath feathered over her parted lips. "A drakon cries only when his heart is breaking. A drakon cries only for love."

Their kiss was a poignant meeting of their hearts. They'd come so close to losing each other. She combed her fingers through his hair, needing to reassure herself he was real and not some figment of her imagination. He lifted his lips, their gazes meeting.

"I love you." All she had to give him were the words. The proof of his love was all around her. It was also stamped on her skin and flowed through her veins.

His mouth came down hard on hers. She tasted fear and hope. Most of all, she tasted love. Tongues tangling, they kissed until they were breathless. She ran her hands over his shoulders and down to his heart that beat against his muscular chest. It was racing as fast as hers.

"You're really okay?" She wasn't sure he'd tell her if anything was wrong if he thought she'd worry.

"I will be." He peppered hot kisses along her jawline, working his way up to her ear. He caught the small hoop in her ear and tugged, sending shivers of desire racing down her arms. "There was something more in the scroll I mentioned."

"Not some weird ritual, I hope?" When he paused, she pulled back. "Please tell me I don't have to run naked through the woods or howl at the moon or anything like that." Talk about a mood killer.

His solemn gaze worried her. "I'm afraid it's far worse."

"Crap." She squared her shoulders, prepared to do whatever she had to. If he was brave enough to risk his life for her, she could do no less. "If I managed to cheat death, I'm sure I can do whatever it is." Faster it was done, the better.

His lips twitched, and he couldn't quite meet her eyes. Her gaze narrowed. "You're putting me on."

"I am, but there is something that was left undone." He traced a finger over the swirl at her neck, following it down to her breast, where it circled into her nipple. He flicked the taut bud, sending sensual heat flooding through her.

She licked her lips, getting an inkling of what it was they had to do. "We shouldn't leave anything undone."

"Is it wrong that I love seeing my mark on you?" If the glow of his eyes was any indication, her drakon really, really loved it.

"Not wrong. Possessive. But that works both ways, buddy. You're mine." His low growl of pleasure vibrated through her. "It covers only half my chest to my waist and halfway down my arm. Is it on my back, too?" She twisted, trying to see.

He groaned and she became very aware of something hard poking into her side.

"Yes. It's on your back. The mark means you have part of me, but the scroll said it should be done while making love."

"We definitely need to follow through." They'd cheated death. It was time to release her old life and embrace the one she'd been given. She'd been given another chance and wasn't about to squander it on second thoughts or regrets. She wrapped her fingers around his thick cock. It pulsed, hard and hot against her palm. "Wouldn't want to leave the job half done." She pumped up and down, running her thumb over the tip, spreading the wetness all around.

Her skin began to tingle. It started at her heart and radiated outward. "Something is happening." She hoped it wasn't a side effect, or worse—the return to that burning sensation. "I'm not going to die again, am I?" Because that would truly suck.

"Tell me exactly what you're feeling." He ran his hands up and down her arms, worry etched on his face. "Talk to me."

"My skin is really sensitive." It was as though someone had turned a light on inside. "I can see…everything." Minute details of her room came into sharp focus. She concentrated, trying to catalog every little thing. "I can hear cars going down the road beyond the property. And there's someone outside. How can I know that?"

"The person outside is the male Maccus sent." His slow smile increased her tingles, sending them straight to her core. "Your senses are enhanced."

She shook her head, trying to dim the cacophony of sound. It pummeled her, relentless and unending. "It's too much." She pressed her hands over her ears. "Make it stop."

He caught her face and stared into her eyes. "Listen to me, Raine. You can control it. Picture a dial in your head. One that controls the volume."

"I can do this." It was either that or be continually bombarded by noise. That would eventually drive her crazy. Building the image took a little time, but she did it. Focusing on the button, she turned it to one side. When the world quieted, going back to normal, she gave a sigh of relief. "I did it."

"I never doubted it. With practice, you'll have total control."

"Is this temporary or will it last?"

His huge shoulders shrugged. "Only time will tell."

She took a deep breath and winced. Sight and sound weren't the only enhanced senses. "I smell rank." Sweaty and sticky, a sure way to turn a man on—not.

"You smell perfect." He started to kiss her, but she turned her head to one side.

"Not happening until I shower." She was drawing the line at that.

Giving her a grin worthy of any pirate, he stood with her in his arms and carried her toward the bathroom. "We can complete the ritual anywhere."

. . .

It worked! It had been a last-ditch effort on his part. Shockingly, he wasn't diminished in any way. If anything, his drakon was stronger.

He hit the light switch with his shoulder, illuminating the room. There was no way to start the shower unless he put her down, something he couldn't bear to do. The urge to keep her close, to protect her, had kicked up to a whole other level. Having lost her, even briefly, was something he'd never forget. It made him want to cherish her all the more.

"Is there a problem?" she asked after about a minute.

"Yes."

A few more seconds. "Care to tell me what?"

"No." He could do this. Had to do this. No way he'd be able to begin to relax until the ritual had been completed the way it'd been written. She seemed fine but he wasn't taking any chances.

That was the impetus to get him moving. It took some maneuvering to get them both in the stall, but he managed. It hadn't been built for two, especially when one of them was as big as him. "Turn on the water."

She kissed his neck before reaching out and turning the knobs. Water blasted down on them. Raine shrieked and then began to laugh, swiping at her eyes.

"Crap." He angled her away from the worst of the blast. "Sorry about that."

"Everything okay in here?" a male voice called.

"Do not take one step through that door," he thundered. It would be a shame to have to kill the male who helped him, but that's what would happen if he saw Raine naked. His dragon growled in agreement.

"I heard her scream. Just checking to make sure some angel didn't sneak past me. I'll be outside."

There were no footsteps, but he sensed the male getting farther away. Raine's face was buried against his neck, her entire body shaking. "Don't be afraid. He won't harm you."

When she tilted her head back, it wasn't fear making her shake, but laughter. "Oh my God. Can you imagine if he'd burst in here?" She slapped at his shoulder and went off into another peal of laughter.

He shook his head, unable to scold her for her inappropriate humor. His own lips twitched.

"Come on, it's funny." She patted his arm. "You have to put me down sometime."

He hated that she was right. Reluctantly, he released her legs, waiting until she was stable before removing his other arm from around her shoulders. The small space meant they were crowded close, their bodies still touching.

She tilted her head back and smiled up at him. "Hi." There was no one else on the planet who lightened his soul as she did. "Come here often?" she continued.

The gold swirls wrapped lovingly around the left side of her torso. If it hadn't worked, he would've lost her.

He dropped to his knees and buried his face against her stomach. His arms went around her, chaining her to him. That's what he'd done. He'd tethered her to him for all time.

"It's okay," she whispered, as she caressed his head and rubbed his shoulders.

He pressed his lips against her water-kissed skin, capturing a droplet on his tongue. The muscles of her stomach contracted. "There wasn't any way to ask. I took the choice away from you." That was something he'd have to live with.

"Listen carefully. I'm never going to regret what you did. This is new territory for both of us. What the fallout from this will be, only time will tell, but I'm grateful to be alive. You saved me. You took a huge risk not knowing what it might do to you. I'm sure we'll hit some bumps along the way, but that's what being part of a couple is about. And, hey, how many women can say they were saved by a drakon? None." Her brow furrowed. "Maybe a couple. There are other drakons in the world, but you know what I mean."

The corners of his lips twitched. Her forgiveness and acceptance loosened the knot in his stomach. The tension in his shoulders eased. His Raine was back, her clever mind taking all sorts of interesting turns.

With that settled, his mind turned to more basic things. He shot to his feet and crowded her against the wall.

She sucked in a breath, her back arching. "The tiles are cold."

"I'll warm you." He took the bar of soap off the shelf and rubbed it between his hands until it lathered.

"I'm cold all over." The sultry tone of her voice, the spicy scent of her arousal wafting above the perfume of the soap, called to him, luring him closer. Blindfolded, he'd pick her out of a crowd of a thousand women. Ten thousand. She was his mate, his perfect match in every way. All her little quirks made her even more unique, precious.

And even though she had concerns about what changes there might be to her body, to her life, she hadn't blamed him. She could have easily cursed him, shunned him. A shudder went through his big body. That would've been almost as bad as losing her to death.

"Hey, you okay?" She pressed her hand against his chest, right over his heart.

"I will be." Starting at her neck and shoulders, he lathered her skin, washing away the stench of desperation and fear that lingered, traced his fingers over the swirling tattoos that covered half of her torso. Primal satisfaction made his chest swell. His cock was as hard as dragon scales. His balls hung low and heavy, but he didn't want to stop, didn't want this moment to end.

Her lips were parted, her breathing ragged. "Don't we have to complete the ritual?"

Her blatant attempt at getting him to hurry made him laugh. "You're in a rush." He massaged her breasts, cupping them and running his thumbs over the tempting nipples. "I'm not."

That was only a partial lie. He wasn't sure how much longer he could hold out. Touching her was the sweetest torture for them both. He smoothed his hands over her hips and delved between her thighs, stroking and caressing before dipping one long finger inside. Her gasp was music to his ears.

Have to taste her. Going down on his knees, he buried his face against her cleft and inhaled her spicy, sweet scent. There really wasn't enough room in the stall for this, but he wasn't about to let that stop him. He lifted one of her legs and draped it over his shoulder, opening her wide.

She was pink and wet and welcoming. He dragged his tongue over her slick folds, paying particular attention to the bud at the apex. Her heel dug into his shoulder as the steam rose around them.

When he smelled blood, his head jerked up. She'd bitten her lip hard enough to make it bleed. He reached up a hand and rubbed his thumb over the small injury.

"Don't want to yell." She was panting heavily. "Don't want unwanted company."

He wanted to curse and laugh but ached too much for either. She was right. This wasn't the time to linger, even if they did have a guard to watch over them. While Maccus had called off the angelic hit squad, there was no telling what might come at them next, and the ritual wasn't complete until they'd made love.

Cursing himself for indulging his whims, he lowered her leg and rose to his full height. He lifted her off the floor and pressed her firmly against the wall, angling his back toward the water to protect her.

Her smile was tremulous as she pushed his wet hair away from his face. "This is going to be fast," he warned. He was too on edge—physically and emotionally—to last long. Her heat bathed the head of his cock as he notched it at her opening. Swallowing hard, he eased inward, not stopping until he was fully sheathed. His lungs expanded as he dragged air into them. Energy pulsed through him from his head to his toes. His tattoos throbbed.

They needed to do everything right. No way was he going to miss a step and lose her down the road. He manifested a claw and dragged it over his heart. "Just a drop more of blood. You've already had more than you should have."

With a solemn nod, she dipped her head and dragged her tongue over his skin. His orgasm hit him hard and fast. On a roar, he tilted his head back, shocked by the intensity. Her cry mingled with his, her sex rippling around his cock. A rainbow shower of light exploded around them before sinking into their skin, adding an extra sizzle of pleasure.

Head tilted back, she stared up at him and blinked. "Holy shit." She slapped her hand over her mouth and began to laugh. He nudged her hand aside and kissed her, tasting her desire, devouring her love.

Her laugh turned to a sweet moan as he began to flex his hips, moving in and out. The first release had only whetted his appetite. Tongues tangling, bodies moving in harmony, he rode her to another release and followed her over.

The water rained over their heated bodies, cooling them.

Raine leaned in and licked his neck. "You taste different now. Spicy and salty."

He caught her chin, tilted her head back, and smiled.

"I'm not sure I like that look."

"Your eyes."

"What about them?" She shimmied against him, trying to get him to set her down. All it succeeded in doing was driving his still hard cock deeper. They both groaned and stilled. "You can't be serious."

"Drakon," he reminded her. He might not need a break, but after all she'd been through, he didn't want to push her. And as pleasant as it was to be alone with her, it was time to focus on the big problem still hanging over them. They still had no idea who was behind all of this.

"The gold of your eyes has changed to the color of the tattoos and they're rimmed with pink." They were his colors. Enthralled, he couldn't look away.

"You're determined to brand me. First tattoos, now this." He might have been worried if she wasn't playing with his hair and smiling. "Seriously, you have to let me down so I can see."

They washed and rinsed quickly in the cool water before shutting it off and stepping out. Raine stared at herself in the mirror. "Wow, I really look different." She poked at the tattoos and leaned forward, studying her eyes.

Standing behind her, he put his hands on her shoulders and stared at their reflection. "You are still the beautiful woman who woke me from my eternal sleep."

"Thank you for saving me." She turned and pressed both palms against his chest. His erection brushed against her stomach. She glanced down and grinned. "I don't think that guy outside will wait a whole lot longer, and I, for one, want to know who he is and what he knows."

Chapter Twenty-Three

Raine was surprised to find the stranger seated at her kitchen table, but that wasn't nearly as shocking as discovering a corner of the roof was missing and a portion of the front wall of her living room caved in.

Obviously, she'd missed a few things after she'd died.

His gaze missed nothing as he studied her from head to toe, making her glad she'd worn a turtleneck sweater to hide her new tattoos. Maybe he already knew. Maybe he had super hearing like Lucius.

Hers was driving her crazy, coming in and out, like someone was playing with the volume. She hadn't mentioned it, not wanting her drakon to worry. It would take time for her to become accustomed to having amped-up senses. Like everything else she'd achieved in her life, she wasn't afraid to put in the work. Not when the reward was worth it—a life with Lucius. The tattoo was cool. The change in eye color a bit disconcerting, but she'd deal.

"I'm Sven." He was big and broad-shouldered with light hair that was cut short. His blue eyes were as cold as ice. A huge battle-axe was propped against the wall behind him. This guy reminded her of Thor from the movies, only much harder and tougher, and his weapon was no prop.

"Ah, thanks for the help earlier." She had no memory of it, but without him, things might not have worked out as well as they had.

Lucius pulled out a chair for her. If he wasn't with her, she might have run. Sven was not a man to cross. He reeked of badass.

Standing beside her, arms crossed over his chest, Lucius nodded at their guest. "You said Maccus sent you. You remind me of someone I used to know."

One corner of his mouth twitched. Or maybe she'd imagined it. This did not seem like a guy who smiled on a regular basis.

"I am Sven Knutson. My father is Bjorn Knutson."

"You claim to be the Viking's son." He leaned forward and planted his hands on the table. It groaned but held under the pressure. "Bjorn's family was all slaughtered centuries ago."

The corners of Sven's eyes tightened and his jaw clenched. "My mother made a deal with the goddess Freya. Eternal servitude in exchange for her children getting a second chance at life."

Now *that* was badass. It was also unfair. "I'm sorry. About your mother."

His hard gaze softened. "All is well. She is with my father now." He glared at Lucius. Or maybe that was his normal expression. He wasn't exactly a lighthearted soul. "Maccus did not tell you?"

"We had other problems to deal with. There was no time to catch up on the news of the Brotherhood." He headed to the kitchen. "I need coffee and food."

Considering the condition of the front corner of her

home, she was grateful they had power. Must've missed the power line running into the house. Good thing, as she'd kill for coffee and chocolate. Her secret stash. Her chair skidded against the floor as she shoved it back.

Sven jumped to his feet, axe in hand. Lucius whirled, eyes blazing and claws out.

Whoa, talk about intense. "Calm down." Holding her hands out in front of her, she sought to ease the tension. Both men were wound tighter than a coiled spring. "Chill, I'm only going for the chocolate." Suiting actions to words, she slowly eased across the room, opened a cupboard door over the refrigerator, and pulled down a bar of ultra-dark chocolate. "I keep it for emergencies. This qualifies."

Both men held their positions, gazes locked. Trust was definitely an issue with these guys. Silently muttering about the stubbornness of men, she opened the bar and broke off two pieces. She held one out to Lucius. "Here, you need this." When he didn't immediately take it, she waved it in front of him. "I don't often offer my chocolate."

"Then I am honored." He took it and stuffed it in his mouth in one bite.

Horrified, she could only watch as he bolted it down. "You don't eat expensive chocolate like that." *He doesn't know any better, he doesn't know any better.* The calming mantra did little to quell her dismay.

He shrugged, totally unrepentant. "I'm hungry." He began dragging every can of soup out of her cupboard.

With a shake of her head, she left him to his work and held out a piece to the Viking. "It doesn't cure all ills, but it doesn't hurt."

He didn't smile, but his shoulders lowered, and the axe head dipped toward the floor as he took the proffered treat. Holding her gaze, he bit off a small piece.

"That's what I'm talking about. You savor it." Then it was

her turn. The tiny sliver of chocolaty goodness melted on her tongue. It tasted slightly different—likely due to the changes in her body—but thankfully, still delicious. That could have been a problem. She could give up most junk food but not chocolate. "So, Sven, what did Maccus tell you?" Someone had to get them talking.

"Maccus never tells anyone very much."

Lucius snorted. "Understatement."

He propped the axe beside him and retook his seat. "He said you had angel problems and that I was to protect you. He went to Heaven to seek answers."

Four pots were slapped on her stove, each filled with a different kind of soup. Bread was toasting. Her stomach growled. She popped another piece of chocolate into her mouth. "Are you a member of the Brotherhood?" Honestly, if she waited for Lucius to ask, she'd be an old lady before they found out anything. She paused with a piece of chocolate halfway to her lips. She wasn't going to age any more. Or if she did, it wouldn't be for a very long time.

"Is something wrong?"

She waved away Sven's concern. "I'm fine." Or she would be when she had time to process. "You were telling me about the Brotherhood."

The corners of his mouth did twitch and his gaze lightened, making him look younger, not as hard. "I am a member of the Brotherhood."

Interested, she leaned forward, resting her elbows on the table and her chin on her hands. A bowl of chicken noodle soup and a plate of toast were slid in front of her. "Eat. You need it."

Her man was starving, but he'd fed her first. He was one in a billion. Gazing up at him, she offered him a smile. "Thank you." He grunted and went back to the stove, grabbed a pot and spoon, and began to eat.

"How are you here, Viking?"

Not exactly subtle, but from all she'd observed, members of the Brotherhood were blunt, bordering on rude. It probably discouraged questions from most people.

She wasn't most people. After inhaling the soup, she munched on some toast. "You said your mother got you a second life. Is this it?"

He shook his head. "The gods twist things to suit themselves."

That wasn't at all ominous. Even though she was still hungry, her stomach was churning too much for comfort. She pushed her plate away.

"Are you unwell?" Lucius was beside her before she lifted her finger from the plate, concern etched on his beloved face.

"We have angels after us and we still don't know why. Sven is right. The powerful often twist things to suit themselves. Do you know anything? You were sent to us for a reason."

"Protection." The cold cynicism was back. "I'm good at killing."

A chill rushed down her spine.

"You should eat." Ignoring their guest, Lucius stroked her face. He was worried about what he'd done, about the changes taking place inside her.

"I will, as soon as this settles. Don't let me stop you." He'd battled and been through even more than she had, giving so much of himself. When he hesitated, she shamelessly used his feelings for her. "I'd feel better if you ate something."

He leaned down, pressing his forehead against hers. "Don't think I don't know what you're doing."

Her drakon was too smart for his own good. Or her good, for that matter, but she wouldn't change him for anything. There was silence as he polished off a half dozen cans of soup, her supply of canned tuna, and a jar of peanut butter along with the rest of the bread.

"How is your father?" he finally asked.

"Well."

Not exactly forthcoming. Curiosity wouldn't allow her to keep her tongue still. "Lucius is a drakon. Maccus a fallen angel. Your father would have to be special to be part of the Brotherhood. So would you."

It wasn't really her business, but these men were a part of Lucius's life. Part of her life now. It was like living in one of the myths she'd been obsessed with since childhood. On one hand, it was unbelievable. On the other, it was almost shocking how easily she slid into it, as if everything in her life until she'd met Lucius had been preparation.

"Bjorn Knutson is the father of Norse werewolves," Lucius told her. "A fierce fighter who has spent his entire existence angry at the world, with good reason."

"Yes!" She pumped her arm. "I knew werewolves were real. I think I've interviewed one or two."

"Woman, you're going to make me old before my time." He snatched her out of her chair and dragged her into his arms. "You need a keeper." It wasn't the first time he'd said that.

"I do not," she protested, even as she snuggled against him. He smelled so good. "I'm a modern, independent woman. A professional. I've taken care of myself my whole life. I have a job, a home." She frowned at the front of her house. "Or I did. What am I going to tell my insurance company?"

"Anything but the truth." He chuckled, his entire body shaking.

He was right about that. The truth would not go over well. She played out scenario after scenario, finally admitting defeat. "I've got nothing."

Lucius kissed her temple. "Don't fret. One of the pink diamonds will pay for any repairs."

Aghast, she whirled around and thumped her fist against

his chest. "We are not selling those diamonds." That's how crazy her life was. She'd forgotten all about them.

He canted his head to one side. "Why not?"

God, he could be obtuse. "They're mine." She rolled her eyes toward Sven, not certain how much Lucius would want him to know. "And they're special." They were drakon tears. Her drakon's tears. They were a symbol of how much he loved her. She'd never give them up.

"If it means that much to you."

"It does. Besides, I have insurance." She'd figure something out.

His pink eyes glowed as he lowered his head. Breathless with anticipation, her lips parted and her heart pounded. Ignoring their avid audience, she went up on her toes to meet him. They'd barely touched when he raised his head. "Maccus is here."

• • •

It meant everything to him that Raine valued his drakon tears. He wanted this situation settled once and for all so he could whisk her away and make love to her without worrying about someone trying to harm her.

Taking her hand, he led her toward the front of the house and outside. Sven followed but stood off to the side, axe ready, gaze watchful.

Maccus stood in the center of the yard, hands on his waist as he surveyed the damage to the house. "You had quite the battle. Two angels are dead. Heaven is not happy with you."

Every muscle in his body tensed. His dragon roared to life, ready to lay waste to any enemies. "They came after us unprovoked."

"Which I pointed out to them." He tilted his head to one side and studied Raine. "She's changed."

Lucius slowly released her and pushed her partially behind him, his protective instincts on alert. "Yes." It wasn't a surprise that his friend would sense the difference. His reaction was the unknown. He'd hate to have to fight him, but no one was taking her from him. She was his mate, the missing piece of his soul.

"I'm happy for you, Brother." The acceptance, heartfelt and immediate, humbled him.

"I'd invite you in, but the living room is a disaster." She waved her hand toward the house.

Birds called to one another in the distance. Morning had dawned. With it came the light, putting the extent of the destruction on full display. The ground was scorched in several places, the surrounding grass a dull brown. Lucius winced at the damage that had been done to Raine's sanctuary. She hadn't complained, not once, but sadness lurked in her eyes.

He'd build her a castle, if she desired, once this was settled. He owned land around the world. Or had. He'd deeded it to the Brotherhood, but they'd give it back without him having to ask.

That's what the Brotherhood was all about.

"We still have a problem."

There would be no future for them until this was settled. "You went to Heaven?" If he found the idea jolting, how much more so was it for Maccus to return to the place he'd been kicked out of?

"I questioned the remaining force that had been sent here. They'd received orders from higher up. Problem is, there's no record of it and no one will admit to it."

"Someone destroyed the evidence." That was smart and spoke of someone in a position of authority.

"What are our options?" she asked. "I don't know about the rest of you, but I'm not willing to sit around and wait to be attacked again. Should we go to Heaven? Is that even possible?"

He'd never say it aloud again, but she did need a protector. She was willing to jump in where most angels would fear to tread.

"It's not possible." Maccus raised his head to the sky. The clouds parted, revealing the sun. "Gabriel, get your ass down here."

A bolt of lightning zigzagged from the sky and hit the ground, followed by a ground-shaking boom. When the brilliant light died, the archangel was there, arms crossed over his chest and a frown on his face. "I don't appreciate being summoned like some servant. I've been busy trying to get to the bottom of your little problem."

"You and Lucifer tried to cause trouble for me and then for the Brotherhood." Lucius didn't trust him. Neither, it seemed, did Maccus.

"I admit to joining forces with Lucifer to try to kill you." He shrugged when Raine gasped. "It was worth a shot." He pointed a finger at Maccus. "I wasn't involved with Lucifer's plots to harm your little friends. I have better things to do."

That rang true. Lucius wanted someone to punish, to blame, to find a way out of this situation. "If not you, then who?" he demanded.

Gabriel sneered. "I don't answer to you, drakon. Nor to you, Viking." He shot Sven a nasty glare.

"Gabriel." Maccus's tone was level and low, but even Lucius heard the annoyance simmering there. Good, he wasn't the only one losing patience with this bullshit.

"I've informed all angels to stay away from the drakon and his little friend. I'm looking for the angel who oversaw the Angel Foundation, but she's proving to be surprisingly resourceful. I'm not sure what else I can do. Quite frankly, I'm tired of the lot of you."

"You're looking for Rivka."

Gabriel swiveled toward Raine, his eyes blazing. "You've seen her?"

Lucius stepped in front of her, groaning in frustration when she peeked around him. "She was here briefly to warn us but left."

"I'll find her," the archangel vowed.

"No." The finality of that one word froze them all in place. "Sven."

The younger man stepped forward to answer Maccus's summons, axe over his shoulder. "You want me to find her."

It wasn't a question. That Maccus would ask Sven to take on the task spoke volumes about his abilities. Bjorn was the best tracker Lucius had ever known. Maybe his son was as good or better.

"Do what you want. I'm done." Gabriel disappeared in a blast of light.

"He does like a show." Raine squinted and then smiled up at him. "Does this mean we're safe?"

Unsure, Lucius looked to Maccus. "Do I need to find a way to Heaven?" Because he would, and when he did, he'd make them all very sorry.

"No. The angels all know what will happen if any of them go after you, but I still want to know the truth."

"As do I." He wouldn't be satisfied until he was confident everyone behind the plot was punished.

"I'll find this Rivka and uncover the truth." Sven nodded at Maccus before turning to him. "Take care of her."

"I will. Thank you for your help, Brother." Lucius held out his arm. The younger male hesitated for a moment before they clasped arms. "Whatever you need, whenever you need it," he vowed.

Sven stepped back and disappeared. That was one hell of a talent.

"Where will you go?" Maccus asked.

"That's up to Raine." Too many choices had been taken away from her.

"I need to get my things packed and put into storage before the house falls down on them." She chewed her bottom lip. "I guess repairs come after that. I'm going to have to start making a list."

"If you need a place to stay while you're deciding what to do, come to New York. I own several apartment buildings." It was a grudging offer, but an offer, nonetheless.

"Bet that hurt," he teased.

"You have no idea. It's all Morrigan's fault. The woman wants to keep all the Brothers around, at least the ones who have women of their own."

"I like Morrigan." Raine was staring at the house. He could almost see the wheels turning in her head. "I'd love to talk to her, learn more about all of you."

Maccus groaned. "On that note, I'm gone." He, too, vanished, leaving him and Raine alone.

"Is it really over?" She shivered and rubbed her hands up and down her arms. "I want to believe it."

"Believe it." He wrapped his arms around her from behind, loving the way her body fit against his. "I failed to protect you." Something that would always haunt him.

She tilted her head back, her eyebrows drawn down. "Please tell me you don't believe that. Lucius, you saved my life."

"You died." And that was all on him. His arms tightened around her, and a muscle worked in his jaw. "You didn't have a choice about what happened after." The tattoo and change in her eyes were proof of that.

"Maybe not, but I did choose to become your mate, to love you." Her acceptance loosened the knot in his stomach. "I have no regrets."

His throat tightened, forcing him to clear it several times

before he could speak. "Let's get a storage pod delivered, pack your things, and get out of here. I want to take you somewhere I can make love to you for hours without worrying about anyone or anything."

"Somewhere they deliver food."

"Anything you want." He turned her in his arms and kissed her. As always, she welcomed him eagerly. He had no idea how he'd gotten so lucky, but he'd spend the rest of his years being grateful.

Raine's phone chimed. The interruption made him frown. "And we're turning off the phones, too." Someone or something was always getting in the way.

"It might be important." She pulled her cell out and then laughed. "There'll be a storage pod and boxes arriving within the hour, courtesy of Morrigan."

The Brotherhood was stronger than ever. Maybe the women had something to do with that. Raine had made him stronger on every level. "We'll get Penelope before we leave." With all the upheaval, her pet would be a comfort, offer some normalcy.

"Can we? Is it safe? I couldn't bear it if something happened to her, but I miss her so much." She was bouncing on her toes, her excitement palpable.

"It's safe." He'd make it that way.

"Awesome." She threw her arms around his neck and nibbled his earlobe. "We have an hour before the pod arrives. Think we can make love without bringing down the rest of the house?"

He lifted her off her feet and carried her toward the house. "I do love a challenge." Raine would offer him one every day for the rest of his life. He couldn't wait.

• • •

Gabriel was still fuming when he arrived in his quarters. The sting of having to answer a summons as though he was nothing more than a lowly clerical angel wasn't going to go away anytime soon. Maybe Maccus and the Brotherhood were off-limits, at least until he found a way around it, but the missing angel fell under his jurisdiction.

All he had to do was find her. And he had to do it before the Brotherhood did. Dead angels told no tales.

Epilogue

"Will they like me?" Raine set her brush down on her dresser and did one last check of her appearance in the mirror. Her makeup was minimal, the slacks and top she wore casual but excellent quality.

It wasn't like her to fret so much. She was used to navigating social situations. Academia was an excellent training ground for such things.

This was different.

Lucius finished buttoning his shirt. "They'll love you. You already know Morrigan."

That was true. They'd become fast friends since she and Lucius had temporarily settled in New York, bonding over how to deal with a stubborn, overprotective paranormal mate. Morrigan had given her great advice. But now she was meeting three other members and their wives who'd traveled to the city just to meet them.

Penelope jumped onto the dresser and nudged her arm. "Meow."

"I'm not paying you enough attention, am I?" She picked

the cat up and snuggled her, letting the deep purring calm her nerves.

"You're spoiling her." He was smiling when he said it, so she didn't take it to heart. Besides, he was worse than she was. Penelope was the proud owner of not one, but two deluxe cat trees and a basket full of new cat toys. Her pet loved Lucius as much as she did.

He'd also been spoiling her. True to his word, they'd spent an entire week in a luxury hotel, doing nothing but eating, sleeping, making love, and talking. It had been heaven. There were still a lot of details to nail down—like where they'd live—but one thing they had was time.

After much discussion, they'd decided that if she did continue to age—although that seemed unlikely given the other changes she'd experienced—she'd use his blood to counteract it. He hadn't pressured her into the decision, even though she could tell he'd wanted to. He'd impressed her with his restraint. They were both learning to navigate their new normal. She wasn't the only one dealing with huge changes.

The more mundane details of life had been handled. All her belongings were in storage and the repairs were almost finished on her house. Money talked, and apparently, Lucius had tons of it.

She'd been forced to rein him in this past month. It had taken a lot of fast talking to convince him she didn't want to buy anything until they knew where they were settling for good. As it was, there were several new outfits in the closet, including the one she was currently wearing. She'd learned not to show an interest in anything when they were out walking around the city streets or it would inevitably end up in her possession.

Her drakon was generous to a fault.

After one final snuggle, she set Penelope on the floor. The feline ambled over to the bed and jumped up, turning in a circle before settling. "Have you heard from Sven?" He'd been searching for several weeks now, but Rivka was proving to be elusive.

"Nothing in the past week, but he thought he was closing in on her."

"He won't hurt her, will he?" That was the last thing she wanted. The angel had tried to help them, whether from a guilty conscience or because she was an innocent pawn in this as Raine had been—there was no way to know unless they could talk with her. "I'm not convinced she was part of the plot against the Brotherhood."

Lucius kissed her neck, sending shivers dancing over her skin. "He won't hurt her. Unless she attacks him," he added. "He'll protect himself."

Not exactly reassuring, but it was the best she could hope for.

He held his fisted hand out in front of her. "This is for you."

"What have you done now?" She held her hands behind her back. "You have to stop buying me things."

"I didn't buy this. Not really." He shrugged as if unconcerned, but the expression on his face told another tale. "If you don't want it, I understand."

She grabbed his arm before he could tuck away the gift. Whatever it was, it was special to him. "I don't mean to sound ungrateful. It's just that you've already given me so much."

His brow furrowed. "Your life was destroyed because of me."

She pressed her hands against his face. "It changed because of you. For the better. I have you and Penelope. Everything else is just details." Her drakon was dealing with a ton of guilt. It was up to her to help him get past it.

His brow smoothed and the twinkle returned to his eyes. He opened his hand and a stunning necklace cascaded through his fingers. Pink diamonds glittered in the light. One of them was set as a pendant, while the rest were part of the chain.

"Your drakon tears." She'd wondered what had happened to them but hadn't wanted to ask.

He shook his head and draped the necklace over her head. "*Your* drakon tears. A drakon cries only when his heart is breaking. A drakon cries only for love."

"I remember." Tears welled in her eyes and trickled down her cheeks. "It's stunning."

"Each drakon's tears are unique." He ran his index finger down the chain where it nestled between her breasts. "Fire drakons shed rubies, water drakons sapphires, air drakons emeralds. The tears of an earth drakon become diamonds. Most are normal diamonds."

"Yours are pink. I love that they match your eyes." The necklace was heavy, a tangible reminder of the terrible time they'd survived, a testament to his love for her.

"They're rare, as you are. I love you, Raine." Taking her in his arms, he kissed her. She tasted love and heat and forever. Wrapping her arms around him, she returned the embrace until they were both breathless.

"Will you take me flying someday?" With everything else happening, there'd been no time.

"I will." He nibbled on the curve of her neck, causing goose bumps to race down her arm. "I can make you fly another way."

His sensual promise had her heart racing and her entire body quivering in anticipation. "Do you think they'll forgive us if we're a bit late?"

"They're going to have to." He swept her into his arms and carried her to the bed. Penelope jumped down and scurried from the room, obviously annoyed with this turn of events. In short order, Raine was naked except for the necklace. The metal and gems were warm against her skin, but not nearly as warm as her drakon, her love.

"I'm so glad I came into your cave and woke you from your sleep."

He nuzzled his nose against hers. "So am I. Not only my body, but also my heart was stone until you. It was meant to be." They made love, slow and easy, tasting and savoring, taking and giving. They ignored the phone when it rang and were an hour late to dinner.

Acknowledgments

It takes many dedicated people to bring a book to life. I am incredibly grateful to all the hardworking and professional staff at Entangled Publishing who had a hand in making this book a reality.

Special thanks to Liz Pelletier, Meredith Johnson, Alethea Spiridon, Heather Riccio, Jessica Turner, and Bree Archer.

Thank you to all the talented authors and loyal readers that I am privileged to call my friends. Your support and encouragement mean so much. I don't know what I'd do without you.

About the Author

Once upon a time N.J. had the idea that she would like to quit her job at the bookstore, sell everything she owned, leave her hometown, and write romance novels in a place where no one knew her. And she did. Two years later, she went back to the bookstore and her hometown and settled in for another seven years. One day she gave notice at her job on a Friday morning. On Sunday afternoon, she received a tentative acceptance for her first erotic romance novel and life would never be the same. N.J. has always been a voracious reader, and now she spends her days writing novels of her own. Vampires, werewolves, dragons, time-travelers, seductive handymen, and next-door neighbors with smoldering good looks—all vie for her attention. It's a tough life, but someone's got to live it.

Discover more romance from Entangled...

PIRATE'S PROTECTOR
a Sentinels of Savannah novel by Lisa Kessler

Immortal pirate Duke Proctor is facing his biggest challenge yet when he meets grumpy mermaid Annika Mare – who's convinced that he's the one who stole her precious comb – that in the wrong hands forces her to do the bidding of its current owner. And when the government gets involved with a hot lead pointing to a dangerous enemy Duke's pirate crew thought to be long defeated, things get *really* complicated.

HUNTER'S HOPE
a Vampire Motorcycle Club novel by Alyssa Day

Firefighter Hunter Evans died saving a life...only to be reborn as a vampire. Now the "nice guy" must conquer the deadly urges threatening to turn him feral. Alice Darlington can see ghosts, a power some want to use for dark purposes. When Hunter's dangerous actions put Alice's life in danger, he vows to protect her from himself and the threat hunting her down. But Hunter doesn't know how long he can keep the beast inside him away from the woman it craves.

Magic Dark, Magic Divine
a Warrior of the Divine Sword novel by A.J. Locke

Waking up after 300 years to a magic-less world, mercenary Pennrae has had to conceal her magical skills. That is until magic-eating monsters descend on New York City causing all kinds of havoc. Paranormal romance readers won't want to miss the stunning first book in A.J. Locke's 'Warrior of the Divine Sword' series.

Nightshade's Bite
a Blood Wars novel by Zoe Forward

Kiera Rossard's secret life just got complicated. She's leader of a rebel vampire society that rescues werewolves during the interspecies war. Everyone wants her dead—vampires and the werewolves who don't know her secret. Starting with notorious vampire killer Michael Durand—the man who sets her blood on fire. So what if vampires bite when they're turned on? And so what if one drop of his blood will kill her? What's life without a little risk?

Made in the USA
Columbia, SC
14 October 2023

24462558R00181